THE COLOR OF DANGER

For some reason, she was sure the color red was a clue, but a solid image hadn't formed yet. Red dress? Red shoes? Red barn? Fingernails painted dragon red? Her imagination ran wild with the possibilities. Unfortunately, red was also the color of fire and blood. She shivered, wishing she could ignore the pictures that filled her mind and not get caught up in the troubles of others.

She shrugged. It was useless to think of stopping. It was a God-given gift, and she was compelled to continue using her psychic powers. She began breathing deeply, relaxing, willing her inner being to open itself to the images that would come. But there were none, only the nagging fear that somewhere, someone needed her help . . .

HIDE AND SEEK

LORRAINE
P. DE SOSA

DIAMOND BOOKS, NEW YORK

HIDE AND SEEK

A Diamond Book / published by arrangement with
the author

PRINTING HISTORY
Diamond edition / February 1992

ISBN: 1-55773-658-8

Diamond Books are published by The Berkley Publishing Group,
200 Madison Avenue, New York, New York 10016.
The name "DIAMOND" and its logo are trademarks
belonging to Charter Communications, Inc.

PRINTED IN THE UNITED STATES OF AMERICA

10 9 8 7 6 5 4 3 2 1

Grateful thanks to everyone who helped get this book published. Leslie Gelbman, who opened the door; my editor, Gail Fortune, who guided me; my enthusiastic agent, Sherry Robb.

Special thanks to my mother, Virginia Passanante, for her love and encouragement; to my brothers and sisters, Donald Pusateri, Robert Pusateri, Kathryne Quentin, Suzanne Hodgkinson, their spouses and families, for their support; and to Teri Quevreaux for laughter between the pages.

In memory of
John A. Passanante

HIDE AND SEEK

prologue

Elizabeth Anderson awoke and sat up in bed. Her head was pounding and she felt nauseous. She took several deep breaths, willing her racing heart to slow down. She recognized the warning signals. It was always like this—ever since she became aware of her psychic powers.

As a teenager she had only been curious about her visions, but when they began to occur more often, she became afraid. She was twenty-five before she found a use for her curious gift, and over the next forty years she had helped many people, solving mysteries where others had failed. Sometimes the ending was happy, other times she had to deliver bad news. There had also been times when she couldn't help; no matter how hard she tried, the visions were too confusing, the images a blur, making no sense at all. And now, in her twilight years, the visions were unwelcomed.

This time it had started with a flash of a car speeding down a dark, twisting road, and she sensed that a child was involved. Something bad was going to happen. Something she couldn't stop.

Elizabeth glanced at the luminous dial of the clock on her nightstand. It was just after two. She raised her hands to her temples, massaging the throbbing pulses, her eyes closed. She felt an overwhelming sense of unhappiness, half-dreading the images that would come, but there were none. It was dawn before she finally fell asleep, the suffocating fear that someone was in danger lingering in the dark reaches of her mind.

friday

I

Emily Mitchelson stepped out of the school van and waved good-bye to her friends. She skipped up the driveway, wondering if her mother had come home from the movie studio yet. She entered the house by the side door, walked into the bright kitchen, and greeted the plump Guatemalan housekeeper.

"Hi, Socorro! Is mommy here?"

"No, *niña*," Socorro said. "She had two scenes to film today."

Emily sighed. She loved her mother very much, but sometimes she wished she could stay home and just be plain Mrs. Mitchelson, not Crystal Smythe, the famous movie star.

"What did you do at camp today?" Socorro asked.

"Look what I made for you," Emily said, handing Socorro a key chain she had made out of stretched rawhide strips.

"*Gracias, niña*. It's just what I needed," Socorro said, beaming at the child. The two long braids which hung down Emily's back were the same strawberry-blonde color as Crystal's, and the blue eyes and gentle features were carbon copies of her mother's. Emily was nine years old, intelligent and vivacious. She was still interested in dolls and thought boys were dumb. She didn't like punk music, and she preferred wearing dresses to blue jeans.

3

"So what else did you do?" Socorro asked, twirling the key chain.

"We played volleyball," Emily said, "and our team won."

"That's good."

Emily shrugged her indifference. "What's for lunch?"

"You wash your hands," Socorro told her, "and I'll fix you a grilled cheese sandwich."

II

They rolled on the bed, the shimmering white satin sheets a stark contrast to their golden tan bodies. He held her in his muscular arms, his hands slowly sliding down her shoulders, over her back. She gazed into his icy blue eyes, tracing a finger over the handsome face, the sculptured nose, the forceful chin, then ran her hands through his dark hair. She arched her back, rising up to meet him, panting her surrender.

"Oh, yes," she gasped. "Yes, my darling. I love you," she said, her voice trembling with desire as his lips closed on hers in a long, passionate kiss.

"Cut. That's a print," snapped Pierre Montbleau as he sank into his chair. "Finally," the director added in a low voice that was harsh with anger, checking his watch. It had been a long morning, and he had thought they would never get through it. The scene had been difficult to shoot, requiring a great deal of patience on his part since his leading man and lady were not on friendly terms. Crystal had actually refused to do the scene, and Pierre had had to use all his powers of persuasion to convince her that it was essential to the storyline. No matter how much she despised Jefferies, in her role as an undercover agent she was supposed to love him.

The cameramen began shutting down the lights on the closed set. Voices called back and forth, laughing and groaning about facing lunch in the Beechwood commissary. It was a standard joke that everything on the menu tasted like stale scripts.

Crystal sat up, quickly pulling the sheet over her breasts, scrutinizing her co-star.

"You're certainly all worked up," she said sarcastically, pointing to the sheet that was sticking up and moving with a mind of its own.

"You do that to me," he said, grinning wickedly, his lips parted to reveal a perfect set of white capped teeth. "How about my coming over to your place tonight, and we can finish what we started."

Crystal glared at him, outraged by his suggestion. John Jefferies was married to Anna Schuller, whose father, Melvin Schuller, owned Beechwood Studios. She would be happy when the film was completed. She had only agreed to do this movie out of loyalty to Melvin. And, of course, for the money. Jefferies might be good-looking, but he was a pest, and his acting was mediocre in her opinion. Luckily, they had one of the best directors in the business, and Pierre was handling Jefferies beautifully. Or as well as anyone could handle her co-star, she thought. This scene had been the worst since she had to play it in the buff. Or at least partially. She wore nude-colored panties, but nothing on top. Throughout her career she had managed to escape frontal nudity shots, and she wasn't about to start now. Not Crystal Smythe. Not for all the money in the world. She shuddered at the thought and turned to accept a rose silk dressing gown from the wardrobe assistant as she slid out of bed.

"What about your wife?" she asked, curious as to just how far he would go.

Jefferies winked broadly at Crystal. "Surely a small problem like that shouldn't stop us from having a little fun? What she doesn't know won't hurt her."

Crystal's voice was a low growl as she tied the sash around her waist and walked off to her dressing room. "Save your charm for the starlets."

The smile on Jefferies' face dissolved in anger. He didn't like being put down, especially in front of an audience—which in this case consisted of at least twenty people who were trying to look busy with equipment and scripts, their eyes downcast, afraid to look at John.

"Pretentious bitch," he muttered to himself, though his voice was strong enough to be heard on the Beechwood back lot. "Always acting like she's hot stuff. Thinks she's better than everyone else. I'd like to . . ."

Pierre approached the bed, a look of disapproval on his face. He was very unhappy. The film was five weeks behind schedule, and he was getting a lot of flak about it. He hadn't wanted this job, especially after he learned that Jefferies was going to be in the movie. Unfortunately, he needed the money. His two ex-wives were squeezing him for alimony, and his present wife was demanding a new car. If he could just get through this movie. Then he could go back to his beloved France for a well-deserved vacation.

He stared at his leading man. John Jefferies was a royal pain in the ass, and most of the delays were his fault. Like disappearing for a week. They finally found him in Tijuana, delirious from drugs and booze. It took them another week just to straighten him out.

"Your father-in-law wishes to speak to you, John. *A son avis, le film est mauvais,*" Pierre said, his dark eyes flashing his contempt.

John pulled on an Oriental kimono, removing cigarettes

and a Dunhill gold lighter from the pocket. "Translation, please."

"Melvin thinks the movie stinks, or rather, that you stink."

"I don't care what he thinks," John said gruffly. "I'm giving it my best shot. Besides, he knows this film will be a winner at the box office. That's all he worries about—the numbers."

Pierre stretched to his full height, five feet, four inches, which he augmented by two-inch lifts in his specially designed shoes. "It will be a winner because we have a good script, and because I am a good director, and because Crystal is a great actress, and because we have a fantastic cast of supporting actors. But you . . . you are just another pretty face, and don't forget, you can be replaced. The only reason you got this role," he spat out viciously, "is because you knocked up Melvin's daughter and she had to marry you."

"My last film grossed plenty."

"You had a very small supporting role. This time you are co-starring. You should try harder."

Pierre's attitude rankled John. "Are you saying there's something wrong with my acting?"

"Non-acting is more like it," Pierre said, his voice rising impatiently. "We have to reshoot every scene you are in at least ten to fifteen times. You blow your lines, you miss your cues, and Crystal has to carry every scene in which you appear together."

John knew the crew was eavesdropping, gathering bits and pieces to feed to the scandal sheet reporters. He lit his cigarette and snapped the lighter shut. "Bullshit! The bitch couldn't act herself out of a bread box."

Pierre shook his head. "As I have told you, Melvin wishes to see you in his office. Now."

"So all right, already," he mumbled. "I'm going."

"And be sure you're here on time Monday. Perhaps you might even study your lines this weekend—that is, if you're not too busy playing stud," Pierre shouted over his shoulder as he clumped off the set.

III

Emily watched Socorro roll out the crust for a lemon meringue pie, one of her favorites. "Did your mother work?" she asked.

"My mother was always working," Socorro replied as she slipped the crust into the pie tin and began fluting the edges. "I had three sisters and four brothers, and my mother had to take care of all of us. We were very poor, and my mother and father worked in the coffee fields. When the coffee was ready to harvest, my brothers and sisters and I helped to pick the beans off the trees."

"My mother isn't poor, but she works all the time."

"Your mother works because it is what she knows how to do best," Socorro said. "Don't you like to go to the movies and see your mother acting?"

"Daddy says mommy likes making movies better than being a mother."

Socorro shook her head. "When did your father say that?"

"When they were fighting. They didn't know I was listening."

Socorro frowned. She knew Emily was proud to be the daughter of someone so famous and beautiful, but the child was deeply disturbed by her parents' separation. Her father was an equally famous screenwriter, but now he lived at their Malibu beach house. Emily couldn't understand why her parents didn't love each other anymore. Although many of her friends' parents were divorced, she still hoped that her mother and father would get back together again. Emily prayed for it every night when she went to bed. Socorro did the same—the child needed both of her parents.

Socorro sat down and pulled Emily into her arms. "Sometimes people say things they don't really mean."

"Do you think they'll get a divorce?"

"No," Socorro said adamantly. "They love each other very much. And they love you, too. Don't you ever forget that."

"Then why do they argue all the time?"

"I don't know why," she admitted, giving Emily a hug. "Now stop asking such crazy questions so I can get my work done."

Socorro stood and put the pie crust into the oven, then began preparing the filling. Emily finished the last of her milk and carried her glass and plate to the sink.

"May I go outside to play?"

"*Sí, niña*," Socorro told her, "but don't go too far."

Emily picked up a book and her Barbie doll and walked outside, being careful not to let the door slam behind her. She walked down the driveway to wait for her mother; sometimes she came home early on Friday.

IV

Crystal returned to her dressing room and took a shower, scrubbing away the smell of John Jefferies, then washed and towel-dried her long strawberry-blonde hair. She spotted a gray hair and pulled it out, then ran her fingers through the soft waves, grateful that God had blessed her with naturally curly hair. No frizzled hair from too many permanents or bleach, but the hot lights, constant washing and drying, teasing, and hair spray had taken their toll.

Crystal checked her watch. She was due back in make-up in an hour for the scene she had to do that afternoon; at least it isn't with Jefferies, she thought. Something about him irritated her, and she'd noticed that everyone else on the set seemed to have a similar reaction. He was always staring at her with those cold, calculating eyes. When he spoke, his voice was a snarl, unfriendly, condescending. He carried a chip on his shoulder that had to weigh a ton. Crystal sensed an air of evilness about him, and it frightened her.

Poor Anna had come to the set one afternoon, and Crystal saw Jefferies rudely push his wife aside, screaming that she should stay home and not come spying on him. Why did Anna put up with it? Crystal wondered. Was she so much in love with him that she could ignore the rudeness?

Crystal sighed and picked up a jar of face cream. She slathered it on, massaging the skin outward, willing the wrinkles and creases to disappear. Love is so damn cruel, she reminded herself. Twice she had chosen the wrong man. Twice she had been burned. She had been completely disillusioned by love—until she met James Mitchelson. He had been so good to her, so sincere, so gentle, so loving. When he proposed she didn't hesitate. She had thought their marriage was perfect, that nothing could ever come between them. How foolish she had been. Though it was difficult, she was finally facing reality, reluctantly admitting that the break-up had been all her fault. She was well aware of the flaws in her personality. She was too strong-willed, and she had pushed Jimmy too far. But she would never tell him that.

Crystal hugged herself; she had made a mistake in letting her career destroy them. Was their marriage just another Hollywood statistic? They'd been separated too long, their only bond was their daughter. Poor Emily, Crystal thought. She's the one who's suffering because her parents are so stubborn. But it's too late now. Too late to be remorseful with so many pressing problems to deal with. The competition was tough, and she had to stay on her toes.

"I'm not going to give up my career now," Crystal said out loud, staring at her reflection in the bathroom mirror, wiping at the tears that welled in her eyes, "even if it means having to cope with a jerk like Jefferies. I've worked too damn hard to get to the top."

She dropped a tissue in the wastebasket and walked into the dressing room. Beechwood Studios believed in pampering its stars. The walls of the spacious room were covered with pale blue moire silk, and the carpet was a perfect match. The sofa, which opened out to a bed, and the plush easy chair were covered in a colorful chintz fabric. Fresh flowers in a cut-glass vase stood on the coffee table. Behind closet doors was ample space to hang clothes, and there was a television, stereo, refrigerator, microwave, and electric coffeepot. The only thing she didn't like about the room was that there were no windows.

Crystal surveyed her home away from home. She had added a few personal touches. A light cashmere throw was draped over one end of the sofa; favorite photographs were on the dressing table; a novel she had begun to read lay open on the end table next to the telephone. Since Crystal spent so much time at the studio, she was glad that her dressing room was so pleasant. It hadn't always been that way. While filming in Australia she'd been assigned a stall in a barn. On some movies it was a mobile trailer, on others, cramped rooms in which you could hardly breathe. Not at Beechwood; here even her bathroom was elaborate, with marble-topped counters and a padded toilet seat.

Crystal laughed. The studio gossips claimed Melvin Schuller had a penchant for padded seats because he suffered from hemorrhoids. Though he seldom came to

Crystal's dressing room, his comfort was assured in case he had to use the loo.

"Toilet," Crystal said out loud, reminding herself once again not to use the British word. It was hard to break old habits, though, and she admitted that sometimes she did it on purpose. It was part of her image. What the public didn't know was that Crystal had spent hours perfecting her English accent.

She stretched out on the sofa and munched on a sandwich of thin slices of chicken breast on rye bread while she went over her lines. Someone knocked on the door.

"Come in," Crystal called out.

Neil Simmons, her personal secretary and confidant, entered the room, smiling broadly.

"How's it going?" he asked, studying Crystal's face. Her wide, cornflower-blue eyes were fringed by pale lashes, and the high cheekbones of her delicate face emphasized the innocent and vulnerable look that had endeared Crystal to her fans. With the right make-up and her accomplished acting skills, she could play any role in the world. Vixen, royalty, sophisticate, southern belle, or Irish lass. Crystal's long hours with vocal coaches had paid off as well; she could imitate any accent.

Neil noticed how the silk dressing gown clung softly to her full curves, how her hips flowed from a narrow waist into long, slim, perfectly formed legs. Like everyone in the industry, Crystal was acutely aware of the importance of staying in shape. She rigorously maintained her perfect figure by exercising for at least a half hour at home each morning. Although various health clubs and promoters of exercise equipment had tried to sign her up as a spokesperson, Crystal refused to endorse anything she didn't personally use.

She had also turned down huge offers for promoting a

trendy clothing line, a perfume bearing her name, and designer eyeglasses.

"I'm an actress. To use a movie star's name on a product is vulgar," Crystal always said.

Neil thought Crystal was a snob at times and that some day she'd be right there with all the other actresses and actors whose faces appeared in the glitzy advertisements of *Vogue* and *Town & Country*. But he kept his opinion to himself, fully aware that he wasn't paid to give advice. His role was companion, secretary, and, when she needed it, a shoulder to cry on.

Crystal tossed her script on the coffee table. "God, Jefferies is such a jerk. We did that scene *ten times* today, and every time he touched me I wanted to throw up."

"Poor baby," Neil said, his voice properly tinged with sympathy. "Do you have another scene with him today?"

"No, thank God," Crystal said, combing her hands through her still-damp hair. "I'm doing the one with the lawyer. Since I'll be wearing a hat, I'm not worried about my hair, but make-up will probably insist on doing something with it."

"Let them earn their bucks," Neil said, clicking his teeth.

Crystal ignored the annoying habit which he had acquired during the past year. She suspected Neil did it on purpose, but she was tired of having to constantly remind him that his little habit was slowly driving her mad.

"You know, I'm thinking of cutting it off."

Neil stared at her, shocked. It was the first time she had ever hinted at doing something so foolish. "Why on earth would you do that? That mane is your trademark."

"I think I need a new image."

"Why do women think they have to cut their hair as soon as they hit forty?"

Crystal smiled coyly. "According to the fan magazines,

I'm only thirty-five. Anyhow, I think I'd look good in short hair."

Neil shook his head. "I don't."

"Remember when Raquel Welch cut hers? And how about Cher? They dared to be different," Crystal said. "Look at Meryl Streep. She has a hundred different hair images. That's why she gets so many roles."

Neil didn't dare suggest the truth—that her rival might be a better actress. Crystal would think it a betrayal on his part.

"Don't be ridiculous. She gets the roles because audiences like her voice," he said, taking the safer route. "Besides which, she's probably just as envious of you."

"Do you really think so?"

"Undoubtedly," Neil said, "and I strongly suggest you leave the tresses alone. You should consider yourself lucky that you have such thick hair."

"I hate it. And I found another gray hair today. I think I should start changing the color now so that people won't notice it so much when I do go gray."

Neil knew she was just fishing for a compliment and a little assurance that she wasn't growing old. "That's insane. It'll be easier to keep up your original color, and no one will ever know."

"You're sure?"

"Trust me," he said while buffing his nails on his coat sleeve. "You forget I was once a hairdresser."

"I haven't forgotten."

"You know, there are several of your contemporaries who are practically bald," he said in a low voice, being playfully mysterious.

"Who?" Crystal prodded, knowing that Neil's information was usually accurate.

"Well, darling, rumor has it that a certain femme fatale,

an over-fifty star who you sat next to at last week's benefit, uses wigs all the time."

Crystal raised an eyebrow in Neil's direction. "Over-sixty, you mean. What I want to know is how many face-lifts she's had."

"I'll have to check with my sources," Neil said, chuckling appreciatively as he adjusted the cuffs of his shirt, making sure the gold cuff links could be seen below the silk jacket sleeves. "One thing for sure, everyone in tinsel town likes to gossip."

"I hope not about me."

"Especially about you," Neil said, glancing in the mirror above Crystal's dressing table. He ran a hand through his perfectly groomed light brown hair, which he streaked to maintain the California surfer look. Satisfied with his appearance, he turned back to Crystal. "Everyone wants to know your secrets, but I'm saving all the hot items for the book I plan to write."

"Gee, thanks," Crystal groaned in mock desperation. Neil often said he was going to write an "unauthorized" biography about her, but Crystal didn't think he would ever actually do it. Sure, he knew her secrets, but she knew some of his, too. Of course she had a lot more to lose, but how could she ever doubt his loyalty? He was the perfect secretary, irreplaceable in her life, and their friendship had lasted through her two marriages.

"What did you do today?" she asked, changing the subject.

Neil sat at the dressing table and reached into his sports jacket for his notebook. He uncapped his gold Cross pen, a gift from Crystal on his last birthday. At least she's generous, he thought, not whiny and pretentious like a lot of other Hollywood stars.

Of course she hadn't always been a star. *He* remembered

when things had been different. When Crystal had worked for *him*. But that was long ago. Before her success, her fame, her money. Their roles had reversed, and for a while it had been fun, but the glamour and glitter of his position had finally worn off. It was time to move on to something else. Neil wanted to be in business for himself, and he had finally found a super location for a health spa. It would cost a great deal of money, but he had three investors ready to take the plunge. All he needed now was to come up with his share. Knowing how Crystal avoided publicity, it would be useless to ask for her support. And a loan was out of the question. No one knew that Crystal had a miserly streak that would make Scrooge look like a spendthrift. She was proud that she had made it to the top without ever borrowing a penny, and she thought everyone else should do likewise. Still he had to figure out how to get the capital he needed. And soon. The option he had on the building was running out. He only had one more week to come up with the money.

He realized Crystal was staring at him, waiting for an answer. He flipped open his notebook, an unnecessary gesture since he knew what was written there, but he felt it gave an air of importance to his job.

"I picked up your new stationery, sent flowers to thank the Schullers for the dinner party, and bought you two dozen pair of hose in various shades at I. Magnin's. They were on sale," he said, knowing that Crystal loved a bargain.

"Any mail?"

"The usual fan mail, the light bill, and two invitations."

"To what?" Crystal asked, leaning back on the sofa, her eyes closed.

"The AIDS celebrity fund-raiser and a housewarming next weekend."

"Whose?"

"The Ballwins. They've having, quote, a small party to celebrate the completion of their weekend hideaway in Santa Barbara. If I know your friends, half of Hollywood will be there," he said wryly. "They invited Emily, too."

Crystal smiled at the prospect. Ted Ballwin was one of Hollywood's premier directors, and his wife Peggy was her closest friend. Their marriage was solid, unmarred by the mad world of the business. They also had five children whom they doted on outrageously. Ted had been around the world, directing films starring beautiful women, but there were never any rumors of affairs surrounding his name. Peggy didn't have a jealous bone in her body; she admired her husband's talent and loved Ted with a grand passion. Peggy was perfectly content to sit at home and take care of their children.

Sometimes Crystal was envious of her friend's happiness. She often wondered why she and Jimmy couldn't have worked things out. She felt guilty about not having returned Peggy's calls, and realized that it had been over a month since their last visit. As always, her schedule had been frantic. There had been meetings with her lawyer, then with her business manager, and she'd been busy on the set with the new movie. What little time she had left she spent with Emily. There just wasn't enough time for her friends.

"I didn't realize the house was so close to being done," she said. "Am I free?"

Neil consulted his notebook. "There's nothing on your agenda."

"Good. Do me a favor. Call Peggy for me and say yes. And be sure she gives you instructions on how to get there. I don't want to drive around in circles looking for the place."

"You'll have to call Jimmy."

Crystal frowned. Since their separation, Emily spent every other weekend at her father's beach house or on his sailboat.

"He'll probably be angry," Crystal remarked, "but I'll deal with him. Besides, he's getting her for the whole month of August. What lousy timing! The movie will be finished by then."

"Don't begrudge Jimmy one month," Neil scolded her. "After all, you've had her the past seven months."

Crystal sighed. "I guess you're right."

"Peggy has probably invited Jimmy so you can all be together. One happy, loving family."

"Fat chance of that happening, but you're right," she admitted. "Jimmy will be invited since he's their friend, too. Peggy has been trying to get us back together. She's so obvious about it."

"Maybe she's doing you a favor."

"I wish everyone would mind their own business," Crystal said impatiently. "Of course I want Jimmy back, but on *my* terms, not his. Why does he have to be so damn stubborn? Why can't he love me without insisting on changing everything?"

"You're emoting, my dear," Neil said, by now used to her outbursts whenever Jimmy's name came up. "Admit it. You blew your little spat into a major argument, and now you don't know how to get yourself out of the mess you created."

Crystal hated it when Neil acted so smug. "You don't know what you're talking about. As you may recall, Jimmy walked out on me!"

"*After* you kicked him out of the house."

"I did not," Crystal said adamantly.

Neil realized he had pushed Crystal too far. She would never admit she had been wrong.

"What about the fund-raiser?" he asked, leading the conversation away from the touchy subject of love.

Crystal studied his once-handsome face. A scar zig-zagged across his forehead, down over one hazel eye, then along his right cheek. Though Crystal had offered to pay for plastic surgery, Neil preferred keeping his scar. He said it gave him character.

"Are you free to go with me?" she asked.

"Yes, I'm free," Neil said grudgingly. He had checked his calendar—he had a party to go to that night—but Crystal's plans always took precedence over his own. That would change soon enough, he thought, once his deal went through. Until then he wouldn't rock the boat.

Crystal smiled to herself, pleased he would be her escort. She hated going anywhere alone, and Neil was the perfect date. He might be gay, but he could play the supermacho role when and if he wanted.

"I suppose I'll have to buy a new evening gown," Crystal said as she took a final bite of her sandwich.

"Perhaps we can shop tomorrow," Neil suggested. Crystal hated to shop alone. She would try on countless dresses, unable to settle on one, then ask him to choose.

Crystal wiped her mouth and tossed the napkin on the table. "I promised Emily I would take her to the zoo this weekend," she said. "I hate to disappoint her, but I guess we can go on Sunday instead. God, I hope it won't be crowded."

A knock on the door interrupted them. "They need you in make-up, Miss Smythe."

"Coming," she called out, then drained her orange juice. "Back to the salt mines."

"Do you want me to wait for you?"

Crystal stood, pulling the sash of her robe tight. "No.

When I finish this scene I'm going home. Tomorrow will be fine."

"I'll be at my place if you need me . . . answering your fan mail." Neil rolled his eyes, feigning exhaustion, as he walked out the door.

Crystal laughed, knowing it was an act. He said he enjoyed reading the letters and replied promptly, including a personal note with her photograph. He even signed her name with a flourish, a practice which was commonplace in the industry.

She was keenly aware of how helpful Neil was, knowing she would be at a loss without him to sort through all the minor daily problems of her life. She picked up her script and followed him out the door. Hopefully the next few hours would race by, and she could get home before the evening rush hour. And after dinner she would play Monopoly with Emily.

"That'll make up for tomorrow," Crystal murmured to herself, assuaging her guilt about neglecting her daughter.

V

Jefferies walked into his dressing room fuming. He slammed the door shut, then crossed to the refrigerator and took the chilled bottle of Stolichnaya from the freezer compartment. He poured himself a hefty drink, drank it down, and refilled the glass.

He took his anger out on the refrigerator, kicking it. Once again Melvin had berated him, this time saying it was *his* fault the movie had fallen behind schedule. Just because he had gone fishing in Baja. If it had been Crystal who had taken off, old Melvin wouldn't be making such a fuss. The fucking Goddamn "star" couldn't do anything wrong. Crystal was perfect. The golden girl.

On the other hand, Melvin had told Jefferies that if he didn't shape up, this would be the last movie he'd ever make at Beechwood Studios. Still he knew he could get other work. The studio's publicity mill had been hard at work building him up, and his agent was getting calls. Soon every producer in town would be knocking at his door. And, hell, he might even take a shot at directing his own movies. If Michael Douglas could star in a film and direct it, too, then why not John Jefferies.

He slumped onto the day bed, which was covered in leopard print silk sheets. Jungle scenes were painted on the walls, and lush tropical plants filled the room. He liked bringing people here, impressing them, especially the extras and would-be starlets, who were all eager to please John Jefferies. He should have been happy. Instead he was miserable.

God! What a mess! It had all started when he'd gone to the Schullers' house for that party. He'd done some coke on the way there, then drank too much champagne. And then, somehow, Anna Schuller had gotten him down to the pool house and raped him. Yeah! It was rape all right; he never would have touched her if he hadn't been drunk. She was ugly then, and she was uglier now. And fat. He shuddered at the thought. Her pregnancy had made her balloon up like a cow. No. More like an elephant.

It was so unfair. He had no interest in being a father and felt absolutely nothing for the child Anna would soon bear. He had only married her because Melvin's goons had broken his finger and told him his face was next. They had been very convincing. So he wound up married to the heir to the throne, except Melvin would probably outlive them all. Or find some way to make sure John Jefferies wouldn't run Beechwood Studios. So who needed the old man and his studio and his money. For over twenty-five years

Jefferies had worked his ass off, playing second- and third-lead roles, but marriage to Anna had fixed that. Melvin gave them an elaborate wedding reception and most of Hollywood came, groveling at the mogul's feet, jumping at a snap of his fingers, paying homage to one of the biggest men in tinsel town. Melvin had taken him aside. "Make my Anna happy and I'll do things for your career."

John had taken it as a warning more than a gift. But the old man had come through. So Melvin gives him a part in a movie starring Crystal, and today he finds out she's making five times his salary! Plus points!

He hated Melvin, but he hated Crystal even more. "What a bitch," he growled, pounding the pillow, the venom eating at him. He was still pissed about the way she had put him down on the set. What was worse was the way she managed to ignore him, like he wasn't there. All sweetness and how-de-do with the other actors, kissing ass with the director, chumming it up with the cameramen so she'd get the best shots. He could see right through her. He'd been working in the industry long enough to know the ropes, and he didn't have to put up with this shit.

He wished he could do something to bring her down a peg or two. Something that would screw up her life so much that she would quit the movie. How sweet it would be to sabotage the film so it couldn't be completed. It would pay Melvin back for putting him down and making him marry Anna. But what could he do that wouldn't put his own career in jeopardy? If only there was a way . . . He'd do anything to wipe that smile off her face, anything to scare the shit out of her. If only Crystal would fall and break a leg. Or have a car crash and die, he thought maliciously.

Or what if her dressing room caught on fire while she was in it. There was plenty of flammable materials on a movie set. Paint thinner would do the trick. If he could figure out how to do it without someone seeing him.

No. It was too dangerous. Too many people around. He might get caught, and he didn't really want to kill her. Just maim her a little, he thought, smiling maliciously. He would think of something else. Something to put a stop to Crystal and the movie. Something horrible.

VI

Emily closed her book and stretched out on the grass. She squinted up at the sky, then stood and picked up her doll. She walked down the street to the Millers' house and rang the doorbell. "Is Mary Sue at home?" she asked the maid.

"No, they went down to Palm Springs for the weekend," the woman answered.

Emily thanked her and started back down the front walk, then stopped to watch the Mexican gardener as he trimmed hedges. She said hello, but he only grunted something in Spanish and ignored her.

Emily returned to her own front yard and sprawled on the ground. She plucked a piece of grass and tried to whistle through it like one of the counselors at camp had shown her, but couldn't quite do it. She was debating whether to go inside to watch television when she noticed the car. It slowed down and stopped at the curb.

"Hi, Emily," the driver called to her.

Emily smiled, recognizing him, and ran to the car. "Hi."

"Your mother has a special surprise planned for you," he said. "I'm supposed to take you to her."

"What kind of a surprise?"

"Can't tell you," he said, "besides, it wouldn't be much of a surprise if you knew, would it?"

"I guess not."

He opened the door for her. "Come on. Get in."

Emily hesitated and turned to look back at the house. "I don't know. Maybe I should tell Socorro."

"Don't worry," he said, smiling broadly. "Your mother already did."

"Oh! Okay," she said, sliding onto the seat, wondering what kind of surprise her mother was planning.

VII

Elizabeth Anderson pricked her finger on the roses she was arranging in an ornate silver vase, but the sting wasn't as annoying as the persistent feeling that something had happened which would involve her somehow. Something bad. Something she couldn't stop.

Every time was different, but she knew that her psychic visions would soon begin, and then she could start piecing the puzzle together. There was only one problem. She was growing old, and it was getting harder and harder to read the clues and find the solution. She wanted to stop, but her brain acted like a magnet, picking up strange signals and messages. Sometimes voices came to her from across long distances, or vivid pictures would flash through her mind. Other times it was just a feeling of ugliness or something evil that wrapped itself around her. By the time Elizabeth was able to put the bits and pieces together, she would be drained of all energy. In the past few years it had only happened twice. Why now? she wondered.

Vague images of a child, a man, and a fast car swirled through her subconscious. Where were they going? Were they in danger? Would the car crash? How could she help them when she didn't know who they were?

Elizabeth closed her eyes, hoping the vision would

continue, but it was a useless effort. The moment had passed.

VIII

Crystal returned to her dressing room elated. The scene had gone well, shot in just four takes. She took off the hat and suit she had worn in the scene and slipped into slim blue jeans and a white silk shirt. She sat at her dressing table, tucked a hand towel inside her shirt collar, and began removing the thick screen make-up. She was looking forward to the weekend. Shopping tomorrow, then maybe she would take Emily to a movie in the evening. She knew how much Emily would like that. Sunday they would go to the zoo and do anything else Emily wanted. It would be a great weekend, and maybe they would barbecue some hamburgers Sunday night. Crystal would have to find time to memorize her dialogue for the scenes on Monday, but like many good actors she was a quick study and learned her lines easily.

She smiled to herself, remembering how her teachers back in Cape Mary, Maine, had been so sure she was cheating on her school tests because she always knew the answers. But it was her total recall of what she read which had helped her become a straight-A student. There had been talk about a scholarship to Wellesley, but Crystal Meghan Smythe knew she had to get away from Cape Mary. She was determined to become a movie star.

Crystal had been born in Folkstone, England, a small town southeast of London on the English Channel, but she had lived there a relatively short time. When she was twelve years old her parents were killed in an automobile crash. After they were buried she went to Cape Mary, Maine, to live with her maternal grandmother.

Although her grandmother was a gentle woman, she was far too old to cope with a young girl. Crystal found comfort in a fantasy world of her own making. When she entered high school, she discovered a new world of make-believe—the stage. She built scenery, painted backdrops, and began acting in class productions. The dream began to grow. She worked at the candy counter of the local movie theater, and night after night she studied the films, acting out the different roles, convinced she could become a movie star. Three days after graduation she was on a bus to Hollywood.

Her grandmother cried and pleaded with her not to go. Crystal hated to leave her, but Cape Mary had nothing to offer other than marriage to Ray Morrill, her high school sweetheart, and he was only interested in football and going to work in the bait-and-tackle shop his father ran down by the cove. It was not the life she wanted.

Crystal had returned to that small Maine town only twice: once to bury her grandmother, and the second time to attend the ceremony renaming the local movie theater in her honor. She usually played down those years in Cape Mary, preferring to let her public believe she had jumped right from the British theater to Hollywood films.

That was far from the truth. It had been a hard struggle. But she had won. She remembered when she arrived in Los Angeles. She had five hundred dollars in her pocket, and although she was slightly anxious, she still felt confident that she would succeed.

She had taken a taxi to the corner of Hollywood and Vine and followed the bronze stars set in the concrete sidewalk, fantasizing that someday one of the stars would bear her name. Stopping in front of Mann's Chinese Theater, Crystal had glanced up at the marquee and pictured her name in lights.

Then she had walked down Hollywood Boulevard to the

small diner she had spotted earlier. She sat at the counter, eating a hamburger while reading the *Hollywood Reporter*. That was when Peggy Mason had asked her to pass the ketchup. When Crystal told her new friend that she wanted to be an actress, Peggy quickly confessed that she, too, had hopes of becoming a movie star.

Peggy was full of advice on how to get started, and she promised Crystal an introduction to her agent. She was soon leading Crystal down the street, on a course that would change her life and finally bring her stardom.

Crystal sighed as she wiped away the last traces of make-up from her face. She didn't like thinking about those early years, especially the ugly parts. It had been a hard climb to fame. There were times when she was ready to admit defeat, yet something had kept her going.

Crystal studied her image in the mirror. She was tired of pretending there was nothing wrong in her life. She needed a rest, to get away for a while so she could think. She missed Jimmy and she wanted him back in her life. Somehow that didn't seem possible unless she was willing to make a compromise. Maybe it was time to seriously consider doing a television series. Her agent was always getting offers, and she had read some scripts. The hours per day were the same, but once committed to a series she'd be less tempted to go from one movie to the next. Most of her movies involved traveling, going on location. At least with a series she'd be able to stay in town, and there would be a break at the end of the season—time to spend with Emily and Jimmy.

Crystal shook her head. "Who am I kidding?" she said to herself. She wasn't ready for a series. Not even made-for-TV movies. She liked being up there on the big screen. She liked being a movie queen. She ran a brush through her hair, then carefully applied lipstick. She stood and gathered

her script and purse. If she hurried, she might beat the
traffic.

IX

"How much farther?" Emily asked, wondering why they
were driving so far away from the city.

"We'll be there soon enough," he said, wishing she
would stop asking questions. When would they get there?
Where was he taking her? How come mommy wasn't
working at the movie studio this afternoon? It was making
him edgy, and he had enough on his mind.

He still didn't know what he was going to do with Emily.
When he saw her walking down the street, it had suddenly
come to him. He would take Emily. That was as far as his
plan went. Now he had to decide what to do. He braked as
he slowed at the freeway turn-off. Traffic had been heavy
but not unusual for a Friday afternoon.

Emily pointed to a road sign. "Is that where we're
going?" she asked. "Are we going to the beach? I didn't
bring my swimsuit."

"No. Not today," he said. "Maybe tomorrow."

Emily set her doll on the dashboard. "When are we going
to get there?" she asked once again.

"Soon," he replied. "Very soon."

X

It was almost seven by the time Crystal pulled into the
garage. She was happy to be home. A five-car accident on
the Hollywood Freeway had stopped traffic, and she had sat
impatiently while tow trucks worked to clear the lanes. She
made a mental note to have the Mercedes tuned up, washed,
and waxed the following morning. She would call Neil and

tell him to meet her at the dealership. She walked into the house, savoring the smell of the roast Socorro had prepared.

"*Buenas tardes*, Socorro. Where's Emily?"

The housekeeper looked up from the salad she was preparing, then glanced at the clock. "I don't know. I guess she is upstairs in her room."

"Dinner smells wonderful, and I'm famished. How soon until it's done?"

"Whenever you're ready. Would you like a cocktail?"

"Yes, please. A martini."

"With three olives?" Socorro smiled, already knowing the answer.

Crystal laughed. "*Sí, por favor*," she replied.

In the twelve years that Socorro had worked as her maid, Crystal had learned passable Spanish. In exchange, Socorro's English was near-perfect, a result of a constant desire to improve herself. The soft Guatemalan accent lingered, a reminder that Socorro had once lived in a foreign land. She often regaled Crystal and Emily with stories of her country, stories that were filled with fascinating customs and beliefs. Crystal had promised Emily that they would go to Guatemala to see the ancient ruins and visit with Socorro's family. But when? Her schedule was so busy, and the summer was half over. Obviously it won't be this year, Crystal thought.

She walked into the hallway, calling for Emily. As always, the Colonial brick house was spotlessly clean, the wood smelling of lemon polish, cut flowers artfully arranged in a vase on the mahogany side table. Getting no response, Crystal climbed the wide stairs that curved up from the foyer and walked into her daughter's bedroom.

Crystal's memory of the barren walls of her bedroom in her grandmother's home had compelled her to paper Emily's room in a delicate rose pattern. White ruffled curtains hung from the window, matching the four-poster bed's canopy. A cornucopia of stuffed animals filled the room, and a two-story Victorian dollhouse sat in the corner. Emily wasn't there. Nor was she in Crystal's bedroom, the guest room, or the office.

Crystal returned to the kitchen. "She's not upstairs. Where do you think she went?"

Socorro dried her hands on a towel. "She came home from camp, ate some lunch, and went outside to play. She must have forgotten what time it is."

Crystal picked up her martini and went into the adjacent den. Although the living room and dining room of the house had been furnished with exquisite antique pieces, the den was the room they used every day. A David Hockney painting, spotlighted by track lighting, hung on the wall behind the gray corduroy sofa. Blue leather-and-chrome easy chairs faced the sofa across a large glass-topped coffee table. A big-screen television, stereo equipment, and books vied for space on the shelves which lined the far wall. The fourth wall had floor-to-ceiling sliding glass doors which opened to the garden.

The Best Actress Oscar which Crystal had won two years earlier sat in the center of the coffee table. Scripts and magazines were strewn haphazardly around it, adding to the lived-in feeling of the room. Crystal patted the head of the golden statue, a superstitious habit she had acquired when she won her first Oscar for Best Supporting Actress. That one was on the living room mantelpiece. Another Best Actress Oscar stood on a pedestal in the dining room. Crystal had told her friends she planned to have one in every room of the house, a statement that might come true since her last film was winning the hearts of everyone who saw it. The producer had already approached her about a two-picture deal. Of course it all depended upon how the Academy members voted, but she thought she stood a good chance. It had been two years since her last win, and another Oscar would assure her future roles. Or at least she hoped so.

Crystal set her martini down on the coffee table and walked out into the garden, wondering where her daughter could be. Emily was usually at the door, waiting to greet her.

Crystal suddenly felt chilled. She hugged herself as fearful images crept in on her sense of contentment. She walked the perimeter of the pool. It was unlikely that Emily had fallen in, and even if she had, Emily was a strong swimmer. She sighed with relief; the pool was empty.

Socorro came to the patio door. "I looked for Emily in the front yard. Here's the book she was reading, but I can't find her."

"I'll call Mary Sue's house. She's probably over there," Crystal said, returning to the den. She sat on the sofa, shifting the needlepoint pillows she had made while in her dressing room waiting to face the cameras. They had duck, quail and pheasant motifs—their designs chosen because Jimmy was an avid hunter.

Crystal reached for the telephone on the end table and dialed Mary Sue's house. The maid informed her that the Millers were out of town, but that Emily had been there earlier. Crystal hung up, puzzled. She sipped her drink nervously, then stood and went into the kitchen. Socorro was whipping mashed potatoes.

"Could you hold dinner for a while? Emily's not at the Millers'," she said, frowning. "I'll check the other neighbors. Maybe she's at one of their houses."

"Shall I go look?"

Crystal shook her head. "No. You stay here; I don't want Emily to come home and not find one of us here."

Crystal went from house to house, ringing bells insistently, getting the same reply: Emily wasn't there. Apprehension swept through Crystal. Finally she returned to the house and checked the garage, but Emily's bike was in the corner.

"My God, where is she?" Crystal groaned, her voice echoing in the silent garage.

She went back into the house, shivering from fear as she walked into the den. There was no putting it off. She grabbed the telephone and punched the number for the Beverly Hills police.

"This is Crystal Smythe. I want to speak to someone about . . . about my daughter." She gulped, feeling the tears roll down her face. "She's missing."

"Crystal Smythe the movie star?" the female voice came back at her, the tone doubtful.

"Yes," she said impatiently. "I need a policeman. My daughter is missing."

"Are you sure she's missing? Have you checked with her friends?"

"Look," Crystal growled angrily, "my daughter is only nine years old, and I've checked with all my neighbors. She's disappeared! I can't find her!"

"I'm sure she'll turn up."

"And if she doesn't? What if she was kidnapped?" Crystal sobbed as new fears crossed her mind.

The operator took her address and promised that a policeman would be sent immediately to investigate. "Try to stay off the telephone, Miss Smythe. Your daughter could be trying to reach you."

"I have call-waiting," she sharply informed her.

"Even so, it's best to keep the lines free."

"Could you please hurry?" Crystal implored the operator, but was answered by the dial tone.

She hung up and stared at her trembling hands, then

reached for her martini and downed the rest, savoring the warming effect. With a start, she realized she wasn't being logical. Emily was probably with Neil.

"He must have changed his mind and come back to the house for her," she said out loud. She picked up the telephone and called Neil's home, ignoring the operator's warning.

"Please be there," she entreated as the phone rang. After the tenth ring, she finally hung up.

Socorro entered the den. "I don't know where Emily is," she said as tears coursed down her chubby cheeks. "I don't understand it. She said she was just going outside to play."

"I called Neil, but he's not at home," Crystal said. "Are you sure he didn't come back here for her?"

Socorro shook her head. "I don't think so. He always tells me when he is going to take her someplace. What are we going to do?" she sobbed.

"The police are on their way. They'll find Emily," Crystal told her, trying to sound convincing, though she was chilled to the bone with fear.

Melvin had told her that she needed more protection, but Crystal didn't want to live behind high walls and steel bars. Rather than keeping people out, it would make her feel she was being locked in. The house had a state-of-the-art security system, and she had believed it was enough to keep prowlers out.

Unfortunately, she hadn't considered the dangers that might lurk outside her home. Crystal had believed Emily was protected because she rode to and from school, and to her summer camp in a school van which stopped in front of the house. Besides, Emily knew she wasn't permitted to wander any farther than the Millers' house, or to the street corner if she was riding her bike. Why hadn't she obeyed?

Crystal couldn't remember if she had ever told Emily not

to speak to strangers. Had Jimmy? Didn't kids learn that in school? Weren't they warned about talking to strangers, about saying no to drugs, and not to . . .

"Dear God, please let her be all right. Please let me find her. Please," Crystal silently prayed.

Then she suddenly thought, what if Jimmy had decided to pick up Emily. What if he had taken her to pay Crystal back. Would he do something as mean as that? Tears coursed down her cheeks as she remembered. Just a week ago they'd argued about their daughter, over something as foolish as letting Emily get her ears pierced. Jimmy was opposed. Crystal said he was being unreasonable, insisting she would have it done. Crystal couldn't understand why they constantly argued, or why they made Emily a pawn in their malicious game. She knew it was wrong—so why did she allow it to happen?

Crystal picked up the phone and called Jimmy. When she reached his answering machine, she cursed and waited for the message to end.

"Call me as soon as you get in. It's urgent," she said angrily, hating talking to a machine.

Crystal stood and began pacing around the room. A flash of light caught her eye, and she turned to the patio doors. The sun was setting, and the automatic timers had switched on, flooding the garden and pool with light, reminding Crystal of the late hour.

"Where is she?" Crystal whispered, frightened by the terrifying thoughts that filled her mind.

The door bell rang, and Crystal rushed through the house to the front door. She welcomed the sight of two uniformed policemen.

"Thank God, you're here. I can't find my daughter," she shouted. "Do something."

"Calm down, Miss Smythe," one of the officers said as

another car pulled into the driveway. They waited for a heavy-set man to join them. His step was energetic, his jowled face marked by deep-brown eyes under bushy eyebrows, his hair shorn close to the scalp.

"I'm Lieutenant Detective Howard Wright, ma'am. You reported that your daughter is missing?"

"Yes. I mean, no. I don't know," Crystal cried. "Emily came home from camp, ate lunch, then went out to play. She hasn't come home."

"Take it easy," Wright said patiently. "Let's think this out. Have you checked with your neighbors?"

"Yes. I asked at every house on the block. No one has seen her except the maid at the Millers' house. Emily went there looking for her girl friend, but she wasn't home," Crystal explained, her voice cracking. "I'm so afraid. Do you think someone has taken her?" she asked, clutching at his jacket sleeve.

"I don't know, ma'am. Could you give me a description of your daughter?" Wright asked.

"She's nine years old, has blonde hair in pigtails, blue eyes, and is four feet tall," Crystal said in a rush, remembering the ruled marks along the closet door that she and Emily periodically made to record her height. "She weighs about seventy-five pounds, and she's wearing a white top and shorts and tennis shoes. Her T-shirt has a picture of a tree and the words 'Camp Hawthorne' on it in green lettering."

"How about a photo?" Wright asked.

"Of course," Crystal said, racing to the den and returning with a photograph. "This one was taken about three months ago."

Wright turned to the two policemen. "You know the routine. Knock on doors, ask permission to search. Check every room, cellar, attic, and backyard of all the houses on the block. Look inside garages and check the cars, too."

The policemen flicked on their flashlights and disappeared down the street. "May I come inside?" Wright asked.

"Yes, please do," Crystal said, leading him back to the den.

She telephoned Neil's house, needing something to do, hoping he might have come home, but there was still no answer. "Damn!" she said as she slammed down the receiver. Neil refused to buy an answering machine, believing that if anyone really needed to speak to him, they could call back. Crystal now realized that she should have insisted that he buy one.

Wright took a pen and notebook out of his pocket. "Who were you calling?" he asked.

"My secretary. He's not at home."

Wright gave her a sidelong glance. "He?"

"Yes, male. His name is Neil Simmons," Crystal snapped. "I thought he was going home."

"Perhaps your daughter is with him?" Wright suggested.

"Yes, I've thought of that, but I don't believe she's with him. When I saw him at the studio this afternoon, he said he was going home. He wouldn't take Emily anywhere without telling me. Or at least I don't think he would," she said as she slumped down on the sofa.

Simmons is probably gay, Wright thought as he wrote the name, address, and phone number in his notebook, adding his special notation for suspect number one. If the officers didn't find the girl, he would cruise by the secretary's home and check him out.

The Lieutenant wandered around the room, admiring the many awards, studying photographs which crowded the bookshelves. Most of them were of Crystal with famous movie celebrities. There was even one with the President at a White House dinner. Others were of Emily at different ages, and several included Crystal and a man who was probably the father, Wright decided.

Socorro entered the room and placed a heavy silver tray on the table. She nervously poured coffee, the cup rattling in the saucer.

"Do you take cream?" she asked Wright.

"No, black. I'm trying to cut down on my calories," he said amicably, trying to ease the tension in the room. He sat on one of the leather chairs and sipped cautiously from the steaming cup, then set it down. He opened his notebook.

"Are you married, Miss Smythe?"

"My husband is James Mitchelson," she said, "but we're separated. I called Jimmy, but he's not at home. I left a message on his answering machine."

"Is it possible that your husband came to pick up your daughter?" he asked.

Crystal clenched and unclenched her hands. "I don't think so. This isn't his weekend, and besides, the last time I spoke to him, I distinctly told him I was taking Emily to the zoo."

Wright noticed the hesitation in her voice. There could be a custody battle going on, he thought, so he wasn't going to rule out the father taking his daughter. It happened often enough, even in Beverly Hills households. The rich and famous were no different from anyone else when it came to legal battles over who got the kids.

"Are you and your husband in a divorce proceeding?"

"No," Crystal said emphatically, resenting his intrusion in her personal life.

Wright sensed her anger. "It's my job to ask."

Crystal realized she was overreacting. She was so afraid of gossip columnists, or worse yet, the nightmare of seeing her name in the scandal sheets. "My husband and I decided a trial separation would be beneficial to our marriage," she said, feeling that an explanation was necessary.

Wright was a fan of Crystal Smythe and felt sorry for her. He certainly didn't want a kidnapping case on his hands. He hoped the kid turned up in the neighborhood. Or even that the father had taken her.

"Have you and your husband fought about who should have custody of your daughter?"

"No. Of course not," Crystal hurriedly assured him. "There has never been any disagreement over Emily. We both love our daughter very much. We didn't want to upset Emily's routine, so she lives here and spends every other weekend with her father. He's been staying at our beach house in Malibu."

Wright listened to the words, but his trained eye told him more. Crystal had flushed bright pink, a sure sign she was lying. Or feeling guilty about something. Obviously she wasn't telling the whole story. Wright added Mitchelson's phone number and address in his notebook. He also made a notation for suspect number two, though he thought it seemed unlikely. He then called the house, but Mitchelson still didn't answer.

The minutes ticked away slowly as Crystal talked about Emily and answered the Lieutenant's questions. At long last the doorbell rang, and Socorro escorted one of the policemen into the den.

Crystal sprang to her feet. "Have you found Emily?"

"We looked everywhere, checked with all the immediate neighbors, but no one has seen her," he informed them.

"We'll assume she's lost and continue searching the area," Wright told Crystal. "It's highly unlikely that we can overlook her in a neighborhood like this."

"What if someone . . . What if a sex . . . sexual

pervert took her?" Crystal asked, stammering over the hateful words.

"It's a remote possibility," Wright said. "But you don't usually find that kind of crime in a neighborhood like this."

Crystal walked to the patio doors and stared out at the garden. The night seemed so black—blacker than she had ever noticed before. The garden lights created mysterious shadows which took on menacing forms. Who had her child? Who had taken her, and why? To rape, to torture, to abuse her? Or maybe for money? She was famous and rich; what better incentive to take her daughter.

"What if she's been kidnapped?" she asked woodenly.

Wright was prepared for that question and wanted to be honest. "We first have to rule out all the other possibilities. Perhaps your daughter is with your secretary or your husband," he explained patiently. "We usually wait twenty-four hours before we start thinking we're dealing with a kidnapper. Then we can narrow the search down, since statistics show that most victims knew their abductor before they were kidnapped."

The hairs on Crystal's arms stood up. "That's all?" she said, turning to him angrily. "Just wait and see?"

Wright knew it didn't seem like enough, but there wasn't much he could do. "I'll send copies of your daughter's photograph to the other divisions, and I'll check with missing persons. We'll round up the known sex offenders in the city and see if they can account for their time this afternoon. We'll also check the hospitals and, um, the morgue," he said, his voice softening.

Crystal's eyes bulged, stunned by what he was saying. "You don't think that Emily . . . that she's dead?" she managed to whisper.

"No, no, of course not," he hastened to assure her. "She's probably with her father or Simmons."

"And if she isn't? What if she *has* been kidnapped?"

"If someone has your daughter, he'll probably be calling you, or sending a ransom note. We usually wait for something to happen before we bring in the FBI."

"Wait? Wait for what? For her body to be found?" Crystal asked hysterically.

Wright sighed; he had to give her some encouragement. "Under the circumstances, you being a famous movie star and all," he said almost apologetically, "I'll request immediate assistance from the FBI."

"Isn't there anything else you can do?" Crystal asked, keenly aware of her pounding heartbeat.

"Please be assured that the Beverly Hills Police Department will do everything in its power to help you," he said. "I'll work on getting a court order for a phone tap, but I hope it won't be necessary. I hope we find her before then."

Wright handed Crystal his card. "My home phone number is written on the back. You can reach me there if I'm not in my office."

Crystal couldn't believe he was leaving. She clutched at his arm. "What should I do?"

"Wait. And pray," he added, wishing there was something more he could tell her. Something to give her hope. "I'll have one of the officers stay here with you," he told her.

"Thank you," Crystal mumbled as tears appeared in her eyes and began tracing a path down her frightened face.

Wright grasped her hand clumsily. "Don't worry, Miss Smythe. We'll find your daughter."

XI

They arrived at the Pacific Coast Highway, and once again traffic slowed to a snail's pace as he drove through town. He tapped his fingers on the steering wheel while he waited for the light to change, then made a left turn. The road curved and wound up into the hills. He finally pulled into the driveway of an old clapboard house.

"We're here," he grunted.

"It's awful dark," Emily said. "How come there's no lights on?"

"We'll fix that in a minute," he said, leading her to the side door. He reached above the door frame and found the key that Wayne kept hidden there. The door opened easily, and he flipped on the light switch.

"There," he said, blinking as the fluorescent light lit up the tiny kitchen. He closed and locked the door, then led Emily into the living room.

"When is mommy going to come?"

"We'll have to wait and see," he said. "You watch television, and I'll see what's in the kitchen for dinner."

Emily studied her surroundings. The carpet was stained and threadbare, the sofa torn in several spots, and the coffee table in front of it was scarred by cigarette burns. A bare bulb hung from the ceiling.

"I don't like it here," she said, returning to the kitchen. "This house smells funny, and it's cold in here."

He sniffed the air. It *did* smell. Wayne was working in the oil fields of Saudi Arabia, and the house had been vacant the past two months. It didn't matter, since he wasn't planning on staying too long. Just long enough to accomplish what he wanted.

"Go watch television," he told her as he began opening the kitchen cabinets. He found cans of soda and beer, tuna fish, Campbell's soup, a bottle of scotch, and an unopened package of Oreos. Not the greatest dinner in the world, he thought, but he would drive down the hill the next day and pick up some food. He connected the refrigerator, filled the ice trays, and began heating the soup. When it was hot, he called Emily into the kitchen and pointed at the table.

"Eat."

She made a face. "Yuk! I don't like pea soup."

"The other choice is cream of mushroom. Would you prefer that?" he asked, his tone condescending.

Emily shook her head. "That's even worse." She sat and dipped her spoon into the soup, wishing she were at home. Socorro had been planning a big roast for dinner, and Emily wanted her lemon meringue pie for dessert, not some dumb store-bought cookies.

She finished the soup, then had some cookies with her soda. She didn't like 7-Up, especially if it was warm, but there was nothing else to drink. She watched him pour himself another drink.

"I thought you said mommy had a surprise for me."

He laughed. "This *is* the surprise. You get to stay here for a few days."

Emily pushed back from the table. "Mommy promised to take me to the zoo."

"She had a change in plans."

"Can I call her?"

"The telephone isn't working," he said gruffly. "You'll just have to stay here."

"I don't want to," she pouted.

"It's time for you to go to bed. Come on."

"Mommy lets me stay up an extra hour on Friday night."

He was losing his patience with her. Crystal spoiled her far too much. "Well mommy isn't here, and I say you're going to bed. Now," he said, pulling on Emily's arm and leading her to the bedroom.

XII

Selma Siegel slowed at the corner of Roxbury and made a right turn. She was looking forward to getting home and fixing herself a tall scotch and soda. It had been a long day, and she just wanted to relax before she had to go to the discotheque opening later that evening. She hummed to herself, pleased with the interview she had just finished with Tom Cruise. She was writing a piece about male Hollywood stars for the *Los Angeles Times*, and Cruise had been the last name on her list. She would spend the weekend working on the article.

She wondered if she could go to the opening wearing the same turquoise jumpsuit or if she should change clothes. The color went well with her copper hair, and all she needed to do was add some jewelry. She was sorry now that she had agreed to go. She probably wouldn't get to bed until after two or three in the morning.

She studied the palatial homes on the palm-lined street. Though most of the houses were set off by floodlights hidden in lush foliage and carefully tended flowerbeds, she noticed that lights also blazed from nearly every window. She could see people standing in doorways, pointing and gesturing. As she neared Crystal Smythe's house, she spotted the police car and slowed to a stop. She wondered what was going on. Selma had started her career as a reporter, and though she now wrote feature articles, she sensed a story in the making.

She parked her car and approached the policemen, flashing her press card. "Hi, fellows. What's up?"

"A lost little girl," the younger policeman answered.

"Crystal Smythe's daughter?"

"Yeah. No sign of her yet," he said.

"Do you know her name?" Selma asked, her heart racing, knowing there could be a big news story developing.

"Emily," he replied and then followed his partner into the house.

Selma waited outside, wishing once again that she had a telephone in her car; she had to get this information phoned in to the paper. The front door opened, and she recognized Lieutenant Wright.

Selma knew that the majority of crimes committed in Beverly Hills were robberies, the thieves drawn to the affluent neighborhood like flies to a dead carcass. Wright was the man they called in when it was a major crime, like murder. His presence emphasized the seriousness of the situation.

"Siegel, *L.A. Times*," she said, planting herself in front of the tall man. "What's the story?"

"There is none," Wright said angrily, not overly fond of prying reporters. If this was more than just a case of a missing child—if it *was* a kidnapping—then the press would be alerted, since that was departmental policy. But for now he didn't need a slew of reporters running through the neighborhood, hindering the search.

Selma knew better and wasn't going to be put off by a closed-mouth cop. "You have to be kidding! Crystal Smythe's daughter is missing, and you say there's no story? There has to be something more—like maybe she was kidnapped."

"No comment," Wright grumbled as he pushed by her and walked to his car.

Selma watched as one of the policemen followed him in the patrol car. So why had the other one stayed inside? she wondered. Something big was definitely happening, and she was the first reporter on the scene. It was *her* story. She

ran back to her car. She would find a telephone, call the
office to let her editor know of a possible front page story,
then return here until they could send someone to cover for
her.

She started humming, thinking how great it would be to
see her byline on the front page of the *Los Angeles Times*.
Interviews were fun to do, but this was real news. If
Crystal's daughter was missing, maybe she'd been taken by
a depraved sex maniac. That would certainly grab the
public's interest. Or better yet, Selma thought, grinning
from ear to ear, if the girl had been kidnapped, the story
could go on for days.

XIII

Elizabeth Anderson frowned and closed the book she was
reading; the words kept running together, and she couldn't
concentrate. She took off her glasses and rubbed her eyes,
then leaned back against the bed pillows. As much as she
tried to ignore the images she was receiving, they persisted
in tormenting her.

She sorted through the pieces of the puzzle. A child and
a man in a speeding car. They were only silhouettes in her
subconscious, but Elizabeth was sure that their destinies
were linked with her own. She would become involved with
them. But where? And when?

For some reason, she was sure the color red was a clue,
but a solid image hadn't formed yet. Red dress? Red shoes?
Red barn? Fingernails painted dragon red? Her imagination
ran wild with the possibilities. Unfortunately, red was also
the color of fire and blood. She shivered, wishing she could
ignore the pictures that filled her mind and not get caught up
in the troubles of others.

She shrugged. It was useless to think of stopping. It was

a God-given gift, and she was compelled to continue using her psychic powers. She began breathing deeply, relaxing, willing her inner being to open itself to the images that would come. But there were none, only the nagging fear that somewhere, someone needed her help.

saturday

I

Crystal glanced at her watch. It was after two in the morning, and she had a throbbing headache. She went into the kitchen and found a bottle of aspirin, then gulped down three pills with a glass of water. Socorro, whose bedroom was off the kitchen, heard the noise and came to investigate.

She stood in the doorway, clutching her robe across her chest. "Is there any news?"

Crystal shook her head. "No, nothing. I'm sorry I woke you."

She reached for the telephone and dialed Jimmy's number, but again his machine picked up. "Call me as soon as you get in," Crystal said, then dialed Neil's home. There was still no answer, and she suspected he was out cruising the bars. Even with the AIDS scare, Neil was ever on the lookout for a new lover. She turned back to Socorro.

"Neither Jimmy nor Neil are at home," she said. "I don't know what else to do. Maybe I should take another walk through the neighborhood. Maybe the police overlooked something."

"You know they looked good," Socorro reminded her. "They checked at every house on this street and asked everyone if they had seen her. Even now there are two policemen going up and down the streets looking for Emily."

"It's not enough. They should have called in more men. Emily could be hurt, and unconscious, unable to call for help."

"There's nothing more we can do but wait and pray. Why don't you go upstairs and lie down. You must get some sleep," Socorro said, her scolding, motherly tone a comfort to Crystal. "I will wake you if the police have found our Emily."

"No. I'll be all right," Crystal assured her. "Go on back to bed."

Crystal returned to the den and stretched out on the sofa. She glanced at the coffee table, noting the nearly empty pack of cigarettes. She decided she was smoking too much and it was causing her headache. She closed her eyes, wishing she could get some rest, yet still unable to. Questions kept flashing across her mind.

Emily wouldn't have spoken to a stranger. She remembered now that Jimmy had warned her of the dangers. Emily must have gone with someone she knows, Crystal reasoned. It *had* to be Jimmy. Or maybe Neil. But if they had her, wouldn't they call? A cold knot of fear gripped her stomach. Who had taken Emily? Was it a stranger? A transient, a passerby, a sexual pervert? Would he rape her, beat her, kill her?

Crystal began to cry, the tears trailing down her cheeks, as she prayed. "I know I haven't been the best mother in the world, but I promise I'll be better. Please, let me find her."

As she waited for news about Emily, she became painfully aware of how slowly the minute hand made its way around the face of her watch. How long before her daughter was safely home? How long must she wait? The police will find Emily, she repeated over and over. Be patient, she reminded herself, though she knew patience had never been one of her virtues. She had always been in a rush, racing for stardom and fame.

Crystal lit cigarette after cigarette, her thoughts returning to her first day in Hollywood, reliving the past . . .

II

Peggy invited Crystal to her apartment above Sunset Boulevard. The building was neo-Spanish with a green slate roof and lots of ornate ironwork fringing the balconies. Peggy pushed back a steel gate and led the way around a small pool and up stairs that were missing several of their brightly painted Mexican tiles.

"Well, this is it," she said, her southern accent as smooth as mulberry wine. "Home, sweet miserable home. The walls are paper thin, and the water pressure is nonexistent."

"As long as there's hot water. I feel so grimy after that long bus ride."

"You can pay half of next month's rent, if that's okay with you."

Crystal happily agreed as she looked at the studio apartment. The floor was covered in black and white checkered linoleum that needed a good scrubbing. An unmade Murphy bed was folded down from one wall. An orange sofa, piled with stuffed animals, stretched along the far wall; the coffee table was made from orange-painted cinderblocks with a thick slab of wood stretched across them. A small kitchenette occupied the far corner, and a lime-green table with two unmatched chairs completed the furnishings.

"It's darling," Crystal said, thinking that Peggy was the worst housekeeper she had ever seen.

"You can sleep on the sofa," Peggy offered, "unless I'm not here. I spend most nights over at my boyfriend's place."

Crystal smiled at her gratefully. "I really appreciate your letting me stay here."

Peggy folded the bed up into the wall and closed the curtains around it. "Well," she drawled, "I know how it is. I came from Texas with a few beauty pageant titles attached to my name, but I soon found out they weren't worth doo-doo. In this town it takes hard work and guts to get anywhere."

Crystal held up her two best dresses. "Where should I hang these?"

Peggy pulled open a door. "The saving grace of this apartment . . . a genuine movie star's closet."

Crystal entered the walk-in closet and stared in awe as Peggy opened mirrored doors. Behind them were drawers, shelves for shoes and clothing.

"This is fabulous," Crystal said, thrilled by her multiple images.

"I think it's weird," Peggy laughed. "Why would anyone put all that money into this closet?"

"I love it. I'll just sleep in here . . . forget the sofa."

Peggy giggled and walked back into the living room. She sat at the dining table and dialed a number.

"Hi. This is Peggy Mason. Any messages?"

Peggy's look of disappointment told the story. Crystal wondered if her new friend ever found work.

"Well, nothing for me today," Peggy admitted with a grin, "but maybe tomorrow. I'll bet just anything that it'll be busy. In fact, I know it will. We've got a whole bunch of things to do."

"Like what?"

"Well, for one thing, you're going to need photos, and then you need an agent, and an answering service of your own," she said, bouncing to her feet. "But that'll wait. Tonight you're going to your first Hollywood party."

"Oh no! I'm a wreck," Crystal moaned.

"Nonsense. All you need is a shower and some make-up and you'll be fine," Peggy insisted. "And wear something sexy. There'll be lots of producers and important people at this party."

"My wardrobe is hardly sexy. Where I come from, sex is a forbidden word," Crystal said. "As you can see, my dresses are very conservative."

"Hmmn, yes, you're right. That blue number is okay for church but not tonight's festivities."

"What'll I do?"

"Maybe you can wear something of mine," Peggy offered. She pulled a black dress out of the closet. "I've added a few pounds since I bought this, so it'll probably fit you."

Crystal held it up. "It needs pressing. Got an iron?"

"In the kitchen cabinet," she replied, rummaging through the drawers. "Here's the belt."

"I don't know if I'm ready," Crystal said as she waited for the iron to heat. "Everyone will probably think I arrived from outer space."

"Don't be silly. If you want to make it in the movies, you gotta have confidence," Peggy said, pulling her sweater over her head. "All you gotta do is flash those baby blue eyes of yours. And for heaven's sake, don't tell people you're from Maine. You tell them you just arrived from England, and they'll be fawning over you. Trust me."

Crystal shook her head. "My grandmother told me to never lie, since one just leads to another."

"That's not lying, honey. That's just stretching the truth," Peggy admonished her. "Besides, you've got that funny way of talking . . . They're just going to love that accent. Now get in there and take your shower. We're going to celebrate your arrival."

III

Crystal awoke slowly, shaking away her memories, then checked her watch. It was six o'clock. Emily had been missing for over twelve hours. Where was she? Why hadn't the police found her? Crystal stood, stretching her tired muscles, stiff from having slept on the sofa. She walked into the kitchen and found Socorro preparing breakfast. A policeman was sitting at the kitchen table, sipping coffee while reading the newspaper. Pictures of Crystal and Emily were on the front page of the *Los Angeles Times*.

Crystal grabbed the newspaper from him. The headline was large and ominous: CRYSTAL SMYTHE'S DAUGHTER MISSING. She began reading.

"Police are searching for nine-year-old Emily Mitchelson, daughter of Oscar-winning actress Crystal Smythe and screenwriter James Mitchelson. There are no clues to the girl's disappearance, but the police are considering the possibility of a kidnapping."

Crystal glanced at the rest of the article, which was little more than a summary of the films she had starred in. The last paragraph gave details of the screenplays Jimmy had written and mentioned Crystal and Jimmy's separation.

She crumpled the newspaper angrily. "Has there been any news?" she asked the policeman. "Why aren't you outside looking for my daughter?"

"We don't think she's anywhere here in the neighborhood, ma'am," he explained. "I'm supposed to wait here for the Lieutenant to show up."

"Let me know the minute he gets here," she told Socorro, then sped upstairs to her bedroom.

She stood under the shower for a long time, letting the hot water beat down on her, then blow-dried her hair. She

walked into her closet and stood contemplating her large
wardrobe, finally choosing pale blue linen slacks and
matching silk shirt, feeling guilty about her indecision over
what to wear.

Emily's closet was filled with pretty clothes, too. Crystal
loved to take her shopping, and Emily enjoyed dressing up.
She was careful with her clothes, hanging them up properly,
showing Socorro any stains or loose buttons that needed
mending.

Crystal smiled, remembering how she and Emily had
worn matching outfits in the mother-daughter charity fash-
ion show. Emily had been so pleased to be modeling with
her mother and was looking forward to doing it again this
year.

Would there be a next time? What if they didn't find her?
How could she go on with life, if her daughter was . . .

Crystal shuddered, unable to complete the thought. She
had to believe that Emily would be found. She crossed
the room and reached for the telephone on the nightstand.
She called Neil's house, but still there was no answer.
Crystal phoned Jimmy next, but he still wasn't home. She
cursed and went back down to the kitchen.

Socorro was removing a tray of hot muffins from the
oven. She poured Crystal a glass of fresh-squeezed orange
juice, then leaned back against the refrigerator. "It's all my
fault," she sobbed, overcome by her guilt.

Crystal put her arm around the maid. "Don't cry,
Socorro. We'll find Emily. I know we will. It's not your
fault."

The telephone startled Crystal. She grabbed the receiver,
praying it would be Emily. "Hello?"

Crystal was disappointed; it was Moss Rogers, her agent.
He had risen early and read the newspaper.

"I don't know anything," she told him impatiently.

"Look, when I have some news, I'll call you . . .
What? . . . Yes, all right. Thanks."

She hung up and turned to the policeman. "That was a
friend. There'll probably be others calling. Friends, I mean.
The telephone number is unlisted of course," Crystal
babbled on nervously, "but there must be dozens of people
who have it."

The doorbell rang, and Crystal ran to the front door,
opening it expectantly. A photographer snapped her photo,
and a reporter with bright-red hair thrust a tape recorder in
her face.

"Have they found your daughter?" Selma Siegel asked
eagerly. "Have the kidnappers contacted you?"

The policeman came to Crystal's rescue. "No questions,"
he snapped, closing the door in the reporter's face. Then he
muttered, "The boss isn't going to be happy about this.
Those reporters could ruin everything. They tend to invent
their own versions of the case rather than giving the actual
facts. Publicity is often murderous in a kidnapping."

Crystal stared at him, his words rekindling her fear. He
thought it was a kidnapping. Crystal knew the statistics.
Kidnapped children were often murdered. Worse yet, what
if Emily was beaten . . . or . . . Crystal began crying.
She couldn't bear the thought of any kind of abuse. Not her
daughter. Please, God, don't let him harm her.

IV

Emily awoke in a strange room. She had a feeling that he
had lied to her. But why? She got out of bed and went into
the bathroom. The early morning sun filtered through a
small barred window set high in the wall. She found an old
toothbrush and some paste and brushed her teeth, then
returned to the bedroom.

The room was as sparsely furnished as the rest of the house. The iron bed and an old steamer trunk under the window were its sole furnishings. A lone light bulb hung from the ceiling. On the trunk was a tray with a package of cookies, two cans of soda, and an opened can of tuna fish.

Emily stared at the food, puzzled, then walked to the door. She turned the handle, but the door was securely locked. She called to him, but there was no reply. Had he left her here alone? When was her mother going to come? Emily thought for a moment. She couldn't understand why she was being punished. Or was it something else? Suddenly she felt afraid. She didn't like this room, and she didn't like being all by herself. Maybe she could get out the window.

Emily pushed the food aside and climbed up on the trunk. She tried raising the sash, but it was firmly stuck from layers of paint. She pressed her face against the dirty glass panes, which were framed in metal. As far as she could tell, the window was high off the ground. She could see mountains and the ocean in the distance. There were some red bushes growing nearby on the hillside, and some trees partially obscured her view of the house below. A lady came out of the house carrying a large ceramic cat. Emily tried waving, then pounding on the window, but the woman was too far away to hear. Emily sadly realized it was unlikely that she'd look up the hill. The lady got into her car and drove away.

Emily considered smashing one of the window panes. But what good would that do? she wondered. It was too small for her to fit through, and what if he came back and saw that she had broken it? He would really be angry.

Emily crawled back into bed, pulled the covers up, and held her doll. What was happening? What had she done wrong? Why was she being treated like this?

She was frightened and began to cry. "Mommy, mommy. Where are you?"

V

Neil slipped the key into the lock, fumbling in his haste, and ran down the steps into the living room. He missed the last riser and fell forward, landing on his elbow. He groaned, reached for the ringing telephone, and said hello breathlessly, but they had already hung up.

He rubbed his elbow, then stood up. It was late, and Crystal would start to wonder where he was. He stripped off his clothes and walked into the bathroom. He shaved while he showered, then dressed in gray sports slacks and a gray-and-yellow-striped Armani silk shirt. He slipped on Gucci loafers and picked up a pale yellow cashmere sweater.

He looked at himself in the mirror, pleased by the reflection he saw. It was all in the timing, he thought. Last night had gone very well, if unexpectedly. Now he had to decide how to handle the situation. He certainly didn't want to make any false moves. If he played his cards right, he'd have everything he ever wanted.

VI

Lieutenant Wright entered the dining room. He found Crystal slumped in her chair, smearing butter on a muffin. "How are you?" he asked.

Crystal looked up, startled, then sprang to her feet. "Have you found her?"

"No," he said, his voice amazingly gentle for a man his size. He accepted a cup of coffee from Socorro, but refused a muffin, patting his stomach. "My wife has me on a strict diet."

"Have there been any phone calls?" he asked her.

"Several, but they were all from friends," she said listlessly. "The phone is driving me crazy. I keep expecting to hear from Emily, or even the kidnapper if that's what's happened to her, but . . ."

Wright nodded, understanding. "I drove down to your husband's house this morning. He wasn't there, but a neighbor spotted me lurking in the bushes and said Mr. Mitchelson had gone sailing."

"He didn't mention it to me," Crystal said, biting on her lower lip. "Perhaps I should call his secretary and find out."

Crystal walked into the den and picked up her address book. She found the number and reached for the telephone. The secretary answered on the second ring.

"Carol? This is Crystal. I hate to bother you on your day off."

"Oh, golly, Mrs. Mitchelson," she shouted in the phone. "I just read about Emily in the newspaper. I'm very sorry. Is there anything I can do for you?"

"Yes," Crystal said anxiously. "Did Jimmy tell you where he was going this weekend?"

"I'm pretty sure he went sailing. Bob Preston called earlier this week, and I think they were planning to go to Catalina."

Crystal mumbled her thanks and called the Preston home. His wife answered the telephone.

"Margie? This is Crystal. I'm trying to locate Jimmy. Is he with Bob?"

"Bob is here in bed with a sprained ankle. He was playing touch football with the kids and took a nasty fall. He's got me running back and forth playing nursemaid. Men!" she guffawed. "They're such pussycats."

"That's too bad," Crystal sympathized. "Listen, can you ask Bob if he knows if Jimmy went sailing?"

"Bob's asleep."

"It's important, Margie," Crystal said tersely. "Please wake him and ask him if Jimmy said anything about taking Emily with him."

"Why?"

"Emily's missing," Crystal blurted out. "It's already in the newspapers."

"What? God, I had no idea," Margie apologized. "I haven't even had time to read the paper this morning. God, this is just awful. What happened?"

"Please, ask Bob if he knows anything," Crystal implored, ignoring the question.

"Sure. Hold on a minute."

Crystal waited impatiently, drumming her fingers on the table. Margie's reply was negative on both counts.

"What do the police say?"

"They searched the neighborhood, but there's no sign of her. The police officer in charge is here now, but there's still no news," Crystal said hastily. "Listen, I can't talk now. I'll let you know when I, um, hear something."

"If I can do anything . . ."

"Thanks." Crystal hesitated. "The police think she may have been kidnapped."

"Don't jump to conclusions. Maybe Jimmy did decide to take her with him after Bob couldn't make it," Margie suggested.

"It's unlikely," Crystal mumbled, "but God, I hope you're right."

Neil noticed the reporters in front of the house and pulled into the garage. He walked through the kitchen door and found a policeman barring his entrance, insisting on seeing some identification. Crystal heard the commotion and came running to the door.

"What the hell is going on?" Neil demanded, his hands on his hips in a defiant pose.

"Neil, where have you been?" Crystal growled, unaware of her harsh tone. "I've been calling and calling you all night long."

"I, uh, went out for a while," he said cautiously, his eyes downcast, "and didn't get home until, uh, very late."

Wright leaned toward Neil. "Where were you?" he asked, taking in the expensive sports clothes, the gold watch, and the Gucci loafers. Wright studied his face; although the scar was faded, it was still nasty-looking. But interesting, he decided. Like a dueling scar.

"That's my business," Neil said, a faint flush coloring his face. "And who the hell are you?"

"Lieutenant Wright, Beverly Hills Police," he answered, poking a finger at Neil's chest, "and believe me, pal, *your* business has become *my* business."

Crystal grasped Neil's arm. "I also called you this morning," she said accusingly. "If you were home, why didn't you answer the damn phone?"

"Sorry. I had it unplugged," he said evenly, well aware that Crystal would suspect he was lying.

Crystal's voice was a hoarse rasp. "Emily's been missing since shortly after she came home from camp. Did you take her anywhere?"

Anxiety raced through his veins. "Of course not. After I left you at the studio, I came here to drop off some things. Around two," he added for Wright's benefit. "Then I went home to work on your fan mail."

The detective realized his hunch had been right. Simmons was definitely gay. Wright noticed the beads of sweat breaking out on Simmons' forehead, a sure sign that he was worried about something—but what? Wright wondered. What was this guy hiding?

"You say you went out again. Would you like to tell us where?" Wright asked, a sarcastic edge to his voice.

Neil considered a moment before answering. He had to be careful; he had a lot at stake. "I stopped at the Stagecoach Inn for a drink and ran into some friends. We spent the evening together."

"What are the names of these friends?" Wright asked, pulling his notebook out of his pocket. He knew that the Stagecoach Inn was a pricey gay bar, frequented by well-to-do men looking for romance.

Neil's eyes narrowed. "I don't remember."

"You don't remember," Wright snickered, "and yet you spent the evening with them?"

"What I mean is they were, uh, new acquaintances," Neil said, feeling the sting of the detective's scorn. "Look, I can give you first names, but I don't really remember anyone's last name. You're wasting your time; I don't have any information for you." He paused, collecting his thoughts. "I also know my rights," he added, "and I don't have to answer your questions."

"Listen, pal. A little girl is missing, and I'm starting to think she was kidnapped. You're a suspect unless you can show me otherwise," Wright growled, losing his patience. "If you don't want to answer my questions here, I'll be happy to have one of my men escort you downtown, and we can talk there."

Neil was alarmed. He had known it wasn't going to be easy. What was funny was the fact that Wright sounded like an actor with bad lines in a "B" movie. No matter what, he still had to tell the policeman something—anything—to get him off his back.

"Look. I had a couple of drinks with friends, and around

midnight I, uh, decided to go for a drive. To Santa Barbara," he lied. "End of story."

Wright didn't like his story; he decided to prod a little further. "And I suppose no one went with you."

"That's right. I was alone," Neil said adamantly.

Wright still wasn't satisfied with Simmons' explanation. "And you didn't stop for gasoline or maybe a cup of coffee?"

"No. I didn't speak to anyone or buy anything," he said, fully aware that his story couldn't be verified.

"What time did you get back?"

Neil frowned with cold fury. "I don't remember," he told the detective. "Like I told you, it was late when I got home. I unplugged the telephone so I could get some sleep."

"Likely story," Wright mumbled.

Neil held his temper. "If you don't have any more questions," he said haughtily, "I'm going upstairs to the office."

Crystal stared at Neil's retreating back, puzzled by his demeanor. She realized that he wasn't telling the truth. She could always tell when something was bothering him. Over the years she had come to know him very well. It was Neil who held her hand through all the bad times, comforted her when the men in her life had been rotten, reveled in her success. Then the day had come when she had been able to repay him for all his kindness.

Neil had allowed his new lover, a stunt man, to move into his apartment. Crystal disliked the guy thoroughly, and despised what he was doing to Neil. The man was a heavy cocaine user, and Neil had become addicted as well. Crystal knew how destructive cocaine was, but she was unable to convince Neil to stop. Soon she was dismayed at the changes in Neil—and alarmed when she would find his face bruised or notice that he had a black eye. She couldn't understand why Neil put up with the abuse, why he refused to kick the man out.

When Neil called her in the middle of the night, his voice barely audible, she had raced to his apartment. She found him lying on the floor in a pool of blood, naked, his body badly beaten. She had almost fainted when she saw his face. His lover had slashed it open with a kitchen knife, and Crystal thought Neil would lose his eye. Crystal rushed him to the hospital to have his ribs set and face stitched. Afterward, she insisted that he come to her house to recuperate.

He recovered from his ordeal, but refused plastic surgery on his face. Crystal thought it was perverse that he would want to keep a souvenir of such a terrible time in his life, but Neil said he needed the scar to remind him to never let himself fall in love again.

Crystal knew he was deeply ashamed, and she worried that his deep depression was getting the best of him. She encouraged him to go back to the salon he owned, but he said he was no longer interested in pampering absentminded females. He kept his anger bottled up inside, and the few times Crystal suggested he see a psychiatrist to discuss his problem, Neil adamantly refused. She finally offered him a job as her personal assistant, and he accepted, much to her relief. He wrapped himself in a shell, and they mutually agreed never again to speak of that time in his life.

Crystal was sure of Neil's loyalty, but she wondered why he was lying. What was he hiding? Had he taken Emily somewhere? What could he hope to gain? She thrust the disturbing thoughts from her mind. She was becoming paranoid. How could she possibly doubt Neil? And yet, something was definitely wrong. She would wait and talk to him later. When they were alone.

• • •

The phone didn't stop ringing, but the calls were never the one Crystal waited for. Friends, directors, producers, actors, and actresses had read the morning newspaper, and they all wanted to help. Neil efficiently fielded the calls, quickly telling everyone that they had been instructed by the police to keep the lines open. He thanked them for their concern, saying Crystal was too upset to talk.

Neil walked into the den. "I see there's been a change of the guard; there's a new policeman on duty. Has there been any word from your Lieutenant Wright?"

Crystal noted the sarcasm in Neil's voice. "Jimmy's boat isn't at the marina. Wright said he would ask the Coast Guard to contact him, but it probably won't help," Crystal said. "You know how Jimmy is; he never turns the radio on. He could be anywhere. He may have changed his mind about going to Catalina; if the wind was good, he might have sailed to Santa Barbara."

"I don't like Wright," Neil told her, "and I didn't like being interrogated by him."

"He was only doing his job," Crystal reminded him, twisting her rings nervously. "Socorro said that the reporters are trampling the flowers."

"It's a three-ring circus out there. Siegel's article in the *Times* has brought out the vultures. There are three camera crews waiting for you to come outside."

Crystal looked up at him. Her eyes were red and swollen. "I can't stand not knowing what's going on."

"Jimmy probably took Emily with him," he said, thinking it best to keep her hopes up.

Crystal shook her head. "No, I still don't think so. It's not like Jimmy to do something like that. We may have our differences," Crystal said, remembering all the silly arguments they'd had over the years, "but certainly not about Emily."

"It's stifling in here," Neil observed as he switched on the overhead fan. He glanced out at the sun-drenched garden. Socorro was watering the potted herbs she grew, her lips moving in constant prayer.

"Damn it! This is driving me crazy. If someone has kidnapped Emily, why hasn't he called?" asked Crystal. "Surely Emily would give him the phone number."

Neil had an explanation. "Maybe he won't call today. After all, the banks are closed until Monday, and don't forget, the longer he waits to contact you, the more readily you'll agree to his terms."

Though she knew without looking, Crystal checked her watch. "Emily's been gone almost twenty hours. This is terrible, just sitting here waiting. I feel so helpless, not knowing what's happening."

"I talked to Melvin," Neil said as he sat down, carefully crossing his legs so he wouldn't wrinkle his slacks. "He's sending over one of his personal bodyguards."

"I don't need a bodyguard."

"He'll help keep the reporters at bay," Neil told her. "Melvin also said not to worry about the movie."

"That's the farthest thing from my mind," she said angrily. "It'll be a relief not to have to face Jefferies, though. God, this movie has been a drain on me. You know he delights in tormenting me." Crystal reached for her cigarettes and lighter. "Sometimes he'll deliberately blow his lines, then smile that evil grin and say he's sorry. God, how I loathe him."

"He *is* strange," Neil agreed. "I've heard that he actually swings both ways."

Crystal was stunned. "What? I don't believe you."

"One of the cameramen on the set insinuated that he and

Jefferies had a very private tête-à-tête a few weeks ago."
Neil laughed. "I don't know if he was making it up, or
bragging."

Crystal noted the cynical tone in Neil's voice. "Poor
Anna. Melvin told me that he's going to tell his daughter to
divorce Jefferies after the baby is born."

"I wonder what Anna will think of that? I would assume
that she loves the jerk."

"I don't think she has anything to say about it."

"Can I get you anything?"

"Maybe some fresh coffee."

"Too much caffeine," Neil admonished her as he rose to
go to the kitchen. "It'll keep you awake tonight."

"Do you really think I'll be able to sleep?" Crystal asked
bitterly. "This is the worse nightmare of my life. Not
knowing if Emily is all right . . . if she's alive."

Neil hesitated in the doorway. "I, uh, have to run some
errands, and then I'm meeting someone for dinner this
evening. Do you mind?"

Crystal looked up at him. Of course she minded. How
could he ask such a question? Why would he want to leave
her when she needed him most? Neil was acting very
strange, and he was avoiding eye contact. She sensed he
was hiding something from her, but what? It didn't make
sense, nothing did.

"There's no reason to wait here. I can always call you if
they find Emily," she said, holding her chin high, forcing
back the anger, feeling that he was deserting her.

Crystal heard the doorbell ring and raced to the front of
the house, praying that the police had brought Emily home.
Her face fell in disappointment when she found Peggy
Ballwin on her doorstep. "It's all right," she told Melvin's
bodyguard. "She's a friend."

Peggy threw her arms around Crystal. "Oh, baby! I can't believe it. I wanted to call," she said in the Texas drawl that still persisted, "but Ted said not to tie up the line. Is there any news?"

"No, nothing," Crystal murmured, as once again the tears gathered and coursed down her cheeks. She let herself be patted and comforted by her dearest friend.

"I just can't believe this is happening," Peggy said as they walked into the den.

"Every time the phone rings, I think it might be Emily calling me to come pick her up," Crystal sobbed.

Peggy sat beside Crystal on the sofa and held her hand. "I know what you're feeling."

Crystal stiffened. "Do you? How can you possibly know?"

Peggy didn't take offense at Crystal's words. They had been friends for a long time, and she understood Crystal more than anyone else, with the possible exception of Jimmy. Underneath Crystal's cold veneer was a warm heart. The hard shell Crystal presented to the public hid a vulnerable and loving person.

"I meant I understand the anxiety you're feeling," Peggy said clumsily. "I'm a mother, too. If it was one of my children, I'd be terrified."

"I'm sorry. I shouldn't have jumped on you, but it's all this uncertainty. Not knowing if Emily's okay. Not knowing if she's been kidnapped," Crystal said in a choked voice, immediately regretting having lashed out at her friend. "I think I'm going mad. I feel like yelling and screaming. I can't stand the thought of someone hurting her."

"You have to think positive. Maybe she hasn't been kidnapped. Maybe Jimmy has her."

Crystal reached for a tissue and wiped her eyes. "I

thought of that and called him, but I think he went sailing. Besides, this isn't his weekend."

"As I recall, Jimmy was very reluctant about giving you custody of Emily. Maybe he finally decided to take things into his own hands."

"What are you talking about?"

"Maybe Jimmy thinks Emily deserves more attention than you give her."

"He has never said anything like that."

"Oh yes he did!" Peggy leaned back against the pillows. "Don't you remember that time when we were at the beach house and he was shouting at you about caring more for your career than your daughter?"

"That was such a long time ago," Crystal said, vaguely remembering the afternoon. "He was taking out his frustration on me. He hadn't written anything worthwhile in ages, and then I received the second Oscar, and the press referred to him as Mr. Smythe. He felt he was losing his identity."

"Well, I still think he took Emily. He probably thinks this will teach you a lesson and that you'll take better care of her."

A frown creased Crystal's forehead. "You know Jimmy better than that. He would let me know he was taking her, if only to upset me."

Peggy shook her head. One of Crystal's irritating habits was constantly putting herself first—in everything. Like thinking that Jimmy would derive some pleasure out of tormenting Crystal by taking their daughter away. "You don't really believe that!" she admonished Crystal.

"Why not? He'd do anything to hurt me. To stop my career."

Peggy mumbled something, but Crystal was alert. "What did you say?"

"You have a really rotten attitude," Peggy said unhappily. "You can't be serious. You can't think that."

"I don't know what to think," Crystal shouted, pressing her hands to her temples, wishing the horrible pounding would go away. She was keenly aware of how petty she was becoming toward Jimmy, and doubly ashamed for having screamed at her friend.

"I'm sorry. I shouldn't take my anger out on you. It's just that I feel so alone. So afraid."

"I'm here, baby," Peggy said softly, wishing she could do something more.

They both fell silent as Crystal leaned back against the welcoming comfort of her friend's arm. Peggy who had stuck by her through everything. Peggy who knew all her secrets, her desires, her wishes and hopes. She closed her eyes, losing herself in her memories.

Crystal remembered how kind Peggy had been to her when she first arrived in Los Angeles—helping her find jobs, make the right contacts. Peggy got her dates with cameramen and grips and, on occasion, an assistant director, but Crystal didn't date any of those men more than once, much less sleep with them. There was too much to do, and she didn't want to get involved. Making the rounds of casting agents was a full-time job, and she spent hours on improving herself.

Crystal's problems began shortly after Peggy got married. That was when she became involved with Richard. Of course she had been very young then and didn't know what she was doing, how evil he was. But still, common sense should have warned her . . .

VII

Peggy burst into the room. "I have absolutely the best news in the world. I'm pregnant!"

Crystal dropped the apple she was eating and jumped to her feet, shrieking her delight. She hugged her friend. "I'm so happy for you. Does Ted know yet?"

"Yes, and we're getting married right away. We're flying to Las Vegas tonight. Can you imagine? Mrs. Theodore Ballwin! I'm so excited."

"This is really great news," Crystal said enthusiastically, watching as Peggy crammed clothes and cosmetics into a large suitcase. For a moment she felt jealous of her friend's good luck, then scolded herself. Peggy never did have the relentless drive to become a movie star. Marriage and motherhood would suit her well.

"Gee, now that I'm leaving I guess you'll have to get another roommate. Do you have enough money for next month's rent?"

Crystal knew exactly how much money she had in her bank account—about two hundred dollars—but she wasn't going to spoil Peggy's happiness with her problems.

"Don't worry about me. I still haven't been paid for last week's work." Five days as an extra was better than nothing, she thought. At least she was earning money.

Peggy snapped her suitcase shut. "Well, I guess this is it. I'll call you as soon as we get back from Vegas."

Crystal dug around in the kitchen cupboard and found a half-empty box of rice. She threw a handful at her friend as she rushed out the door. "Be happy."

"I will," Peggy called over her shoulder.

Crystal walked into the dressing room, picking up Peggy's discarded clothes, rearranging hangers, trying not to feel as if she had been deserted. She felt a strange emptiness, missing Peggy already. She was really on her own now, she thought, as she stared at her reflection in the multiple closet mirrors.

"Well, isn't that what you wanted, dummy?" she asked herself. She had left nice, safe Cape Mary to be discovered, to become a movie star. When would it happen? When would she get her break?

She knew she had talent, and her acting teacher had used her in two class productions. But when were all the singing, dancing, diction classes going to start paying off? She would do anything to get a real chance at a role—even if it meant a tryst on the proverbial casting couch. Unfortunately, she had never been inside a studio office, much less met a producer. When would someone notice she had talent?

She glanced around the room; the silence was unnerving. Crystal decided she needed some sunshine to cheer her up, so she slipped into a bikini and walked down to the pool.

Richard Cummings, who occupied the corner apartment on her floor, was stretched out on a chaise lounge. Crystal had seen him around the building, but they had never spoken. Peggy had warned her to stay away from him, claiming that he dealt drugs when he couldn't get any movie work. Crystal wondered if it was true. She thought he was one of the most handsome men she had ever seen. He had curly chestnut hair framing a narrow face, and his mustache emphasized the thin nose. He was very tan, which made his turquoise eyes seem translucent.

"Hi," he said, glancing up at Crystal. "My name is Richard."

"Yes, I know. My roommate told me your name," she said as she began slathering oil on her barely clad body. "I'm Crystal Smythe."

"Your accent is strange," he said. "I'll bet you're not from California."

"That's right," Crystal admitted. "I was born in England."

"So what brings you to tinsel town?"

"I'm an actress," she said.

"No kidding! I'm an actor," Richard said, reluctantly tearing his eyes away from her breasts. "How're things going?"

"Nothing to write home about. I've been filling in with modeling jobs at department stores, which helps pay the bills. Although my agent has landed me work as an extra, I haven't been discovered. I keep hoping to get some lines, since the extra pay would help, and maybe someone will take notice that I can act, too."

"Who's your agent?"

"Moss Rogers. Who's yours?"

"Jodie LeVitus. She says she's got a supporting role for me in the next Burt Reynolds film."

Crystal sat up. "No kidding?"

"It's not for sure yet, but I'm going for a screen test on Thursday." Richard grinned at her, turning on the charm. "I'll see if there's anything in it for you."

Crystal had heard that line often before, but she still hoped it was true. Besides, she decided she would like to know him better.

Richard glanced at his watch and sprang to his feet. "I've got to go," he said, flexing his muscles for her. "Catch you later."

Crystal watched him saunter away. She wondered if it was true about the Reynolds movie. That's the type of break I need, she thought, as she slipped into her favorite dream of stardom.

• • •

Two weeks passed before she saw Richard again. He was sitting by the pool, reading the sports page. She smiled at him as she sat in the lounge chair next to his. "How did your screen test go?"

He shrugged indifferently. "Aw, they turned me down. Reynolds couldn't cut the competition. Said I was too good-looking."

Crystal suspected he was lying, or at least exaggerating the truth, but kept her opinion to herself. "I know what you mean. The kids in my acting class say that if you're ugly or have a wart on your nose, you can always get a job as a character actor. But heaven help the rest of us."

"No work, huh?" He glanced long and hard at Crystal, thinking she would be a pleasant diversion.

"I've been demonstrating perfumes at department stores, but last week I had two days' work over at Paramount. I played a nun one day and a hooker the next," she said, grinning mischievously.

"At least it's something."

"Not enough, though. What I earn barely covers my classes, phone service, clothes, and make-up." She pointed to the classified section of the newspaper. "I'm looking for a job now. I may have to put my acting career on the back burner for a while."

"That's a shame. What kind of work are you looking for?"

"Mostly part-time work, telephone sales, that sort of thing. Or maybe I could be a cocktail waitress. I wouldn't mind working in one of those classy bars where the tipping is good."

"Have you ever worked as a waitress?"

"No, but I'm willing to do anything to pay the rent and put food on the table," Crystal said, a serious look on her face. "I want to be an actress, but not a starving one. I'm tired of eating spaghetti. What I want is a nice juicy steak."

Richard winked at her, laying on the charm. "I can fix that. I've got a couple of T-bones in the freezer. Come on over to my place tonight, and I'll grill you a steak so big, you won't be hungry for a week."

Crystal awoke in Richard's bed, her head throbbing; she had drunk too much cheap red wine the night before. She sat up slowly, her mouth dry. She looked down at Richard, her eyes traveling over his slim body, the hairy chest, the way the hairs crept down to his crotch.

Though she had lost her virginity to Ray Morrill, her high school sweetheart, the setting had been the back seat of his father's car, and it was a clumsy and inadequate experience. Then there was Bobby, one of the fellows in her acting class. They'd dated a few times, and one crazy night she had allowed him to make love to her.

Crystal hadn't realized how little she knew about sex until Richard made love to her. He had shown her what good sex was, and she had been an avid pupil. She reached out and touched him, boldly, almost possessively. He opened his eyes and broke into a wide, open smile.

Crystal crept into his arms, seeking his caress, forgetting her headache as his fingers searched between her legs, rekindling the tingling sensation.

"Do you like that, babe?" he grunted.

"Oh, yes," she sighed.

Richard persuaded Crystal to move into his apartment. She continued working as an extra, and occasionally even had a line or two of dialogue, but her career wasn't progressing as quickly as she wanted. Everyone had advice: change agents, change your hair color, get a nose job.

Crystal ignored their suggestions, waiting for her break. She knew that the odds were stacked against her, that it was a question of luck, but she spent hours wondering when it would happen.

"Don't worry, babe," Richard consoled her when she came back from yet another fruitless round of casting agents' offices. "You'll make it."

"It's so damn discouraging," she moaned. "I'm a good actress, but no one bothers to find out."

"They will."

"When?"

"It'll happen. Don't worry so much. Someday you'll be the biggest star in Hollywood," Richard said, picking up the television guide.

"Do you really think so? You're not just saying that to make me feel good?"

Richard thumbed through the pages and began screening the listings. "Flip the TV on channel five. There's a program I want to watch."

"I asked you a question!" Crystal snapped at him. "Why can't we talk? Why do you have to turn the damn television on the minute I have something important to discuss?"

Richard looked up at her. He liked having Crystal around; she was a good cook, could iron his shirts right, and was one hell of a lay. But all she did was bitch about her career. Shit. He had a career, too, not that she ever asked. He'd even had six lines in that Michael Caine movie. They'd got cut, but it wasn't every day you got to be in a film with a big star like Caine.

"I'm tired," he said. "It's been a long day, so turn the TV on, will you?"

Crystal did so angrily and flopped into the upholstered chair. It was covered in faded chintz, and its stuffing had started to come out at the seams. She looked around at the room she called home. The sofa was a fold-out bed, its mattress lumpy. The coffee table was scarred where Richard had carelessly let his cigarettes burn down, falling out of overflowing ashtrays. He never bothered to empty them, and she worried that someday he'd set the place on fire. Though she tried to keep things neat, Richard was a slob.

Home! It was a dump, but she had nowhere else to go. At least Richard let her spend her money on her classes and clothes. She felt guilty about not contributing to the household expenses, but on the other hand, rent was paid for with the money he made from selling drugs. She knew it was wrong, but Richard convinced her that he was careful, only dealing to fellow actors, to people he knew. It was a rotten way to live, she thought, but someday she would become a star—and everything would be different. Someday.

Crystal became a slave to Richard's lovemaking. He made love to her in his car, at the movies, and one night in the swimming pool, not caring if the neighbors saw or heard them.

They smoked grass constantly, and he gave her coke, too. And there were pills to take: one to fly by, one to come down by.

Peggy was disappointed by the change in her friend. Crystal had lost too much weight and looked like a zombie. She ventured to voice her opinion of Richard, but Crystal wouldn't listen to any criticism of him.

"You have Ted, and soon you'll have your baby," she said impatiently. "I have no one but Richard."

"You'll always have me as a friend," Peggy assured her, "but I still think you're wasting your time on this guy. What happened to your career?"

"Don't worry. I'm working."

Peggy sighed. There was no way she could convince Crystal that Richard was ruining her. "Well, if you ever change your mind . . . like if you want to leave him or something . . ."

"I won't," Crystal said emphatically and then changed the subject.

A few days later she was making dinner when Richard came flying into the apartment, whistling happily.

"Have I got good news, babe!" he said, throwing his arms around her waist and squeezing her tight. "I was talking to this producer friend of mine, and I showed him your pictures. He's mad about you and wants you in his next movie."

Crystal stared at him. "Are you serious? When? What's the name of it? Who's going to be in it?" she questioned him excitedly.

"I'm your co-star," Richard said, patting her on the behind, then letting her go. He opened the refrigerator and took out a beer.

Crystal hugged herself as she danced around the room. "I can't believe it. Me! Starring in a movie."

"I promised you that I'd get you some roles," Richard said as he sank down onto the sofa. He gulped his beer, then reached for the box where he kept his grass and began rolling a joint.

"What kind of a movie is it?" Crystal asked, returning to the preparation of their dinner.

"You'll find out tomorrow evening. We're going to meet with my friend."

"Tomorrow! Oh my gosh! I wish I had more time. My hair needs a trim, and look at my nails."

"Your hair's fine, and you can do your nails in the morning," Richard said, lighting the joint.

"I just wish I had more time to prepare," she said. "What do you think I should wear?"

"I don't think it makes much difference," he said, inhaling deeply. "Here, have a hit."

Crystal sat beside him and accepted the joint. "I can't wait to tell Peggy."

"She'll be surprised, that's for sure," Richard said, grinning at her.

"You still haven't told me the name of the movie."

"What difference does it make?" Richard said. "The important thing is that you're going to be a star."

Richard gave her some pills to calm her nerves before they went to their meeting with his friend. They drove down Sunset Boulevard and pulled into the driveway of a seedy motel.

"What are we doing here?" Crystal asked.

"Meeting my friend," he said, pulling out a small bottle and a tiny spoon. He snorted some coke, then insisted that Crystal do likewise. "Here. This will get you up."

She felt the rush to her head and the tingling sensation. "Wow! What a rush!"

"Yeah, I know. It's good stuff," he said, recapping the bottle. "Now look. This guy is going to pay us big bucks, so you have to agree with anything he wants. This is your big break, babe."

"Yes," Crystal said breathlessly, her eyes sparkling, her cheeks flushed.

"Good girl," he said. "Come on. Let's get the show on the road."

Richard led her to room twenty-three, knocked on the

door twice, and entered. He greeted a short, balding man who was bending over a movie camera on a tripod.

"We're all set to go, Marty. This is Crystal."

Crystal smiled at him shyly. "It's a pleasure to meet you."

"Yeah. Same likewise," Marty said. "Okay, strip down and do your thing. And I want solid action."

Richard laughed. "You're going to love it."

Crystal froze, the shock reversing the effect of the cocaine. "What's going on?" she demanded, eyeing the short man warily.

Richard grasped her arm. "After we make this flick you'll be a star, babe. Come on, take the clothes off."

"What kind of star? A porno star?" she shrieked.

"The money is good, and a lot of people started in porno," Richard whispered as he pulled his pants off. "Even Marilyn Monroe did a skin-flick."

"I'm not going to do it," she hissed back at him. "This isn't the kind of movie I want to make."

"Cut the jabbering," Marty growled, wondering why Richard hadn't explained things. "I ain't got all day. Let's get the show started."

Richard turned to him. "Give me a minute."

Marty was angry. He'd given Cummings up-front money and paid for two hours at the motel. "Look, girlie, all you gotta do is spread your legs. Lover boy will do the rest."

"I can't do it," she whispered.

Richard glared at Crystal. "What difference does it make if we do it in private or on the screen," he said angrily. "What do you think I've been keeping you around for? Get undressed."

Crystal stared at him in disbelief. She had actually thought he loved her. How could she have been so dumb? The horror of what she was becoming made her blush with

shame. She felt degraded, humiliated. She had trusted
Richard, loved him, but he was only using her.

"You'll have to get someone else," she stuttered, the
tears rolling down her face as she backed out of the room
and fled.

VIII

The sun was setting when the FBI arrived. Wright directed
the investigators to set up shop in the living room.

"Is this really necessary?" Crystal asked, watching in
dismay as the sofa was pushed back to make way for a card
table.

"They need somewhere to put their equipment," Wright
said. "We're lucky the FBI has decided to get involved so
quickly, since we still don't know if Emily has actually been
kidnapped."

"What good will all this do?" Crystal asked.

"Let me introduce you to Agent Gerald Willis. He's in
charge of the FBI investigation."

A tall, skinny man bowed his head to Crystal. His skin
was ghostly pale, as if he spent all his time indoors. His suit
jacket was rumpled, and Crystal's alert eye caught a
glimpse of mismatched socks under trouser legs that were
far too short. His shoes were scuffed as well. She wondered
if he was wearing some sort of disguise. No one could
possibly be that disorganized, she thought.

"We'll try to trace the ransom call when it comes in,"
Willis said in a no-nonsense manner. "It'll be important that
you keep him on the phone long enough for us to get a good
fix."

Crystal nodded. "Yes. I understand."

"Good," Willis said, plugging a headset into the telephone. "We'll be recording his call, of course, so even if he

hangs up before we can trace him, we'll still have something to work with."

"How will that help?"

"What we do is take the tape to the lab to analyze it.
You'd be surprised at what we can learn once we sort out all
the background sounds. Sometimes we can pick up a clue to
the kidnapper's location. Modern technology is really something else, you know," he said, his tone haughty. "We can
also use the recording for voice prints, and those can be real
important in the courtroom when we want to establish
someone's identity. You just never know what you're going
to learn from these tapes. Why just last week I was working
on a case where . . ."

He droned on and on, and Crystal feigned interest, but
her head was spinning. She had to get away from the man
and his grating voice. "Would you excuse me? I have a
headache."

"Bit of a snob, isn't she," Willis observed after Crystal
had departed.

"Not at all," Wright replied, irritated by his attitude.
"Miss Smythe is really quite nice. And she's been damn
patient, considering she's under a great deal of strain. What
the hell did you expect? An invitation to tea?"

Willis threw his hands up in the air. "I give up. Okay?"

Wright shrugged his shoulders. "You're supposed to be
the expert. You tell me how she's supposed to act when her
daughter is missing and we have no idea if she's been
kidnapped or not."

"I'm going back to the office," Willis's assistant said.
"Want anything?"

"Bring me back a pizza," Willis said as he sprawled on
the brocade sofa.

"The maid here will be happy to fix you something to
eat," Wright told him.

"I don't want to impose on her ladyship's hospitality."

"Cut that out," Wright growled.

"Just joking," Willis said, "but I really do want a pizza."
He handed some money to the other agent. "Make it double
everything, will you?"

Willis loosened his tie. "Okay. Tell me what you think.
Who done it?"

Wright sat opposite Willis. "I have two names on my
suspect list, both which are highly improbable. The first one
is the husband, James Mitchelson. He and Crystal have a
trial separation. He may have taken the child to gain
custody, but Crystal says he wouldn't do anything like
that."

"Crystal? So you're on a first name basis. How cozy."

Wright bridled at the insinuation. He knew he wasn't
going to like working with Willis, but he had no choice. He
had to cooperate if they were going to find Emily.

"Miss Smythe is what I call her," he said. "And wipe the
sneer off your face. We haven't been able to locate her
husband, though it seems he might be out sailing. His boat
isn't at the marina."

"Who's the other suspect?"

"Miss Smythe's secretary. His name is Neil Simmons."

"Why do you think he did it?"

"Maybe money. Maybe he's jealous of all this."

"So what do you know about him?"

Wright gave Willis a brief history of the secretary. "What
bothers me is that he has a very flimsy excuse for the time
when Emily disappeared. He was very nervous when I
questioned him. My instincts tell me he's lying. I've
decided to put a tail on him."

"Okay. What else?"

"So far, that's it."

"Hmmph! That's it, huh?" he repeated, adding to

Wright's irritation. "You Beverly Hills cops sure got cushy jobs. Babysitting all these movie stars and the rich and famous, protecting their multi-million dollar homes and plastic-surgery faces. A kidnapping just isn't up your alley, is it?"

Wright stood up, controlling his anger. "You play with your toys. I'm going back to my office to do some real work," he said, getting in his own swipe at the agent before he left the room.

IX

Emily glanced at the door, listening to him turn the lock. He had several bags in his hands and carried them to the trunk next to the bed. Emily watched as he placed the food on the trunk. There was Kentucky Fried Chicken, milk, sodas, cookies, crackers, peanut butter, and jelly. He silently placed paper plates, napkins, and plastic utensils next to the food.

The chicken was still warm and gave off an inviting aroma, making Emily realize that she was very hungry. "Why have you kept me locked up all day?" she demanded.

"Because I don't have a babysitter for you. This way you can't get into trouble."

"When's mommy coming? I don't want to stay here anymore. Why can't I go home?"

"She told me to tell you that she had to work late at the studio. She'll be here tomorrow," he said as he pulled a blue T-shirt out of a bag. "Here. Put this on. The one you're wearing needs washing."

Then he carried the television set into the bedroom, turned it on, and adjusted the rabbit ears. The black and white picture was snowy, but the sound was okay.

"The reception around here sucks," he said as he picked

up Emily's camp shirt and walked out the door, "but it'll keep you company while I'm gone."

"When are you coming back?"

"Tomorrow," he said. "With your mother."

"Please don't leave me alone," she pleaded.

"You'll be all right," he said. "There's plenty of food if you get hungry."

"No. Please. Don't go," she screamed as he turned and walked out of the room and locked the door.

Emily sat in stunned silence. She sensed that he had lied to her. Mommy hardly ever worked on the weekends. Was she being punished? Why? What had she done? Mommy never left her alone. She always had Socorro to take care of her.

Emily crawled on the bed, pulled her doll into the tight circle of her arms, and began to cry.

"Mommy, mommy, where are you?" she sobbed.

X

Elizabeth stood at the window, studying the dark ocean. Her home had been built in the late thirties and was situated on a bluff above Sausalito. There was no fog today, affording a view of Alcatraz Island and the city across the bay. The hills were starting to sparkle as dusk stole away the sunlight. Streetlights blurred with the soft amber of house lights and the neon glare of shops and restaurants. The view normally had a calming effect on her, but she had felt uneasy all day. She hadn't received any new images, nothing about the child, except the sensation of traveling down a dark tunnel. It was an obstacle vision, one she would have to overcome if the images persisted. Only then would she be able to help the child.

She sipped her vodka-on-the-rocks, rehashing the day's

events, searching for a clue. She had been working on her memoirs, a compilation of the more complicated cases in which she had assisted the police by using her psychic powers. She felt tired. Faces of the people she had helped, or had been unable to help, flashed across her mind. Elizabeth was seventy-two years old and had been a psychic investigator almost all her adult life. She enjoyed the feeling of accomplishment that her unusual power gave her.

It hadn't always been that way.

Elizabeth sighed and turned back to the girl who sat quietly waiting to continue, her pencil poised above her steno pad. Jennifer Elkins was a graduate student who had agreed to work as Elizabeth's secretary in exchange for material for her master's thesis on parapsychology. So far the relationship had been quite satisfactory for both. Elizabeth had little patience for writing, and Jennifer was an eager student.

"I'm sorry. What did you ask?" Elizabeth said.

"I said I need some background. When was the first time you actually had a psychic experience?"

"I was eleven years old," Elizabeth recalled. "I foresaw my grandfather's death and told my mother about the vision."

"What did she say?"

"Mother laughed and said it was just my overactive imagination. Grandfather died unexpectedly three days later."

"Did that frighten you?"

"No. I was just curious. There were other incidents after that—dreams which had a sense of reality, images of events that actually happened at a later date."

"Like what?"

"I became quite adept at finding lost objects," Elizabeth said, the memories flooding back. "One afternoon I was sitting in the living room, working on a jigsaw puzzle. A neighbor, Mrs. Sovinsky, was having tea with my mother, lamenting about her lost wedding ring. She had searched everywhere, and her husband had even taken the kitchen drain apart to look for it. So I told her it was in the basement, underneath the washing machine, where it had fallen while she was doing the laundry. In those days washing machines were quite monstrous. Difficult to use, and your clothes often got chewed up. I hated having to put the clothes through the wringer."

Jennifer smiled politely, accustomed to Elizabeth's rambling stories. "What happened next?" she prodded.

"Mrs. Sovinsky set her teacup down and turned indignantly to my mother, demanding an explanation. Mother shrugged and told her that I had a kind of sixth sense about those things. I remember her words: 'If my daughter says it's there, it's there.' "

Elizabeth laughed, remembering her mother's expression. "Anyhow, the following morning Mrs. Sovinsky reported that the ring had been found—right where I said it would be. Mrs. Sovinsky was sure that I'd stolen the ring and later put it under the washing machine. The neighbors thought it was just a lucky guess. I knew better, and my mother believed in me, and she told me about my Aunt Sophie, who also had the power. I guess I inherited it."

"How did you feel?" Jennifer asked, pleased that the psychic was confiding in her.

"Excited," Elizabeth admitted, "but my mother warned me to be careful. She didn't want people to think I was a freak, so she told me not to talk about it."

"What did you do?"

"I had no one to confide in. The girls in my classes at school were only interested in talking about boys and hairstyles. I found the public library more to my liking.

That's where I read about psychic phenomena, and about
Edgar Cayce, who used his psychic power to diagnose
illnesses. Since he was a firm believer in reincarnation, I
devoured every book I could find on the subject."

"What did you learn?"

"I'm not sure. I kept wondering if my present life was a
continuation of a previous life and if I was Aunt Sophie's
reincarnation." Elizabeth laughed, amused by the thought.
"I never have figured that out."

"So tell me more about yourself," Jennifer prompted, not
wanting to break the magic spell of the moment. Elizabeth
was usually reluctant to speak about her personal feelings.

"I married Bill Anderson, the older brother of a high
school classmate. When World War II broke out, he earned
his pilot's wings and then was based in San Diego. I moved
from Bakersfield so I could be near him.

"I was happy living by the sea. It was strange, but I
sensed that my psychic powers were stronger now. I was
still studying reincarnation and wondered if it had anything
to do with my previous life, since my Aunt Sophie had lived
by the ocean. Anyhow, my visions increased, and I became
fearful for Bill's life. I knew something was going to
happen to him."

Elizabeth closed her eyes, as if blotting out the memory.
"I tried to live with my fears," she continued, "but the day
came, a Wednesday—the exact hour is etched in my
mind—when I saw Bill's plane crash."

"How awful!"

"The shock was overwhelming. I rushed to the navy
base, hoping against hope that my vision was incorrect. It
wasn't."

Jennifer leaned forward in her seat. "How were you able
to go on with life? Didn't you hate your psychic power?"

"It was difficult. I was torn with grief and had to get

away from there. That's when I moved to San Francisco and bought this house."

Elizabeth looked around the room. It was filled with ghostly reminders of her past. There was far too much furniture in the combined living-dining room, but she couldn't part with anything. The people she helped always found a way to thank her. Every table top was cluttered with mementos. It was a mismatched room, a memorial to the work she had done.

But not all the stories had happy endings. Often the results were tragic, but the parents, friends, sons, and daughters were always grateful. No matter how long the person had been lost or dead, they had to know the truth.

"I'm tired," Elizabeth said. "Do you mind if we stop for today?"

Elizabeth watched Jennifer leave, admiring her light step, wishing she was young again.

Elizabeth's reputation had steadily grown over the years. The police were always asking her to help with the difficult cases, the kidnappings and the murders. Her only request had been anonymity, but unfortunately, reporters constantly wrote articles about her. Elizabeth had been besieged by so many people who had lost faith in the police and considered her their last hope for finding a missing relative. Sometimes she was able to help, sometimes she was too late.

It had been a lonely life. She never remarried, unable to bear the thought that if she did meet someone, she might "see" his death, too.

Elizabeth had always felt compelled to take on more cases than she could handle, having decided her God-given gift was meant to help humanity. She despised those psychics who tricked people into spending their money for information, pretending they held the key to life.

Sometimes she disliked her power. When she went to

bed, a strange, fog-like trance would overcome her subconscious. Sometimes she awoke in a sweat, with chilling thoughts filling her head: visions of a major earthquake, an image of an air collision that would soon take place, awareness of the impending death of a famous person. Elizabeth knew a psychic couldn't, shouldn't, try to shape destiny. That's why she didn't try to warn someone when she "saw" President Kennedy's assassination before it happened. Not that they would have believed her. She had hoped and prayed that she was wrong, then wept as she watched the news footage of that sad day in Dallas. She had visioned countless disasters, been pulled apart by the images, and felt utterly helpless knowing she couldn't prevent the dreadful things that would happen.

She also knew that as she got older, her powers were diminishing. It was taking her longer and longer to solve cases, and she felt constantly tired. She would gladly quit, but the powers that ruled her subconscious wouldn't let her. Elizabeth sighed. Whatever was bothering her now would soon reveal itself. She walked into the kitchen.

After dinner Elizabeth went to bed and tried to read, but was unable to concentrate on the words. She fell asleep and slowly became caught up in a vivid dream. She was traveling on a road, going through a dark tunnel of trees. She felt afraid, apprehensive, watching for a sign. The car finally stopped in front of a small house.

Elizabeth struggled to free herself from the dream, but it drew her in deeper. She approached the house slowly, sensing the child's fear. She entered the house, stumbling in the dark, afraid of what awaited her there. Her hand trembled as it opened the door to a dark room.

And then she heard the child's voice call out to her over and over. "Mommy, mommy, where are you?"

With a start, the dream ended, and Elizabeth woke up.

She switched on the nightstand light and picked up her pad and pen. She wrote down her impressions, but something eluded her. What was the meaning of the dream? she wondered. Was the child alone? Where was the man? Could this be connected to her earlier images of the color red?

Once again Elizabeth realized she was getting old. She knew she was losing her power, which was why she couldn't get a true picture. Yet, though her "awareness" was fading, she was sure of one thing—the child was real, and she was afraid. She needed help.

Elizabeth didn't want to become involved, but it was too late. She was reluctantly being drawn into the mystery. She leaned back against the pillows, and flicked the light off. She closed her eyes, thinking that perhaps the answer would come in another dream, but it was a long while before she fell asleep.

sunday

I

John Jefferies reread the newspaper article about Crystal and Emily.

"God damn it!" he growled to himself. "That bitch got a huge write-up about starring in Melvin Schuller's new spy-thriller but they didn't even mention my name."

He angrily wadded the newspaper in a ball and threw it at Anna's black French poodle. It yelped and ran out of the room.

Anna looked up from the social pages she was reading. "What's wrong, sweetheart?"

John eyed Anna with disgust. Her mousy brown hair was cut in short curls that emphasized her chubby cheeks. Her skin was blotchy, and the buttons of her housecoat bulged over her extended stomach. She had devoured a huge stack of pancakes and was now eating greasy sausage patties.

Melvin threw parties at his palatial home at least two or three evenings every week so he could screen new movies for his friends. On the weekends he had pool and tennis parties. And of course John was expected to accompany Anna to all these affairs. It embarrassed John to have to be anywhere near her. If he had to suffer through this sham of a marriage, why the hell couldn't she fix herself up?

"I thought the doctor told you to stop stuffing yourself,"

he spat out at her. "If you don't give a damn about the way you look, you could at least think about the baby. Don't blame me if the kid comes out deformed."

Anna winced at his profanity. "Momma says she weighed the same as I do when she was carrying me."

"Momma says," he mimicked. "I'm tired of hearing what momma says."

Anna's eyes filled with tears. "I don't know what's bothering you. I had hoped that we could at least have a quiet Sunday together."

"God! You are such a whiner," he said, lighting a cigarette as he turned to stare out the window.

Anna stood and came to his side. "Daddy says that the kidnapping is going to slow down production on your film. Even if they do find Emily, Crystal isn't going to want to return to the set right away."

"Isn't that too bad," he snickered. "Crystal thinks she's so hot. Well, let me tell you something. She's finally getting what she deserves."

"That's a mean thing to say."

"What do you know about anything? You don't have to work with her. The bitch is always stepping on my lines."

Anna ventured a hand to John's shoulder, letting her fingers slide across the fine hairs on the back of his neck. "Daddy says they plan to shoot around Crystal's scenes."

"This film will never be completed."

Anna was puzzled. "Why not?"

"Because Crystal will never get her daughter back," he said harshly.

"That's ridiculous," Anna said, though she wondered if he could be right. She decided to press her point. "At any rate, I guess they won't need you on the set this week since all the scenes you have left are with her."

"So?" he said, shrugging off Anna's hand and standing.

"I thought maybe we could do something together. I'd like to go shopping for the baby's room," she said.

John stubbed his cigarette out. "No can do. I have to go somewhere."

"Where?"

"What business is it of yours?" he asked, infuriated that she was always meddling in his affairs. He was half-tempted to tell her—to see how she would react—but of course he couldn't. He would have to be careful. He had a lot to lose if anything went wrong. In a few more days all his worries would be over, and Crystal would become just a bad memory.

"I'm your wife," she said with a pout. "I think I'm entitled to know where you're going. What if I need you?"

"You'll survive."

"It isn't easy being pregnant; you should be more considerate of me. The doctor says my time is very near. If anything should go wrong, I need to know where you are." She paused, studying his handsome face. "Speaking of which, where were you yesterday?" she demanded. "I called all over town looking for you."

John stared at Anna, his blue eyes turning cold, surprised by her sudden assertiveness. "How dare you! Where I go and what I do in my free time is my business. Get that through your thick head," he shouted at her as he stomped from the room.

Anna slumped in his chair, crying. She hated him. She had thought marriage would be beautiful and that he would learn to love her, especially with the baby on the way. His baby. But he never even came near her now, refusing to sleep in the same bedroom. She had told him the doctor said it was okay to make love, but John refused to do so.

Her mother said she had to be patient with him, that he would come around after the baby was born, but Anna wasn't sure. He was always running off somewhere without her. Like when he went to Tijuana. Daddy hired a detective to find John and bring him back. It hadn't helped since he wouldn't stay at home. He had lots of excuses for where he went, and she was tired of hearing them.

Anna picked up John's fork and began eating what was left of his pancakes. She wondered if she should ask her father to have the detective follow John again. He was acting like he had something to hide, and she wanted to know what it was.

II

Emily pushed the hands away. "No, no, no . . ." she screamed, and then awoke from the terrifying dream.

She had become entangled in the blanket, and she struggled to free herself, panting, her heart pounding.

"Mommy?" she called out, but was answered only by an ugly silence. She sat up. "Mommy?" she called once again, this time her voice a bare whisper.

Emily sighed deeply, realizing that she was still alone in the strange little room. She crawled from under the covers and stood on the trunk. She could see the sun bouncing off glass chimes hanging from the cat lady's porch.

Dreadful thoughts filled her mind. He had said mommy was coming this morning. Where was she? When would she arrive? What if he had been lying? What if mommy wasn't ever going to come? Didn't mommy love her anymore?

Emily was scared and began to cry. She angrily pounded on the window with her fists. "Mommy, mommy, where are you?" she screamed with a wrenching sob.

III

Once again Crystal had spent the night on the sofa in the den, praying and crying, waiting for something to happen. At dawn she stumbled into the kitchen, where Socorro insisted she have some toast and juice. She glanced through the newspaper, but the words were a blur. Socorro finally convinced Crystal to go up to her bedroom to rest. Crystal meekly obeyed and fell across the bed. She slept fitfully and awoke exhausted, feeling drained of all energy, her head pounding as if she had drunk too much the night before. A shower and fresh clothes did little to make her feel better. She brushed her hair vigorously and tied it back with an elastic. She studied her tired face, then used make-up to disguise the dark circles under her red-rimmed eyes. She decided it was useless to bother putting on eye shadow or mascara; if she cried again, it would just be a mess.

Crystal paced back and forth, her movements repeated in the mirrors which covered every wall of the bedroom. Jimmy had teased her about the mirrors, saying she was vain, laughing at her attempt to explain how the mirrors enlarged the room. Secretly she knew he enjoyed watching their bodies as they moved together when they made love. Crystal shivered. That was such a long time ago, she thought, realizing how desperately she needed to be with Jimmy now. To feel his arms around her. To help her find Emily.

Noise filtered in from the street. She walked to the window and pulled back the curtains. A television crew was carelessly trampling the flowers which bordered the sidewalk. A pack of reporters had gathered in front of the house, cameras in hand, waiting for her to step outside. Several neighbors stood huddled together, and she could hear scraps of their conversation. The words "neighborhood watch" made her want to lean out the window to shout: "Too late. Where were you when my daughter was taken?"

She saw more cars stopping, lured by the television cameras. The passengers joined the crowd, eager for a glimpse of Crystal.

Crystal watched Melvin's bodyguard argue briefly, then escort a protesting teenager down the driveway, where he joined his friends in a convertible. The girls had short green and purple hair that stood on end, while the boys sported long ponytails. She could see them passing a cigarette, undoubtedly marijuana. They laughed and poked each other, then finally drove away, the wheels of the car squealing, the car stereo blaring.

Crystal saw Lieutenant Wright pull into the driveway, and she hurried downstairs. Neil had already opened the front door, and Socorro hovered nearby.

"Have you found her?" Crystal asked anxiously.

Wright fumbled nervously with his hat, choosing his words carefully. "I got a call from the West Hollywood Sheriff's Department. They found a little girl who matches the description."

Crystal's eyes grew large. "Oh, thank God!" Then her facial muscles tightened when she saw the look on his face.

There was no gentle way to break the news. Wright grasped Crystal's arm firmly. "The girl they found is dead."

Crystal swayed back, his words slamming into her. "No," she screamed. "No, no. It's not true. It can't be Emily."

"It is all my fault," Socorro gasped as she made the sign of the cross over her chest and began praying in Spanish.

Neil threw his arms around Crystal, rocking her gently, his eyes on Wright. "There has to be a mistake," he said emphatically. "Why do you think it's Emily?"

Wright studied the secretary. He had run a check on him but hadn't been able to find out anything. He would keep probing. As far as he was concerned, Simmons was the number-one suspect. He had had every opportunity to do it, and the child undoubtedly trusted Simmons and would go anywhere with him. As to why, the motive had to be ransom money. The financial gain would certainly outweigh any risk involved. Unless of course the dead child was Emily.

He addressed Crystal. "The girl has blonde hair, blue eyes, and is about the right age." She'd been raped, but Wright didn't think he should mention that. Not yet. He took the easy way out. "The body, uh, had no clothes on when it was found. Since we have no other missing children reports, we think it might be her."

"You think?" Neil said.

"The girl was discovered in a dumpster. We can't be sure until someone comes with me to the morgue to identify the body. She was, uh, kind of beaten up," Wright said, avoiding the truth. The West Hollywood police said the girl's face was bashed in, making it hard to base an identification solely on photographs.

Crystal slumped in Neil's arms, sobbing, the terrible feeling of loss tearing her apart. "My God, why? Why? Why?" she repeated over and over. "Why Emily? Why my baby?"

Wright helped Neil carry Crystal into the den. He walked to the bar in the corner and poured her a large brandy, carrying it back to the sofa. "Sip this," he said softly.

Crystal rocked on the sofa, her hands clutching the brandy glass tightly, crooning Emily's name over and over. Neil clumsily patted her shoulder. It was the first time he had ever seen Crystal lose control.

He stood slowly. He didn't want to go to the morgue, but someone had to, and he'd be a coward if he didn't. "You stay here. I'll go with Lieutenant Wright and check this out," he told her. "This is all a mistake. It *can't* be Emily."

Crystal looked up at Neil, her eyes brimming with tears, wanting to believe he was right but too tired to hope. She nodded wordlessly, then fell back against the cushions, drained.

"I'll be back as soon as I can," Neil promised, then turned to Wright. "Okay. Let's get this over with."

Socorro shook her head. "I'm so sorry. I should have been watching her," she sobbed. "I love Miss Emily; she's like a daughter to me. I would never do anything to hurt her."

"I know, Socorro. I know," Crystal said. Her heart felt like it would burst, and a huge lump welled in her throat. She stood up wearily, a sickening knot tightening her stomach. She patted Socorro on the shoulder, aware of the maid's suffering. "It's not your fault. Please believe that," she said. "I'm going upstairs to lie down. I don't want to be disturbed."

She climbed the steps slowly and entered Emily's bedroom. She fell across the bed, crying, praying that it wasn't true. That the dead girl wasn't Emily. That it was all a mistake, like Neil said. She was thankful he had gone to the morgue. That's something I could never do, she thought. But Neil is strong. He'll take care of everything.

Neil. Her good friend, her support, helping her once again . . . like he had done so long ago . . .

IV

When Crystal fled from Richard she took a chance and returned to the apartment. She hastily packed her clothes and make-up, picked up her portfolio, and slipped back out into the night, praying that Richard wouldn't come looking for her. She caught a bus and rode it to the end of the line, getting off in Santa Monica. She found a diner that was open and drank coffee for hours that night, wondering what she should do.

Her hands shook uncontrollably as she lit one cigarette after another, wondering how she could have been so stupid. Why had she thought Richard loved her? She realized she had confused sex with love and vowed to herself that she would never be used again. Because she had believed Richard's lies, her dream of being a movie star had washed down the drain, along with her self-respect.

Crystal thought of calling Peggy, but she had a husband and a baby to take care of. Why hadn't she listened to her friend's warning about Richard? Why had she let herself get involved with a man who sold drugs? Was she a coke head? Was she a grass freak? The cold realization of what she had become was brutally shocking. She had chosen easy street—and learned a bitter lesson.

She remembered a time back in Cape Mary when she had suffered a deep disappointment. Her favorite teacher had chosen another girl for the starring role in the school play, a part Crystal had worked hard to get for herself. She had stormed into the house, tossing her books on the kitchen table as she collapsed in a chair, sobbing. Her grandmother had been alarmed.

"What is it? What's wrong?"

"I didn't get the part. They gave it to that dumb Barbara Ann."

Her grandmother held her hand. "You're going to find out that you can't always get what you want, honey. Life is that way. Sometimes you win, sometimes you lose."

"But I'm better than Barbara Ann," Crystal cried.

"Then the next time you'll get the part."

"I wanted this one," Crystal said stubbornly.

"Don't be ungracious. There's always a tomorrow," her grandmother told her. "If you really want to succeed, you have to remember that."

After that, her grandmother's words became Crystal's motto. She learned to deal with disappointment, to look forward instead of backward. To have hope for a brighter future.

Crystal finally realized there was no point in berating herself for her involvement with Richard. It had happened, and now it was over. Done with. Finished.

"There's always a tomorrow," she repeated over and over, realizing she would have to make a fresh start. She had come to Hollywood to be a star, and she was going to do it. But first she would need a job to get back on her feet. She glanced out the window and saw that the morning fog was clearing. It was time to get on with her life.

She washed and changed clothes in the diner bathroom, then went out into the street, dragging her suitcase. She had walked three blocks when she saw the small sign in a beauty shop window: RECEPTIONIST NEEDED IMMEDIATELY. She waited until eight when a tall man came around the corner of the building and approached the door.

"Are you the owner?" she asked timidly.

"Yes. Do you want an appointment?"

"No. I want a job. I really need one," she added.

Neil Simmons noted the frightened eyes. He sensed that she was running from something or someone. He led her into the shop and she told him about arriving in Hollywood, trying to be an actress, and confessed that she had gotten involved with a man who had promised her the moon—and had given her nothing.

Neil liked her crisp English accent, the way she stood proudly, her honesty. He decided to hire her, even agreeing to allow her to sleep in the back room until she could find an apartment.

Crystal enjoyed working for Neil Simmons. The patrons were a mixed group, including many older women who had come to Hollywood to be movie stars but had never made it. Find yourself a husband was their advice. Neil had a different opinion. He styled Crystal's hair, showed her new ways to use make-up, and encouraged her to pursue her acting career.

"You have to put the past behind you. Everyone makes mistakes . . . but that's part of the growing process," he told her.

Crystal knew Neil was right. Richard had been the wrong man for her, but she was free of him, and she vowed it would never happen again. She saved her money, returned to her acting classes, and asked Moss Rogers for help. The agent didn't let her down. He found work for her as an extra. After that came the small speaking roles, and she began earning enough to give up her job with Neil. She learned and she grew, and finally got her break. Peggy convinced her husband that Crystal would be perfect in the new movie he was going to direct, insisting that Ted arrange a screen test for her. He was hesitant, but took the chance anyway, realizing he really had nothing to lose. He was glad, since the rest was history.

Crystal was sensational in the role, playing the part of the wife of a southern sharecropper. She had learned how to cope with disappointment in her personal life and used it to play the bittersweet role.

Neil prepared a celebration dinner at his apartment. They had finished eating and were sitting on the terrace, enjoying the balmy weather and the sumptuous view of the city lights.

"It's a dream come true," Crystal said, kicking her shoes off.

"It's only the beginning. You're going to be the biggest star in Hollywood. I know it."

"I couldn't have done it without your help," she said modestly.

Neil refilled their champagne glasses. "So many people come to tinsel town filled with dreams of being famous. When they do find work as an extra, they get paid peanuts, since only the stars make megabucks. The extras struggle to make ends meet, always hoping to be discovered, then wind up working in mundane jobs as waiters, shoe clerks . . ."

"Beauty parlor receptionists?" Crystal interrupted.

Neil laughed. "Yes. But it wasn't your destiny to remain one."

"I was lucky; I made the right friends."

"That has something to do with it. Plus being able to act. You've got a special quality—call it a radiance—that makes you stand out. Star quality."

"Do you really think so?"

"I know it."

Her next role was that of a schoolteacher in a suspense story. Crystal studiously prepared for the part. She'd been lucky with her first film. It was now time to prove she was an actress. She immersed herself in the character, becoming the timid, innocent Miss Perkins who falls in love with a street hustler. Her efforts paid off. She won an Academy Award nomination for Best Supporting Actress. The offers came pouring in to her agent.

"You see!" Moss gurgled, jabbing his cigar in the air. "I told you I would make you a star. The first day you walked into my office, I knew you had potential."

Crystal smiled to herself. In the beginning Moss hardly

earned his ten percent. No. It hadn't been Moss who made her a star, but Crystal didn't say so to the wiry little man who sat behind the huge marble-topped desk. It amused her to let him have his own dream. Besides, she needed him. Now more than ever. There were so many decisions to make, so many things she didn't understand about contracts. And she really did like Moss.

"You're going to be big, sweetheart, and you're going to be rich," Moss pronounced.

Crystal giggled, finding him amusing. "What I need is work."

"Did you read the new Scott Biggam script that I sent you? Melvin Schuller is producing."

"Yes, I read it, and I like it."

"Word is out that they've already cast the lead, but you would be great as the wife," he said. "I think it's a better role, and it'll show off your talents."

"That's exactly what I was thinking."

"Good. Good. I think we can make a deal. Tomorrow," he added. "Tonight, though, we're going to a big party at Melvin's house. I want you to buy something sexy to wear."

"Why the fuss?"

Moss held up his hand, counting on his fingers. "First, Melvin Schuller owns a major studio. Two, there will be some important people there that I want you to meet. Three, you spend too much time at home."

"I go out."

"With that hairdresser," he grumbled. "That's no life for a woman. You need a real man in your life."

Crystal stifled a laugh and stood, smoothing her suede skirt. Moss was a strange father figure, but his intentions were well-meaning. "I appreciate your concern, Moss, but suppose you worry about getting me the right films, and I'll take care of the rest."

Crystal bought a white silk dress that plunged seductively and draped over her hips. Then she purchased a white fox jacket to complete the look. Neil had brushed her hair up and pinned a white orchid among the cascading tendrils. She splurged on diamond and pearl earrings and wore her mother's solitaire engagement ring.

Now she stood at the party, nervously twisting her mother's ring, looking for Moss. He had said they were leaving, but somehow he had disappeared, and Crystal found herself trapped in a conversation with an obnoxious drunk who kept asking for her phone number.

"Crystal, *amor*," a dark-haired man interrupted in a deep Spanish-accented voice. "I have been looking for you everywhere. Our car is waiting," he said, grasping her arm firmly and leading her away.

"Who are you?" she whispered, curious about her handsome savior.

"Julio Goldman," he said, bowing gallantly. "Your humble admirer and devout fan."

"Thanks for the rescue," she said, waving to Moss, who was standing by the front door. "That man was getting on my nerves."

"Wait," he commanded.

Crystal was mesmerized both by his tone and the way his eyes caressed her. "I'm sorry. I really must leave," she apologized.

"This can't be. I meet the most beautiful woman in the world, and then she deserts me? No, no. You must promise that you will join me for breakfast in the morning."

Crystal looked into his black, piercing eyes, drawn to this strange, attractive man. She felt a blush come to her cheeks.

He's just like all the others, she thought. He isn't interested in me. He just wants to be seen with a movie star.

He arrogantly assumed that her silence was acceptance. "Good. The Polo Lounge at ten," he said, bending over her hand to kiss it, then snapped his heels at attention before spinning away.

Crystal didn't keep the appointment, but that didn't stop Julio. A few days later she awoke to the sound of someone banging on her front door. She glanced at her clock and saw it was just six.

"Now who on earth . . . ?" she mumbled to herself, grabbing her robe and rushing down the steps. She had recently purchased the two-bedroom bungalow in Laurel Canyon, and her only visitors had been Peggy and Ted, Neil, and Moss.

She opened the door and found Julio standing before her, clutching dozens of roses in his arms.

"How did you find me?" Crystal asked, dumbfounded, wondering if her hair was a total mess.

"Nothing is secret in this town, *querida*," he said, beaming wickedly. He held out the dewy roses. "These, my sweet, delicate flower, are for you, compliments of the Beverly Hills park system."

Crystal's jaw dropped. "You stole them?"

"Merely removed them from the gas-fumed beds of Santa Monica Boulevard so that their beauty and fragrance would not be lost."

Crystal was enchanted by his melodic voice. "I think you've had one drink too many."

He cocked an eyebrow at her. "I am drunk on your beauty, fair lady. I was so very disappointed by your nonappearance at breakfast. But I am a man of great patience. Today you cannot refuse me."

"I guess I can't," she laughed.

"Good. Now hurry and get dressed, my flower."

"Where are we going?"

"We must hurry to Santa Barbara."

"Santa Barbara? Why there?"

"Because I am scheduled to play in a polo game this afternoon. It's an exhibition match. My countrymen against yours."

"Exactly which country is that?"

"*Mi querida, Argentina, naturalmente*," he said in his lilting Spanish. "While we drive to Santa Barbara I will tell you everything about my home in Buenos Aires. My family raises cattle and horses, and I . . . I play polo. Now please, do hurry and dress. We'll have breakfast at the Biltmore Hotel in Santa Barbara. They have the most delicious . . ."

Julio talked nonstop. He regaled her with stories of growing up in Buenos Aires, his family's vast land holdings, his life in England as a student and later as a *bon vivant* on the French Riviera.

Though his conversation was generously sprinkled with the names of famous people—presidents, princes and princesses, European and American movie personalities—he spoke of them unpretentiously, like old friends. Crystal was totally charmed by his easy manner and pleased that he didn't ask her inane questions. She hated when people asked how it felt to be a movie star or work with some famous actor.

The waiter approached the table, refilled their coffee cups, and removed the empty breakfast plates.

"I've never been to a polo game," Crystal said.

"It's great fun, quite colorful, and it's the sport of kings.

Horses charging down the field, the wind in your face, your shirt sticking to your back."

"You paint an exciting picture," she said.

Julio signaled to the waiter for the check. "It's really quite thrilling. Nothing quite like it," he boasted. "I hope you learn to enjoy polo, since I play quite often and expect you'll attend all my future matches to cheer me on."

Crystal's romance with the South American playboy was a fairy tale come true; she had found her Prince Charming. He took her to elegant restaurants, sent flowers to her home and her dressing room on the set of her new movie, bought her beautiful jewelry. He was a true gallant, escorting her home by ten in the evening so she could get her rest. The newspapers and magazines featured photographs of them attending movie premiers, going to art shows, enjoying all the best parties. The gossip columnists speculated on when the wedding bells would ring.

Crystal secretly enjoyed the lavish attention but was perplexed by one thing: why hadn't he made any advances?

"I don't understand it, Peggy. He never kisses me."

"Never?"

"Pecks on the cheek, on the forehead, or on the wrist. Not that they don't excite me," Crystal hastily added. "But . . . he has never actually taken me into his arms and kissed me passionately. He seems to be holding back for some reason."

Peggy leaned back against the sofa cushions and giggled with amusement. She was expecting her third child and was in her final month. She patted her stomach. "This is the result of passion. Be thankful that you've finally met a gentleman."

"I think he's just a bit *too* much a gentleman," Crystal said wryly. "He's a *latino*. He's supposed to be passionate."

"I think I read somewhere that a Latin man will bed anyone in sight, but not the woman he intends to marry."

"That's ridiculous," Crystal chided her friend. "Anyway, Julio says that when I finish the movie, he wants to take me to Argentina to meet his family."

"Ah ha! Then I imagine he's getting ready to pop the question."

Crystal absently twirled a strand of her long hair. "Do you really think so?"

"Why not? I mean, I do assume that the two of you are madly in love," Peggy said, happy for her friend. "Or at least that's what I've been reading in the supermarket scandal sheets."

Crystal stood and began pacing around the room. "I think so. It just seems strange to me that he hasn't been more aggressive."

"Oh for goodness sake! Since you've got the hots for the guy, why don't *you* seduce him?"

"I've tried."

Peggy laughed. "Maybe I could get Ted to direct. This movie will be titled: 'Crystal's Seduction.' Opening scene: a glowing fire, champagne on a low table, Julio lounging comfortably on the floor atop a polar bear rug. The camera pans the room, stops on Crystal standing in the doorway, silhouetted by the hall light, wearing a daringly sexy and very transparent black nightgown . . ."

"Stop!" Crystal shouted, doubling up with laughter. "I think I can handle the rest of the scene," she gasped.

"Then do it and stop talking about it," Peggy chuckled. "And don't forget. I want a full report the next day."

The following weekend Crystal invited Julio to her house for dinner. She wore a frilly ivory lace blouse with a black silk skirt and pinned the gold butterfly which Julio had given her over her left breast. She splashed herself lavishly with her favorite perfume and brushed her hair hard to make it shine. She had studied cookbooks, debated over the menu, finally deciding on veal piccata and pasta, a green salad, and cheese with fruit for dessert.

Julio raved over the meal. "I didn't realize you were such a good cook," he said as they walked into the living room.

Crystal poured brandy, then sat on the sofa beside him. "I like to putter around the kitchen, but I never have enough time. When I come home from the studio, I'm too exhausted."

"It's not important," Julio said. "You need all your energy for the movies you star in so gloriously."

Crystal moved closer to Julio. She draped her arm across the back of the sofa and casually began stroking the back of his head and neck. It was time to take the initiative, she thought, and make her fantasy come true.

Julio broke the subtle contact and leaned forward to place his brandy glass on the table.

Crystal wasn't deterred. She felt sure that he wanted her but didn't know how to ask. Or perhaps he was reluctant to make the first move. This time she rested a hand on his thigh. "Julio, darling, I am extremely fond of you, but there's something that's bothering me. There are times you seem so distant." She paused a moment, weighing her next words. "I wonder if you really do care for me as much as you say."

"Have I given you any reason to doubt my devotion?" he asked, covering her hand with his own, immobilizing it.

Crystal laughed nervously. "No, of course not. But you treat me like . . . like a school girl!"

"Surely you are joking!"

"What I mean is that you don't seem to realize that I have

sexual needs and desires. I'm not a virgin, you know," Crystal said, her embarrassment turning to annoyance.

He tensed, turning to her. "I, too, have certain sexual needs and desires," Julio said, "but I was afraid of offending you. I wanted you to be sure."

"Oh, I'm sure," Crystal said, pressing against him, lifting her face to his.

Julio kissed her, soft gentle kisses at first, then more aggressively, bruising her lips. His hands roamed freely over her body.

Crystal shivered with anticipation as she fumbled with his belt buckle, found his zipper and reached inside his pants.

Julio groaned and pushed her back on the pillows. "I've wanted you for a long time," he said as he tore her panties off.

Crystal moaned, excited by his sudden assertiveness. "We should go into the bedroom," she whispered.

He crouched over her. "No, here, now," he said, losing all control.

He lay heaving upon her. Crystal was surprised and disappointed by how quickly it was over. She decided that in the excitement of the moment, Julio had simply overlooked her needs. A few minutes rest is all he needs, she thought, and then we can try again.

She smiled and stroked his face. "Julio, darling . . . ?"

"That was good," he said, springing to his feet. He began tucking his shirt inside his pants. "I must leave you now."

Crystal stared at him, not understanding. "Why?"

He grinned at her. "Don't you have to be at the studio tomorrow morning?"

"Yes, but it's still early."

He laughed. "Get your beauty rest, *querida*. You have a movie to complete."

She was confused. He turned from cold to hot to cold so

quickly. "When will I see you?" she asked, feeling beg-
garly, resenting having to ask.

"I'm flying to Dallas to look at some horses," he said as
he walked to the front door. He pursed his lips and blew her
a kiss across the room. "We'll get together next weekend,"
he said as he walked out the door.

Crystal was like a zombie the following week. She
flubbed her lines, missed her cues, and had to reshoot her
scenes over and over.

She had a sinking feeling that she had offended Julio. She
decided to consult Peggy. They met at the Bel Air Hotel.
Crystal sat opposite Peggy dejectedly, picking at her veal
chop and wild rice while drinking two martinis—something
she seldom did in the middle of the day.

Eventually the conversation turned to Julio. Crystal
poured out her heart to Peggy, telling her all her fears. "I
don't know what to do," she admitted.

Peggy told her she was worrying unnecessarily. "You're
being foolish. Julio was probably embarrassed by his lack
of control and that's why he disappeared."

"Do you really think so?" Crystal asked, still not
convinced.

"Yes. You wait and see. The next time you're together
will be different."

And it was. Julio took her out to dinner, and he was as
attentive as ever, showering her with compliments, holding
her hand, laughing and joking. Afterward, they went back
to her house, and Julio followed Crystal to her bedroom.

"Nice," he observed as he walked around the room,
picking up photographs, opening trinket boxes, smelling
her perfumes.

Crystal walked to him and put her arms around his waist.

She looked up into his dark eyes, waiting. Julio bent to kiss her.

"You are so beautiful," he said. He stepped back, studying her.

"Julio . . . ?"

"Don't move," he said. He swiftly removed his clothes, then walked to the chaise lounge and stretched out on it. "Now you may undress," he told her. "Slowly, seductively."

Crystal smiled at him; she understood. If he wanted a show, she would give him one to remember. Using all her seductive skills, she let the black silk dress glide down over her hips. She was glad she was wearing a black garter belt and nylons, knowing that the picture she presented was even more appealing. She posed and turned coyly, improvising her striptease. She slowly removed her lace bra and cupped her breasts.

She looked at Julio. Sliding her underpants down over her thighs, she stepped out of them gracefully. Then she moved toward him.

His eyes glistened as she approached.

Crystal bent over, pretending to smooth her nylons, presenting her backside to him. He suddenly smacked her on the behind, and Crystal stood up, startled.

"Go sit on the edge of the bed," he commanded.

She did as he asked, waiting expectantly. He hadn't moved. She started to take off her high heels, but he told her to leave them on.

Julio licked his lips. "Arouse yourself."

Crystal stared into his eyes, excited by the game they were playing. Her hands did as he bade.

"Please, my darling, please make love to me," she pleaded.

Silently he rolled her over on her stomach. "You want it now, don't you," he said in a rough voice.

"Yes, please," she panted as she felt him positioning himself between her legs. In an instant she was filled with horror. "No, not that way," she screamed.

He ignored her screams, groaning and repeating her name over and over. He finally collapsed on top of her, his breath coming in gasps. Crystal slowly mustered her strength to push him away and rolled on her side, crying. This wasn't the way she wanted to make love. Why had he been so cruel? Why had he used her so horribly? Why couldn't it have been beautiful? A joining of two souls, like she had imagined and wished for.

As if reading her mind, Julio reached out and wrapped his arms around her. "Crystal, *amor*. You excite me so much," he whispered. "More than any woman I have ever known."

"You hurt me," she sobbed.

"I lost my mind, *querida*. You must forgive me. I never want to hurt you," he swore, stroking her back. "I want you to be my wife. I want you at my side always. Will you marry me?"

Crystal turned and studied Julio. He seemed so sincere, so caring, and yet . . . she was puzzled. Perhaps his moment's madness had been her own doing, she rationalized. She shouldn't have been so convincing in her striptease act, she decided. And in a way, she, too, had enjoyed their game until . . .

She shuddered. She would never let that happen again. She would have to be patient with Julio, show him how much pleasure she could give him without pain involved. And yes, there would be time. He wanted her for his wife.

She wiped away her tears and smiled expectantly at him. "Yes, Julio, I'll marry you."

• • •

As soon as the film was completed Crystal began assembling a trousseau.

"I don't know why you can't get married here," Neil complained.

Crystal turned slowly, studying the exquisitely beaded wedding gown in the full-length mirror. "Julio says his family would be disappointed. And don't forget, I did ask you to come to the wedding."

"Impossible," Neil moaned. "Apart from the ghastly cost of flying to the other end of the world, I simply can't get away. I'll be up to my elbows in hair spray at the National Hairdressers' Convention."

"When we get back, I plan to have a small party so my friends can properly congratulate the groom."

"Small consolation," Neil said, lifting the veil from the folds of tissue and placing it on Crystal's head.

"Well, what do you think?" Crystal asked.

Neil stepped back, one arm folded across his chest, the hand of the other raised thoughtfully to his chin. "Not bad."

"Gee, thanks." Crystal rolled her eyes upward.

"I wish you and Peggy and Ted were going to be with me. It's kind of scary."

"You're having second thoughts? You can change your mind, you know."

Crystal stared at her image in the mirror. She had to admit she was edgy. But why? Was she being hasty? She hadn't made love with Julio since the night he proposed. He said he wanted to wait until they were married, but Crystal couldn't understand why or what difference it would make.

With a start she realized how silly she was being. It seemed that all she had on her mind was sex. Marriage has to be based on more: on love. Did she love Julio? She had asked herself that question countless times, and she still wasn't sure. Perhaps it was just marriage jitters. Lots of brides had doubts before they marched down the aisle. And there were probably men who did, too. After all, it was a big step. Crystal sighed. It was too late now. She was committed to the marriage. If she changed her mind now, everyone would laugh at her.

She turned to Neil, holding out her hands to him. "No, of course not. I'm sure I want to get married. Now help me out of this dress. I'm meeting Julio for cocktails, and you must do something creative with my hair."

The wedding took place at the Goldman hacienda, culminating two weeks of whirlwind activity. There had been horseback riding across the vast ranch, shopping excursions to the glamorous boutiques of Buenos Aires, luncheons, tea parties, elegant dinner parties, and balls.

The reception was the largest event of all. Crystal was sure she danced with every man at the party. She was relieved when her new sister-in-law finally accompanied her to change into her traveling clothes.

It was past midnight when Julio and Crystal arrived at the hotel in Buenos Aires. A fire had been lit in their suite, and a light supper waited. Crystal went into the bedroom and changed into a white lace nightgown, a gift from Peggy. She sprayed herself with perfume, freshened her lipstick, and joined Julio in the sitting room. Julio poured champagne, and they sat in front of the fire, the flames the only light in the room. Crystal yawned, stretching her feet toward the warmth.

"Tired?" he asked.

"A bit. I'm so glad it's all over. I think I have lockjaw from smiling so much."

"Everyone kept telling me what a lucky man I am. They all agree that you're the most beautiful woman in the world."

Crystal smiled and reached out a hand to caress Julio's face. "I'm the lucky one—to have found you."

Crystal waited for him to say something, but he was silent, lost in his own thoughts. She wanted him to hold her in his arms, to feel his touch, to taste his lips. She stood and slowly began to remove her nightgown, letting it slide over her hips. She stepped out of the gown, proud of her body, and held her arms out to Julio.

"I want to make love with you," she whispered, her eyes glued to his face.

Julio looked up at her. "The first time that I saw you, I knew you were the one for me. I had waited so long to find the perfect woman. For someone who could understand me, who would understand my special needs, who would give me pleasure."

Crystal trembled. It has been a long time since they had made love, and she was ready for him. "I want to please you," she whispered.

He stood, holding his hand out to her. "Do you? Would you do anything I asked?"

Crystal blushed, remembering the last time. "I'll do anything that gives us both pleasure, as long as it doesn't hurt."

Julio led Crystal into the bedroom and told her to lie in the center of the four-poster bed. "Let's pretend," he said, "that I am an Arab prince, and you are my slave."

He opened the suitcase and took out four silk cords. Crystal eyed them suspiciously. "What are those for?"

"It's part of the game. Come on," he teased, "you said you would do anything. Don't you love me?"

"Of course I love you," Crystal said. But she was dismayed. This wasn't how she had anticipated spending her honeymoon.

"Then play my game. I promise I won't hurt you."

Crystal knew she should say no, but she didn't want to hurt his feelings. She reluctantly agreed, allowing Julio to spread her arms and legs, then tie them to the four posters of the bed.

"I'll be back in a moment," he said, then disappeared into the bathroom with his suitcase. When he emerged, he was dressed in a loose caftan.

"I am Prince Ahmed, and you are my slave," he said, approaching the bed.

"Yes, master," Crystal giggled, falling into the game. "How may I please you?"

"You have been a bad slave."

"What have I done that should give displeasure to my master?" Crystal said, noting the stern look on Julio's face and trying not to laugh.

"I saw you with the palace guard."

"No, master, it wasn't me," she said, feeling light-headed. She realized she had drunk too much champagne, and now that she was stretched out in bed, she was starting to feel the effects.

"You lie," Julio said, whipping off his caftan.

Julio poised over her and poured oil into the palm of his hand. Crystal squirmed as he began rubbing her body with it. She felt herself becoming aroused as his hands possessively explored her body.

"Oh, God, Julio! What is that stuff? It's making me so hot!"

"Do not speak to me thus, slave," he said as he picked up a vibrator.

Crystal was stunned. Her eyes were glued to his, wondering if she had made a mistake. When would this game end?

"Tonight you will know pleasures that only I can teach

you," he said. "From now on you will do everything that I command."

Julio used Crystal, bringing her to the edge, then pulling away so that he could savor her moans of frustration.

Crystal was alarmed. The game, as he called it, wasn't finished. What was wrong with him? Where was the sweet, loving man that she had thought she was marrying, she wondered, as he assaulted her body over and over. She struggled against the cords that bound her to the bed, wanting the nightmare to end.

Crystal glanced up at his face. He's mad, she thought, as she suffered the abuse, afraid to say anything, afraid that he would never stop.

When he had satisfied himself, he collapsed on her. "Oh, God, was that ever good," he grunted.

Crystal was infuriated. She seethed silently with rage while waiting for his breathing to return to normal. She finally summoned her courage to speak. "May I go to the bathroom, please?"

Julio looked at her, smiling broadly. "*Ay querida*," he said, untying her bonds. "How thoughtless of me."

Crystal picked up her suitcase and walked into the bathroom, fighting back her tears. She showered and washed her hair, disgusted and ashamed, wondering how she could have been so wrong. Why had she thought he loved her? Why had she believed she was in love with Julio? She considered her options: life with a man she despised or going back to Hollywood and facing the scandal. She decided the latter would be easier to bear. She was Hollywood's golden girl. Her public would forgive her mistake. Moss would find the right role for her, and she would act her heart out. And she would forget the horror of this evening.

"There's always a tomorrow," she whispered to the

frightened image in the mirror, reminding herself, as she had done so many times in her life, that there was still hope.

When Crystal walked back into the bedroom she was fully dressed and had composed herself. She put her suitcase on the dresser and began packing the clothes she had worn earlier.

"I'm leaving," she calmly told Julio.

He jumped out of bed. "What did you say?"

Crystal looked at him with contempt, laughing, her shoulders shaking uncontrollably. "I'll bet anything that you can't make love normally like most men." She paused, then smiled smugly. "Wouldn't the gossip columnists like to know the truth? What a great headline: 'World-famous playboy likes kinky sex.'"

Julio reached out and slapped her hard. "I trusted you with my secret. You will never tell anyone."

Crystal touched her cheek; it was hot and she could feel a welt rising. "How dare you strike me," she said, thinking the words were like those in a script she had read. "No. You're not a man. Not a real man."

He shrugged his shoulders. "It was only a game."

"You should see a psychiatrist," Crystal said, snapping her suitcase shut.

"Where are you going?"

"Isn't it obvious? This marriage is over before it begins."

Julio was alarmed. He couldn't let her leave. He couldn't face the scandal. The newspapers would destroy him, his family would be outraged. "You can't mean it."

"But I do. I want an annulment."

"You would embarrass me in front of my family and friends? I thought you loved me."

"No. I loved an illusion," she said wryly. "I never want to see you again."

Julio felt ill. His parents had wanted him to marry an

Argentine girl; they would never forgive him. How could he
have misjudged her so? He had thought Crystal would
understand. After all, she was a famous movie star, and
there were undoubtedly things in her past she hadn't
revealed to him.

"Why play Miss Innocent with me?" he stormed at her.
"I'll bet you've put out plenty for all your producer and
director friends."

"You're pathetic," Crystal said. "I never realized how
narrow-minded you were."

"You're the one who's being narrow-minded."

Crystal realized it was pointless to continue the conversation. She picked up her purse and suitcase. "Get some
help, Julio," she said.

Julio glared at her. "I'm warning you, if you should ever
mention this, to anyone, I'll make you pay. Somehow,
somewhere, I'll make your life miserable."

Ignoring his threat, Crystal walked out of the room and
down the hallway, relieved to be away from him. "Why?
Why? Why?" she repeated over and over as she waited for
the elevator, wondering how she could have made such a
terrible mistake.

"Never again," she vowed. "I will never trust a man
again."

V

"*There's always a tomorrow. There's always a tomorrow,*"
Crystal repeated aloud, awakening from her nap with a
start. A voice was calling to her, bringing her back from the
past. She sat up slowly, frightened by the ugly memories.
And then she remembered. Neil. He was back from the
morgue where he had . . .

"Crystal, Crystal, where are you?"

Crystal walked to the landing and leaned over the railing. "Was it Emily?" she whispered.

Neil looked up at Crystal. "No, thank God! It wasn't her. The little girl wasn't Emily."

Crystal's heartbeat quickened, the awful fear she had held inside slowly changing to hope. She raced down the steps and grasped Neil's shoulders. "It's not her?" she asked, her voice trembling with excitement.

He shook his head. The morgue had been terrifying, and he had felt as if the walls were closing in on him. He was still unsettled by what he had seen. The dead girl had been sexually abused and badly mutilated, but he didn't think Crystal would want to hear the gory details.

Wright watched the tension drain from Crystal's face. She was relieved, and so was he, but for how long? How soon would it be before he had to return to the morgue to look at another child's bruised and battered body? "I'm sorry we had to upset you," he said, "but we had to be sure."

"I was afraid, and yet I couldn't believe that Emily was dead. I had this . . . I feel that Emily is all right. I don't know how to explain it." Crystal paused, trying to put words to her feelings. "I think it's something only a mother could sense. Or a father," she added. "Do you have children?"

"No. My wife and I haven't been blessed. But I think I understand. We have a dog—a mutt, actually—who is real friendly. He'll let anyone pet him. Anyhow, one night he got out of the backyard. I thought we'd never see him again. But not my wife. She was sure he would come back."

"Did he?"

Wright laughed. "Yes. And he brought home a girl friend. We still have both of them. They're kind of like our children. It's funny how you can become attached to dogs."

Crystal was surprised by the Lieutenant's friendly attitude. It made her feel better to know he was a sensitive man. "Emily has always wanted a dog, but I thought it would be too much trouble," she told him. "Maybe I'll get her a dog when she comes back."

"I bet she would like that," Wright said, then turned his attention back to business. He jerked his head toward the living room, where Willis's assistant was reading a magazine. "I take it there haven't been any phone calls?"

"No," she said. "It's so strange. If Emily has been kidnapped, why hasn't he made contact?"

"I'd feel a lot better if we could locate your husband. There's still a chance that Emily could be with him."

"No. I don't think so. I've told you that Jimmy would never do anything to hurt me," Crystal said. "It has to be someone else."

"You could help by making a list of people you know who might want to harm you or your daughter."

"I can't think of anyone who would be so cruel."

"That's what you want to believe, but I'll bet there are people who are jealous of you. Hairdressers, shopkeepers, maids, co-stars," he told her. "If you set your mind to it, maybe you could come up with a few names. Then the FBI would have something to go on. They could run names through their computers, maybe find someone who has a criminal background. You never know."

"I'll try," Crystal promised. "But what about you?"

"I'm doing what I can, but you have to understand that there are just over a hundred officers in the Beverly Hills Police Department. And only twenty-five detectives, of which two specialize in missing children cases like this. Myself and another man."

"I didn't realize," Crystal said feebly.

"If this were a homicide, I could enlist some of the other

detectives. Don't worry," he hastily assured her, "we'll find Emily. All we need is a lead."

"I want you to know that I appreciate all your help."

"Thank me when we get Emily back," the detective told her. "I'm going to my office for a while, and then I'll be at home. If you hear anything, please call me."

Crystal finally sat down to a late lunch. Though not hungry, she perfunctorily ate the grilled chicken and steamed vegetables Socorro placed before her. Then she carried her coffee into the den and sat on the sofa.

"I've been thinking," she said in a soft voice. "When Emily comes home, I'm going to take her to Knotts Berry Farm. She wants to see the dinosaurs. Do you know what she wants to be when she grows up?"

"No, what?" Neil asked, though he knew already. It was all Emily talked about. He poured brandy into a snifter and carried it to Crystal.

"A paleontologist! She wants to study fossil bones. Can you imagine?" Crystal said, smiling at the thought. "I didn't even know what a paleontologist was. Don't you think that's wonderful? Emily is so smart."

"Yeah. She sure is," Neil said. He glanced at his watch; it was getting late. "Uh, I have to go home. I need a shower, and I want to change clothes."

"What?" Crystal turned to him. "You're not staying?"

He hesitated before answering, choosing his words carefully. "I'm sorry. It's just that the morgue was a very trying experience. I need to, um, have some time to myself."

Crystal was grateful that he had gone to the morgue for her, but she was angry that he wanted to leave. He was acting completely out of character, and she couldn't understand why. Didn't he know how much she needed him? She didn't want to be alone, but she couldn't force him to stay. He had his own life to lead.

"Where is Emily?" she asked, her voice hoarse, her eyes searching Neil's for an answer.

He hesitated in the doorway. "We'll find her," Neil assured her. "We'll find Emily."

VI

Emily flipped the television dial. The reception was only good on three channels, and there was a baseball game on one of them. She saw that a news program had just begun on another and was about to change the dial when her photograph appeared on the screen.

She was shocked as she listened to the newscaster's comments. He was saying that she might have been kidnapped. How could that be? Didn't they know where she was? Why didn't they ask her mother?

After showing a few pictures of her mother, a commercial came on. Emily was confused. Was it true? Had he lied to her? Had she been kidnapped? Emily waited for the commercials to end and turned her attention back to what the newscaster was saying, but none of the other stories were about her.

She was afraid and began to cry. Why would he want to kidnap her? It couldn't be true. He said her mother was going to come. He said that she had planned a special surprise. It was just a game he was playing, and mommy would come soon and take her home.

Emily crawled under the bed covers, shivering from fear. "Mommy, mommy, where are you?" she sobbed as tears coursed down her cheeks.

VII

Lieutenant Howard Wright sat in his favorite chair. He had just eaten dinner with his wife for the first time in a week. He quietly picked up the newspaper, glanced at the headlines, then turned to the sports section.

Virginia asked, "Can I get you anything?"

"No, thanks. It's good to sit back and do nothing," he said, glancing fondly at his wife.

"Is there anything new on the Emily Mitchelson case?"

He shook his head. "Nothing useful."

"You mean you still don't have any clues?"

"Not a damn one. It's been forty-eight hours now, and no word. I think the secretary might be involved."

"Why?"

"When he went with me to the morgue to check on a body, he said something odd."

"What?" Virginia asked, intrigued.

"He said that it wasn't Emily, even before we got there, and he sounded convincing. Maybe he knows more than he's letting on. Maybe he took the girl somewhere. Only thing is . . . I can't figure out what his motive could be."

"You must be wrong. You told me that he and Crystal have been friends for years."

"Yeah. Well, friends become enemies."

"You're so . . . so . . . darn skeptical," Virginia said, shaking her head.

"That's my job, remember?"

"How about Emily's father? Maybe she's with him."

"We still haven't been able to contact him."

"Poor Crystal," Virginia said, pushing her needle through the material as she embroidered. "This must be horrible for her."

"It'll get worse if we don't find Emily soon," Wright said, turning back to his newspaper.

VIII

He drove slowly, thinking. He had only taken Emily to scare Crystal, to teach her a lesson. But now the newspapers were calling it a kidnapping.

He laughed. The best movie plots were often based on real life dramas. He was the producer and director of this strange turn of events. How would he write the story? Who would play Crystal, Emily, himself? How would the movie end? What should he do next?

He glanced down at the manila envelope into which he had stuffed Emily's T-shirt. He would drop it off at the studio. At least that way Crystal would have proof that Emily was alive and well. The question was, how far should he take the game?

IX

Elizabeth was watching the late night news, riveted by the story of the disappearance of Crystal Smythe's daughter, Emily. She flipped the television dial to see what the other news channels had to say. She was puzzled. Something about the story bothered her.

She turned the television off and walked to the patio windows, staring outside at the fog that enveloped the hillside.

Then she heard the voice again, "Mommy, mommy, where are you?"

Elizabeth leaned her head against the cool glass, her eyes closed, trying to focus on the voice, but it had gone. Was it possible? Could it be Emily? Occasionally it came to her this way, but it had been a long time since that happened. How could she be sure?

She paced back and forth, undecided. She walked back to the coffee table and picked up the newspaper, turning to the page with Emily's photograph. Elizabeth felt a sudden stabbing fear. She was sure now, but she wondered what Crystal Smythe would think if she turned up on her doorstep and said she could hear Emily's voice.

She would think I'm insane, Elizabeth mused. No. She couldn't do that, but she *could* contact the police. She checked the newspaper article and noted the detective's name who was in charge of the investigation. Elizabeth made up her mind. Tomorrow she would fly to Los Angeles. She would find Emily.

monday

I

Crystal lay back against the bed pillows, sipping her coffee. She was exhausted both physically and emotionally. Never in her life had she experienced so much pain and sorrow. She had been too young to comprehend the terrible loss of her parents, and when her grandmother died she had long been expecting it. She wondered how other people coped with losing someone they loved. Crystal had acted the part in several of her movies, but she realized how ill-prepared she was for the real thing.

She shuddered. She had to stop thinking gloomy thoughts. She had to think positive. The police would find Emily. The FBI would capture the kidnapper. Emily would be home today, and they would laugh and cry and hug each other. And later she and Emily would go to the pizza parlor and eat tons of pizza with everything on it, and . . .

No. Not with everything. Emily hated anchovies. She always picked them off her pizza. But she likes root beer, Crystal remembered, with vanilla ice cream floating in it. When they went shopping Emily always wanted to stop for a floater. Crystal would say no, but Emily would insist, knowing her mother all too well. Crystal always gave in, unable to deny Emily her special treat.

Crystal got out of bed and padded across the hallway to Emily's bedroom. She opened the closet and started pushing hangers aside. What will Emily want to wear? Not the pink dress; no, not the blue, it's too dressy. Yes. The white sailor dress with the navy-blue tie. Jimmy bought it for her, choosing it himself. Yes. Emily likes this one.

She carried the dress to Emily's bed and laid it out. She'll be so excited, have so much to tell me, she'll . . .

Crystal collapsed on the bed, crushing the dress in her arms. "Oh, baby, where are you?" she cried. "Where are you?"

II

Lieutenant Wright pulled into the driveway of Crystal's house and shut off the engine. Only one car was parked at the curb, a reporter sitting on the hood, talking to a man with a video camera. The rest of the reporters and the contingent of television crews hadn't arrived yet. Maybe they had lost interest in a story that had no clues, no suspects, no body. They'd be back, though, at the slightest sign of any new developments. Unfortunately, tragedy sold newspapers and fueled television news programs.

Wright sighed, leaning back in his seat. He didn't want to go inside. No children had been found during the night, no one had called to say they saw the man who did it. He had nothing to tell Crystal. Her daughter had simply disappeared. There was still the possibility that Emily was with her father. According to Mitchelson's secretary, he had recently sold a screenplay and had a meeting on Tuesday to discuss some scene changes. It was highly unlikely that he would suddenly disappear with his daughter when he had something so important scheduled on his calendar.

Then there was Simmons. He was hiding something, but what? Could he have taken Emily somewhere? Maybe he had a grudge against Crystal. Was he jealous of his employer? What was his motive?

Nothing made sense. The sexual pervert theory wasn't really probable. Willis had pointed out that that type of crime was usually committed in a busy neighborhood, often near a school, where victims would be easy to find and where the perpetrator wouldn't be noticed. Who would chance taking Emily in broad daylight in a neighborhood of multi-million dollar homes, where chauffeurs and maids were on constant alert for prowlers?

Or maybe they weren't. Maybe the wealthy thought no one would dare attack them. Was Crystal so used to admiring fans that she considered herself immune to the evil of the real world? Wright sighed. He couldn't figure it out. Someone had taken the child, but why? If it *was* a kidnapping, why hadn't anyone contacted Crystal? Perhaps a ransom note will arrive in today's mail, he thought.

Bees hummed in the air, and the smell of freshly mowed grass drifted on the wind. He watched as the gardener came around to the front of the house and started to clip the hydrangeas. He laughed to himself. Now there's a job; working outside every day, tending already perfectly manicured lawns . . .

Wright sat upright. The gardener! Why hadn't he thought of it before. He climbed out of the car and approached the man, tipping his hat back on his head.

"Police," Wright said, flashing his badge. "What's your name?"

The gardener looked at the badge, then promptly bowed his head. "Juan. Juan Morales."

"You work here on Fridays?"

Morales shook his head. "No work here. Work there," he said, pointing down the street.

Wright pulled out a copy of Emily's photograph. "Do you know this little girl?"

"She live here, this house."

"Did you see her on Friday?"

The Mexican scratched his head, his eyes squinting as he tried to remember. "I see her go to white house. Talk to maid there. Then she go home." He paused, searching his memory. "Then I see her wave to man in car, and then she go away with him."

Wright was shaking with excitement. He finally had a witness. "What kind of car?"

Morales shrugged his shoulders. "I think maybe it was a blue car."

"Do you know the make? Ford? Chevrolet?"

"Don't know," Morales said, then smiled. "It had two doors, and I seen the commercials on television."

"Which commercial? Who was in it?"

"*Quién sabe*?" Morales mumbled. "I don't remember. It was too long ago."

Wright decided it was useless to question him any further. He'd get photographs of different car models to show to the gardener, and maybe that would jog his memory. He said thanks and hurried up the front walk, excited by this new piece of information. Emily had known the man. Now they had a lead.

III

Julio Goldman sat at his favorite table in the Polo Lounge of the Beverly Hills Hotel. He always enjoyed having breakfast in this room, greeting friends, observing studio heads confer with lawyers, agents, and stars, speculating about what type of deals were being made. He had ordered his usual breakfast of fresh fruit, toast, and coffee. He placed a cigarette in his gold holder and lit it, savoring his first of the day.

He glanced around the room. He loved being here, surrounded by power people. There was no place quite like it. The Beverly Hills Hotel was his favorite place.

Not that he could afford to live here any longer. His father was old and wanted him to come back to Argentina, to take an active role in the many family businesses. Julio had argued that his brothers were doing an excellent job. His father became angry and cut back his allowance, and now Julio was reduced to living in an apartment instead of the hotel. It was a spiteful thing to do, but Julio saw no reason to return to a country that still had a foot in the past century. Though the landscape had changed with modern buildings, and technology boosted the economy, the country was still run by a privileged few, including his father and his cronies. What was so deplorable was that their sense of justice was based on a feudal system thinly guised as democracy. Julio wanted nothing to do with politics, and living on a lesser allowance was more agreeable than being in Buenos Aires.

The fast pace of tinsel town was more to his taste. He liked the glamour and excitement of the film and music industries. He was a voyeur of the ups and downs of all the famous people. But more important, he enjoyed a certain amount of celebrity as a polo player. He was part of it all. Luckily, he had good friends who allowed him to keep his polo ponies at their stable. Unfortunately, he had one small problem: He hated not being able to entertain as he would like, often turning down invitations because he couldn't return them. It was an embarrassing situation, but he hoped to soon correct that. He had spent the evening working on his plan, now all he had to do was iron out a few details.

He glanced once again at the newspaper headline. POLICE

BAFFLED BY DISAPPEARANCE OF STAR'S DAUGHTER. He read the article, taking pleasure in the paragraph about himself. "Miss Smythe's first husband was handsome Julio Goldman, the darling of the jet-setters. He divides his time between his estate in Argentina and the polo fields of Palm Beach and Santa Barbara."

He set the newspaper aside, remembering how much he had loved and adored Crystal. But she had ruined everything; she laughed at him, ridiculed him. He was sure she had told his secret to many people. There had been times at large social gatherings that he could feel people's eyes on him. He was sure that they were all wondering, guessing, knowing his shame. In the years since, he had never dared allow himself to get that close to a woman. When he needed to satisfy his cravings for the bizarre, he sought a prostitute.

It was unavoidable that he meet Crystal on occasion, but always there was tension between them. He had recently encountered her at a party for his godson. Crystal arrived to pick up Emily. There had been so many children at the party that he hadn't realized the cute little girl with pigtails was Crystal's daughter.

Crystal had been civil enough, presenting Emily to him, conversing about mutual friends. Emily had waited patiently, even shaking his hand good-bye, which had impressed him. He'd been surprised by Crystal's change of heart, her supposed friendly attitude, but there was no hiding the contempt in her eyes. He knew it was her way of reminding him that she couldn't stand the sight of him. Even after all these years, she could make him feel inadequate. It was then he realized how much he really hated her. He began thinking of ways he could humiliate her, hurt her, repay her for . . .

"Hi, I'm Selma Siegel, a reporter for the *Times*," a

red-headed woman said, interrupting his thoughts as she thrust her press card in his face.

Julio sat back in his chair. "What do you want?" he said irritably.

"I noticed you were reading the article about your former wife. I was the first person to write about the kidnapping," she gushed on, "and I was wondering if you might have some comments, Mr. Goldman."

"I have nothing to say."

"But surely you must have an opinion. I know your marriage only lasted about a day and a half, but still . . . you *were* married to Hollywood's leading lady."

"That was a very long time ago," he said, rankled by her impertinence.

"My readers would love to read about you," she said, hoping to play up to his vanity. "And I'd bet they'd give anything to know the inside scoop about your marriage."

"I prefer not to discuss that period of my life."

"Then perhaps a few comments about the kidnapping?"

Wouldn't the world be surprised if his true feelings were made known, he thought. He'd like to tell Siegel that he hated his former wife, that he was happy Crystal was so miserable, that . . .

He snapped out of his mood. Unfortunately, that would arouse the reporter's suspicions. No. He couldn't afford to draw that kind of attention to himself.

He forced a smile. "I only have a few moments, but I suppose I could answer some of your questions."

IV

Jimmy rang the bell, then unlocked the door and entered his former residence. A policeman barred his entrance.

"I'm James Mitchelson, Crystal Smythe's husband," he explained. "What's going on?"

Crystal entered the hallway and seeing Jimmy rushed to his side. "Where have you been?" she demanded angrily. "Why didn't you call me?"

"I was out sailing. I didn't arrive home until this morning and found your message on the machine," he answered awkwardly, surprised by Crystal's outburst. "I tried calling, but I kept getting a busy signal. I figured there was something wrong with the phone, so I decided to drive here."

He paused, noticing the haggard look on Crystal's face, the tears welling in her eyes. "What is it? What's wrong?" he asked, sensing it was bad news. He had a sudden, ugly premonition. "Has something happened to Emily?"

"She's missing," Crystal sobbed.

Jimmy was stunned by the news. He gripped Crystal's shoulders. "When? How did it happen?"

"It happened some time Friday afternoon after she got home from summer camp," Crystal said, wiping her eyes with a crumpled tissue. "It's been in the newspapers and on the news."

Fearful thoughts raced through his mind. "I told you I went sailing. I haven't turned the radio on since I left town. I didn't know."

"I'll bet you didn't," Wright said sarcastically.

The hairs on Jimmy's neck stood on end. He turned to the tall man, riled by his impertinent tone. "Who are you?"

"I'm Lieutenant Wright, Beverly Hills police," he said, "and I'm investigating the disappearance of your daughter. I think it's a little odd you wouldn't at least tune in your marine radio. The Coast Guard has been trying to contact you."

"I've been working on a new screenplay and needed time to think," Jimmy explained brusquely. "That's why I went sailing—to have some peace and quiet."

"Hmmmph!" Wright grunted. "What about your car radio?"

"When I'm driving on the freeway I listen to taped music," Jimmy said. "So I didn't know, for God's sake. Does that make me a suspect or something?"

Jimmy was gripped by an alarming thought, his words echoing in his ears. He gulped hard, fighting back the bile that rose in his throat, infuriated. "How the hell can you think I would take my daughter anywhere without advising her mother?"

"It's my job to ask." Wright walked to the front door and glanced out at the driveway. A red station wagon was parked behind his own car. "That your wagon out there?"

"Yes, of course it is," Jimmy said, disturbed by the policeman's unfriendly attitude.

"Do you have any other cars?"

"No, that's the only one," Jimmy replied testily. "Could you please tell me what you're doing to find Emily?"

Wright nodded toward the living room. "Those gentlemen are with the FBI, and they're monitoring all incoming phone calls. The consensus is that we're dealing with a kidnapping."

"What? You don't know?" Jimmy asked, totally disarmed. "I don't understand what's happening."

It didn't take long for Wright to explain what little information he had. "We're fairly sure Emily knew the man, which means Miss Smythe, or you, must know him, too. I thought maybe you'd hired someone to pick up your daughter," he said, flushing slightly, feeling foolish for being so suspicious. He could tell now that Mitchelson was genuinely surprised and as upset as his wife.

"I've been racking my brain," Crystal said, tormented by her confusion, "but I can't think of anyone who would want to do this. The only explanation I have is that Emily is used to people picking her up. Whoever it was must have known that and convinced her . . ."

"Damn it," Jimmy exploded. "This wouldn't have happened if you had let her come live with me."

Crystal glared at Jimmy, shocked by his outburst. "Are you blaming me?"

"If you had been home instead of at the studio . . ."

Wright cleared his throat. "Arguing isn't going to solve anything. We have to work together."

Crystal turned to the policeman, embarrassed. "I'm sorry."

"What can we do?" Jimmy asked, equally dismayed by their emotional display.

"Not a whole lot," Wright mumbled. "We have to wait for some kind of contact. We've given instructions to the post office to hold all mail for this address." He noticed the surprised look on Mitchelson's face. "Your mail is sorted in the morning, but not delivered until the afternoon," he explained patiently. "If a ransom note *has* been sent, there's always the remote possibility that there'll be some identifiable fingerprints."

Jimmy shook his head. "I still can't believe this is happening. What kind of madman are we dealing with?"

"That's what we hope to find out," Wright said. "I'm going to my office, but I'll have my men question the neighbors again. They're not the type of people who commit this sort of crime, but I do want to question the household help. I want to be sure we haven't overlooked anything. And maybe we'll get lucky; someone else might have seen the blue car."

V

Charlie Fischer had been a gate guard at Beechwood Studios for over forty years. He was up for retirement, a prospect he wasn't looking forward to. He was worried about what he was going to do with himself all day long. His job as gate guard was important, and it was his whole life. He knew all the big stars and studio executives by name. He knew who their children were. He knew the agents, the directors, and most of the behind-the-scenes people, too. The ones that he didn't know had to wait at the gate while he checked their names on the admission lists on his clipboard. Or if they were extras, they darned well better know the name of the movie they were making and on what lot they'd be filming if they wanted into his studio.

That was the way Charlie Fischer thought of Beechwood. It was his domain, and no one got past the gate without his okay. And there were plenty who tried. He'd heard just about every story in the world.

He was usually one of the first people to arrive at the studio, along with the others who really ran things. The mechanics and engineers, the electricians, the kitchen employees—the backbone of a major corporation like Beechwood. Soon after that the extras started to pour in, followed by make-up people, then the stars, directors, producers . . . and another movie would be made. Charlie was proud to be a part of it all.

He left his post briefly to use the Porta-John that was parked around the corner of sound stage three. When he returned and stepped inside his guardhouse his foot hit a package. He bent down and picked up the manila envelope. He turned it over. Crystal Smythe's name was written on it with a black marker pen. People were always leaving things at the guardhouse, expecting him to be a delivery boy. Didn't they know he had to stay at his post?

He lifted the envelope flap and partially pulled out a T-shirt with green lettering on it. He saw the word "Hawthorne" and guessed a fan had sent it to Crystal. They were always sending stuff to their favorite stars. He pushed the shirt back inside and considered what he should do with the envelope.

He could send it over to Crystal's dressing room, but Charlie figured that probably wasn't such a good idea. Since Miss Smythe's daughter was missing, or maybe even kidnapped, she wouldn't be coming into the studio. There was gossip about the movie being suspended . . . maybe even halted indefinitely.

The sound of a car approaching the gate drew Charlie's attention. He recognized the chauffeur-driven limousine of one of the vice-presidents. Charlie tossed the manila envelope on the shelf and stepped outside to tip his hat and open the gate.

He watched from across the street, sitting in the car pretending to read a newspaper. He had taken the chance of dropping the package right on the doorstep, then waited to see what Charlie would do.

The minutes ticked away slowly, and he got out and put another quarter into the parking meter. He waited some more, expecting the police to show up any minute.

He finally realized nothing was going to happen. Dumb old Charlie hadn't figured it out. Unless he called and told the idiot what was in the envelope, it would just sit there and rot. The hell with it. He had to get moving. It was time to put the next phase of the kidnapping into operation.

VI

Selma Siegel was very pleased. She had another exclusive, thanks to the alert eyes of the rookie reporter assigned to cover the Smythe house for her. B.J. Hunter was fresh out of college, but he was learning the ropes fast. He had spotted Lieutenant Wright questioning the gardener and then put two and two together. After the detective went inside the house, B.J. followed the gardener to the side of the house and asked some of his own questions.

"You're sure we can't get anything else out of Morales?" asked Selma.

"I squeezed hard," B.J. said, "but he clammed up. He swears all he knows is that the man was driving a blue car. And that Emily appeared to know him."

He tilted the rearview mirror of Selma's car to check his heavily moussed flattop. "I couldn't believe it. There I was, all alone, except for some creep who had his eye on the front door watching for Crystal to come outside," B.J. said breathlessly. "He's a big fan of Crystal's."

"Skip the side bars."

B.J. nodded toward the crowd of reporters that had gathered. "Those goons didn't show up until noon."

"Anyone else?"

"The husband arrived. I recognized him from the photo you gave me."

Selma reclaimed her rearview mirror. "Okay. You did good. I'm on my way to the office. The gardener's account will give some life to this story."

B.J. opened the car door. "What do you want me to do?"

"Have you seen the secretary?"

"He left here shortly after the detective."

"Okay. If the maid comes out, follow her, try to get her to talk. Ditto for the secretary if he returns. Maybe we'll get lucky and find out what's going on inside."

VII

Elizabeth paid the taxi driver and carried her small suitcase up the steps of the Beverly Hills Municipal Court House.

The baroque building with its gingerbread trimming was a landmark often photographed by tourists and had appeared in countless films. The grounds were immaculate, the palm trees limp sentinels in the muggy heat. Elizabeth pushed through the wide doors and entered the marble hallway. A sign on the wall indicated that the police department was to her right. She walked past walls decorated with photographs of Hollywood, Los Angeles, and Beverly Hills dating from the 1930's. She approached the information desk.

"Hello. My name is Elizabeth Anderson. I believe I may be of some help in the Emily Mitchelson kidnapping," she said to the officer behind the barred window. "You know," she said in response to the officer's astonished stare, "Crystal Smythe's daughter."

The police sergeant looked at her, not sure if he should believe her or not. "You saw the person who took the girl?"

"Well, no, not exactly," Elizabeth said, setting her suitcase down. "I think I'd like to speak to the detective in charge of the case."

"That would be Lieutenant Wright," the policeman said, betting to himself that the elderly lady standing before him was hoping there would be a reward for information.

"May I see him, please?"

"If you'll have a seat, I'll inform the Lieutenant that you're here."

Elizabeth sat on a wooden bench and waited, studying her surroundings. Although it was a large building, the police department seemed crammed into a very small space. She noted how the desks were crowded together, partitioned by small formica panels. She had visited police departments all across the country, and it seemed there was never enough room. Telephones rang incessantly, and people hurried in and out the door. Elizabeth watched with interest, accustomed to waiting. She caught the sergeant staring at her and she smiled. He blushed and looked down at the papers on his desk. Nearly fifteen minutes passed before Elizabeth was finally admitted into the inner confines and directed down a dark hallway to Wright's office.

His office was as crowded as the rest of the department. Filing drawers and cabinets lined one wall, and a worn sofa claimed the other. Incongruously, a patchwork quilt was thrown across the back of the sofa. Elizabeth sensed that the detective occasionally rested there when he was bogged down with cases and couldn't go home to sleep. Colored push pins were strewn across the maps and charts which hung on the gray walls. Behind the desk a window opened on a dark, tiny courtyard. An air conditioner rattled noisily in its casing, doing little to cool the tiny room. Wright was sitting in shirtsleeves, but he rose to his feet and pulled on his jacket as Elizabeth entered the room. She set her suitcase down and walked to his desk.

"How do you do?" she said, extending her hand. "I'm Elizabeth Anderson, and I believe I may be of some help in that kidnapping case involving Crystal Smythe's daughter."

"Good. We need all the help we can get," Wright said, shaking her hand. He indicated the chair facing his cluttered desk. "Please be seated."

"Thank you," Elizabeth said, settling down in the chair, eyeing the man in front of her. Would he be receptive to her plan? she wondered. She searched his eyes; they seemed friendly. She plunged in.

"I'm a psychic investigator, and I have often worked with the San Francisco Police Department."

"For how long?" Wright asked bluntly.

Elizabeth was taken aback by his manner. "About forty-five years," she said proudly.

"How did you get started?"

"The police had an unsolved case of a missing woman.

There were plenty of witnesses who had seen her quarreling with her husband and thought he had killed her. They found the car, but their only clue was a bloodstained scarf they discovered in the trunk. They questioned the husband repeatedly, convinced he had slain her, but without a body, they were unable to prove murder.

"Although I was only a secretary at the time, I had a strong premonition that I held the key and felt I could help. I asked the detectives to give me a photograph of the woman. Then I held her scarf in my hands. The impressions came tumbling before me. At first I got just vague images. I was starting to wonder what I was doing, but then I received some fairly clear pictures and was able to pinpoint the area where they would find the body."

"And you took the police there?"

"No one believed me! They thought I was insane," Elizabeth said with a smile. "Psychic investigators were just starting to work with the police. It took me several days to explain myself."

"How?"

"I showed them some books I had about psychics."

"That convinced them?"

"Not exactly. But they were curious and decided to follow up on my suggestions by sending a couple of men out to investigate."

"Did they find the woman?"

"It took awhile, but eventually we did. I had a very strong image that she was buried in a shallow grave near Mill Valley. The detectives asked me to be more specific, so I decided to go with them. I was hoping that once I was in the right area, I would get some fresh images. I was also praying that I wouldn't make a complete fool of myself."

"What happened?"

The memories came flooding back. "We drove slowly

through town, and then I saw the triple peaks of Mount
Tamalpais. It suddenly became clear to me. I told the
detectives that they would find the body up there, about
midway up the hiking trail."

"What were you feeling?"

"Mostly scared that I might be wrong," she admitted.
"Anyhow, we went on foot, and more images flooded my
mind. I could sense the woman's unhappiness with her
husband. It was just like watching television. I heard her
accuse him of seeing another woman. They began to argue
and . . ." Elizabeth grimaced, a pain shooting across her
cheek as she remembered . . . "Something unusual happened. I was reliving those moments—and I actually felt the
woman's pain when he slapped her."

"Does that happen often? Actually feeling the pain?"

"Sometimes, when it's been a very violent murder.
Sometimes the pain is so terrible that I wish I hadn't become
involved. But something makes me continue. I can't ignore
it when the victim keeps calling out to me for help. Other
psychics have written of the same phenomena."

Wright toyed with a pencil. "How did the woman die?"

"She fell backward, hitting her head on a rock. She was
still breathing, but then he dragged her . . . down behind
some trees, where he strangled her with his belt." Elizabeth
paused, her hand at her throat as the ugly memories brought
back the sick feeling.

Wright noticed the unconscious movement. "How did the
police prove that the man murdered his wife?"

"He used a stone to dig a shallow grave and covered it
with dead brush and tree limbs. When the police dug up the
grave, the belt was still wrapped around her throat,"
Elizabeth explained. "The belt buckle had an initial on it, a
very distinctive design, and several people identified it. The

D.A. eventually found a photograph of the man in which he was wearing the belt."

Wright was impressed. "Is that the way you usually work when you're investigating a murder?"

"Every time is different," she admitted. "If you have any doubts about my capabilities, you can check with Christopher Swatt at the Los Angeles police headquarters. He'll verify my accomplishments."

Though they'd never worked together, Wright was well aware of Swatt's reputation. He was the wonder kid, known for his flashy clothes, fancy cars, and his jet-set life-style. He was also a good detective, and some of his case records were required reading for new recruits.

He smiled wryly at the lady in front of him. "I've never worked with a psychic investigator before, but I've read departmental reports on cases where they've been involved."

"What's your opinion?"

It was Wright's turn to study the woman before him. Would he offend her? She was smiling pleasantly, as if genuinely interested in hearing what he had to say.

"To tell the truth, I don't put much store by psychics," he said, leaning back comfortably in his chair. "In the cases that I reviewed, most were resolved by good police work and the, er, psychic's conclusions were, uh, shall we say, pure conjecture."

The phone rang and he answered it, said yes, okay, and good-bye. A man of few words, Elizabeth decided. She realized that the detective's mind was already made up on the subject. A nonbeliever. A skeptic. She smiled to herself, knowing how she would convince him.

"No matter what you think, Lieutenant, I believe I can help."

"How?"

"Unfortunately, or fortunately as the case may be, I can read thought transmissions. I've been able to do it since I was a child."

"You're joking. You can read anyone's mind?"

"I suppose I can, but I assure you, Lieutenant, I don't make a habit of it. Only when I have to convince someone I can do it. I'll demonstrate," she offered. "I'll bet you carry your wallet in the right back pocket of your pants."

Wright gaped at her. "Now how did you know that?"

"Elementary, to paraphrase Sherlock Holmes," Elizabeth twittered, enjoying his momentary discomfort. "I noticed that you're right-handed, so it's logical that you would carry your wallet there."

"And I suppose you're going to tell me what's in it," he smirked.

Elizabeth leaned back in the chair and closed her eyes. "There's a photograph of your wife playing with your two dogs in your wallet."

Wright sat up and felt his back pocket. His wallet was where it should be. He pulled it out and looked. The photograph was tucked behind his detective's badge. There was no way she could have seen it.

"Do you do magic tricks, too?" he asked.

"No," Elizabeth said, laughing softly, happy she had guessed correctly. "There's no magic involved. Your thoughts automatically were directed to the photograph, and I read your mind."

Wright shook his head, amazed. "I'm impressed."

"A psychic *sees* the past, present, or future. The technical term for what I do is 'psychometry,'" she said, relishing her role of teacher. "I use my sixth sense to measure the flux—or electro-magnetic radiation that comes from another person."

"How do you do that?" Wright asked, feeling like an idiot for asking.

"Sometimes by touching an object that was used or worn by the person," she replied, "or, as I told you, by thought transference."

Wright shrugged his shoulders. "So you've got this power. What does that have to do with the kidnapping? Assuming that it *is* a kidnapping."

Elizabeth was shocked. "You don't know? It's been days now. You must know something by now."

"There's been no ransom note," he said defensively. "However, we do have a few leads we're checking."

Elizabeth nodded, understanding police jargon enough to know that he probably had very little to go on but wasn't about to admit it. "That puts a crimp in things. I had hoped there would be a clue or two. Tangible evidence. Something I could touch, hold in my hands," she said. "Oh, well, I guess I'll have to do without."

"Do what?"

"Why, assist you, of course," she replied patiently. "In any way beneficial to the case."

Wright wasn't convinced. "Why do you think you can help?"

"For the past few days I've had this odd feeling that I just can't shake. I'm sure it has something to do with Emily, and I know she's alive."

"How do you know that?"

"I've heard her voice."

Wright stared at her, more confused than ever. "You what?"

"When I go to sleep I hear Emily's voice," she said, hoping she didn't sound like a complete fool. "I'm sure it's her."

"What makes you so sure?"

"I don't know exactly. I read in the newspaper today that Emily's birthday is the same as mine. That could explain it."

"Explain what?" he said, his voice filled with exasperation.

"It makes sense," Elizabeth said, ignoring Wright's interruption. "Since our birthdays fall on the same day, our lives are probably parallel."

"I don't understand all that mumble-jumble."

Elizabeth stood and began pacing the small room, her hands shoved into the deep pockets of her purple cotton dress. A small bunch of silk violets were pinned to the bodice, and Wright noticed that she smelled vaguely of violets, the same cologne his grandmother had used.

"Since Emily and I are astrologically in sync, I'm able to tune in to her thoughts," she explained patiently. "I suppose that's too complicated for you to understand."

Farfetched is more like it, he thought, then grimaced, afraid she had read his mind. One thing for sure, she had been right about the photograph in his wallet. So maybe she *did* have unusual powers.

"What do you propose?" he asked, mildly curious.

"I'm sure I can help you find Emily, but to do so I think I should go to her home . . . to where she was last seen," Elizabeth said, sensing the detective's hesitancy. "I suppose you would call it 'the scene of the crime.' "

Wright leaned back in his swivel chair, rocking, thinking. The only thing he had to go on was the gardener's account of what had happened, and his boss was already on his back for not finding the answers. Maybe the psychic lady *could* help, even if she did sound a little out of tune with the world. At any rate, he thought, he had nothing to lose. But first he would call the San Francisco Police Department to make sure she was legit. And a call to Swatt might clarify things, too, he decided.

"All right. I'll phone Emily's parents and tell them we're coming over," he told her. "You might as well wait for me in the lobby, since I may be awhile."

Elizabeth picked up her suitcase and walked to the door. She stopped and turned to Wright, guessing what he was thinking.

"Tell Christopher Swatt hello for me," she said, enjoying the startled look on Wright's face as she left his office.

VIII

He unlocked the door and entered the bedroom. Emily was watching television.

"I brought you some hamburgers," he said, setting them on the trunk under the window. He reached into a K-Mart shopping bag and pulled out a box of crayons and a coloring book. "I bought you something to draw with. That'll keep you busy."

"You lied to me," Emily said, her face contorted with anger. "My mother isn't coming to get me. My mother doesn't even know where I am."

He looked down at her, a mocking smile on his face. "Well, well, well. You've finally figured it out."

"I saw it on television," she said. "They say that I've been kidnapped."

"That's right, and I'll bet your mother will pay anything to get you back." He snickered. "How much do you think you're worth?"

Emily remembered seeing a movie on television about some kids who got kidnapped and their school bus was buried underground. She couldn't remember how the movie had ended.

"I don't know," she said. "A million dollars?"

He laughed. "I wonder just how much she's willing to cough up." He hadn't planned this, but now that he had come this far, it was time to take action. "Eat your hamburgers before they get cold," he commanded and walked out of the room, locking the door behind him.

He paced around the living room. He hadn't realized what he was doing at the time. If he was caught, he would be sent to prison. He had no choice, so why shouldn't he benefit from it? He walked into the kitchen and placed a shopping bag on the table. He opened the bag and took out the surgical gloves, paper, scissors, glue, envelopes, and magazines.

He worked slowly, first writing the message, then rewording it until he was satisfied. He put the gloves on and began searching through the magazines, looking for the right letters and phrases. He cut them out carefully, then glued them on a clean piece of paper. He admired his handiwork, then pondered about addressing the envelope. Crystal might recognize his handwriting. He laughed and returned to the bedroom.

"Here. Sign this and write your mom's name and address on this envelope," he told Emily.

"What's it for?"

"You want to go home, don't you? Well, now that you know you've been kidnapped, we're going to have to send a ransom note to your mother," he explained patiently, knowing he'd have to keep Emily happy if she was going to cooperate. "When your mother sees your handwriting, she'll know it's from you."

He watched her print the envelope, then instructed her to lick and seal it. He had read somewhere that the police could make an identification from saliva. He wondered if it was true.

Emily looked up at him, hating him. "When my mother pays, can I go home?"

He stared down at her. "Sure, kid," he said, wondering what the hell he was going to do with her. But he knew.

IX

Crystal and Jimmy were on the terrace, seated at a glass-and-wrought-iron table. A light breeze took the edge off the heat. Socorro had served them a late lunch, but neither had eaten much, moving the forks around on their plates, picking at the food.

"It just doesn't make sense," Jimmy said, pounding his fist on the table. "Why hasn't he contacted us?"

Crystal lit a cigarette, inhaling deeply. "We shouldn't overlook the possibility that the kidnapper could be a woman."

"I thought the gardener said it was a man."

"He could be wrong, especially since he isn't even sure about the car."

Jimmy frowned. "That FBI guy . . . what's his name . . ."

"Willis?"

"Yeah. He said the kidnapper is probably someone you know."

Crystal immediately took offense. "Why the hell can't it be one of *your* friends?" she asked angrily.

"All *my* friends, are also yours," Jimmy reminded her. "And I don't have any enemies. I haven't stepped on any toes. I write screenplays. I sell one, and I write another. No one's interested in me."

"What enemies?" Crystal spat out.

"Come off it, Crystal. You know what I mean. There must be at least twenty female stars in this town who would be glad to see your career come to a standstill." He paused, remembering how pushy Crystal could be when she wanted a certain movie role or if she wasn't happy with her co-stars or a film crew. "Let's not forget the erstwhile director of that film you did in Rome," Jimmy said, his expression bordering on mockery.

"What do you mean?"

Jimmy sipped his beer before answering. "As I recall, he did meet Emily. Maybe he took her so he could get back at you."

Crystal frowned. The director, Victorio Marsala, had been fired from the movie at Crystal's insistence. He had been impossible to work with, a demanding, mean little man who had made every day on the set a miserable one.

"Is Victorio in this country?"

"Don't you ever read the trade papers?" Jimmy said. "He's been all over town practically begging for a job. He hasn't worked since you bad-mouthed him. Word is out that he's broke."

Crystal stubbed out her cigarette. "Such a vain, stupid little man."

"It wouldn't hurt to have Lieutenant Wright check him out."

"I suppose you're right." Crystal sighed uneasily and sat back in her chair. She *had* stepped on a few toes during her career, but who hadn't? You had to be tough to survive. She was a survivor, but then so was Jimmy. He'd had his ups and downs, and he knew it was a dog-eat-dog business. There were no guarantees that a screenplay would sell.

Crystal studied Jimmy, thinking he had changed a lot. He was balding now, his reddish-brown hair far too long and pulled back in a ponytail, as if that could make up for what he lacked on top. He was thinner, too, his cheeks gaunt under cover of a beard liberally peppered with gray. The marks of time were there, but the brown eyes which had drawn her to him were still gentle and loving.

She realized with a jolt that their tenth anniversary had gone by, and she hadn't remembered. How sad, she thought. We were so sure we were going to beat the odds on Hollywood marriages. We were going to be together for the rest of our lives. They had promised each other to always resolve their problems without arguing. That seemed like such a long time ago. She remembered when it all began. Peggy and Ted were having a housewarming to show off their new home in the Trousdale Estates area . . .

X

"The house is lovely," Crystal said, stroking the cushions of a plump easy chair. "I like the big sofas and the large coffee table, and I absolutely adore the Santa Fe scheme . . . all sand and desert colors."

"Nice sturdy stuff," Peggy laughed. "With three kids and another on the way, we decided antiques and crystal doo-dads weren't for us."

They entered the den and joined Ted at the bar. He was mixing drinks and telling a story to a small group of people. They laughed politely, making room for Crystal and Peggy. Ted made the introductions.

". . . our neighbor, David Mark; Chris Anderson, the realtor who talked us into buying this monstrosity; and the man next to you is Jimmy Mitchelson."

"Nice to meet you," Crystal said graciously, extending her hand to each.

"Jimmy has written a fabulous screenplay which Ted is going to direct," Peggy informed her.

Crystal accepted a drink from Ted and listened politely to the conversation. She finally excused herself, weaved her way through the guests, warmly greeting those she knew, and walked outside to the pool. She sank down on a chaise lounge and kicked off her shoes, happy to be off her feet. She had just returned from location in Athens, and she still hadn't recovered from jet lag. She stretched back against the cushions, watching the two oldest Ballwin children splash noisily in the shallow end of the pool while their nanny tried to coax them out.

"Great kids," commented Mitchelson as he sat on a lounge beside her own. "Do you have any?"

"No. Not yet," Crystal replied. "If I ever remarry, I plan to have some. What about you?"

Jimmy smiled sheepishly at her. "No kids. No wife. Still single. I doubt there are many women in this world who could live with a writer. I have this ungodly habit of waking up at four-thirty or five in the morning. I jog, make coffee, then hit the typewriter."

"I get up around the same time. I need a couple of jolts of caffeine to start my motor before I can go to the studio," she said. "How long do you work?"

"My creative juices dry up around noon. I waste my afternoons daydreaming, going to long, boring meetings at the studios, and worrying how I'll pay the mortgage."

Crystal laughed appreciatively, discreetly studying him. He was handsome, almost rugged looking, and she felt attracted to him. She wondered if he was a good lover, then blushed at her thoughts. After her divorce from Julio she had thrown herself into her work, thinking she could erase the bad memories. Though she had been asked out by several eligible men, she was hesitant about getting involved again. She finally went to a psychiatrist, and through patient counseling she was able to come to grips with her feelings.

She started dating, had two affairs, both with co-stars,

but after the initial fascination and sexual attraction wore off, Crystal was relieved to be free of them and retreated back to her solitary life. She was determined that no man would ever use her again—nor interfere with her career.

"You know," Jimmy said, leaning forward, "I would love to write something special just for you."

"You're joking!"

"No. I'm serious." He offered her a cigarette, then lit his own. "Tell me something. How do you see yourself? What kind of role would you like to play if you had the opportunity?"

"I don't know," Crystal said, regarding him with growing curiosity. She thought a moment. "When I was a teenager I went to the movies every day and played all the roles. Scarlett O'Hara, Dorothy in Oz, Bette Davis as Queen Elizabeth, Ingrid Bergman in Casablanca; the list goes on and on."

"But there must be something you would really like to do."

"I've never done comedy. But I'd be willing to try," she said, grinning mischievously. "I don't want to be limited to dramatic roles."

"Then I'll write a comedy for you."

"How can you do that? I thought you had to start with the plot."

"Sometimes I build a plot around a character."

"I envy writers, but they rarely get the recognition they deserve."

"I'm rewarded when I see a famous movie star speaking my lines on the big screen. And I certainly can't complain about the money, though not everything I write sells. Of course a little recognition wouldn't hurt, either," he admitted. "I spend hours dreaming of winning an Oscar. I even have my acceptance speech memorized."

Crystal smiled at him. "Doesn't everyone in this business?"

Crystal enjoyed talking to Jimmy. He led the conversation, asking about her favorite food, restaurants, books, taking a genuine interest in what he had to say. Before leaving the party they had exchanged telephone numbers.

Within days they were dating and talking on the telephone for hours on end. Jimmy was unlike any other man she had known. He was warm and caring, intelligent and funny—and a very private person. Over the next few months she discovered that he preferred small, intimate restaurants over the pretentious places most of her colleagues gathered. They often went to his house in Malibu, where they spent the day walking on the beach and later barbecued steaks. Afterward, they would sit on the deck, enjoying the soft whisper of the waves on the beach, counting stars, talking about their dreams and desires.

The first time he made love to her she was unexpectedly pleased. He overwhelmed her with love and gentle caring, making sure she derived as much pleasure from their lovemaking as he did. And afterward, he held her in his arms, caressing her, until her trembling ceased.

As time passed, Crystal realized she was falling in love with this wonderful man. Yet when he began speaking about a future together, she was wary; she had made two mistakes in her life and didn't want or need a third. But when he held her in his arms and kissed her, she felt all her reservations melt away.

Jimmy took his time. He sensed that Crystal wasn't ready for commitment. He thought he understood her reticence, why she had built a wall around her feelings. He'd had a bad experience himself, barely surviving a tumultuous three-year romance with a photographer. She had dropped him without a thought when she was offered a wire-service job in the Middle East.

He'd been hurt, then slowly relieved that the affair had ended, realizing that they had nothing in common other than sex. After that he steered clear of women, not wanting to get involved. Until he met Crystal. He sensed that she was different and felt sure that one day she would be his wife.

He waited patiently for Crystal to complete her current film. The wrap party was a tearful affair held on the vast sound stage. Photographs were taken and promises made to keep in touch. Jimmy finally led Crystal away for a quiet dinner at Chasens. Afterward, they drove to his house for a nightcap. Jimmy lit a fire and poured brandy into large snifters.

"I'll be right back," he said and disappeared into the bedroom.

Crystal kicked off her shoes and stretched out on the sofa. Secretly she was glad the movie was over. Though she hated to admit it, she was tired and needed a rest. She had been considering going away for a vacation, but the thought of traveling from one place to another, packing bags, checking in and out of hotels was too exhausting. And she didn't want to leave Jimmy. It would be nice to spend some time with him.

Jimmy returned to the living room, carrying a long package. "This is for you."

Crystal smiled and began tearing the wrappings from the long, thin box. She looked puzzled as she withdrew a fishing rod. "What on earth!"

"You said you wanted to get away. I thought you might like to go fishing with me."

"You're joking," she said, totally amused. "I don't know anything about fishing."

"You said you came from a fishing village."

"That doesn't mean I know anything about fishing."

"I'll teach you," he said, digging into his pants pocket. "All you have to do is put some bait on the hook, cast your rod, and let nature take its course. Here's a little bait."

Crystal looked at his hand. He was holding a beautiful ring in his palm, the square-cut emerald set with diamond clusters on either side. She was speechless. She stared up at Jimmy, a flush coming to her cheeks as she realized what he was offering. She smiled and held out her hand to him.

He pulled Crystal to her feet and slipped the ring on her finger. "A perfect fit. And I thought a fishing trip would be the perfect honeymoon."

"I wasn't expecting this," she said hesitantly.

"I love you," Jimmy said, bending to kiss her.

Crystal leaned back in the comfortable circle of his arms. "This is happening too fast."

"How long does it take to fall in love?" he asked huskily.

Crystal stared up into his warm eyes, losing herself in their depths. It had really happened. This time it was for real. He wanted her; he loved her; he would take care of her.

They had been married three months when Crystal learned she was expecting a child. Jimmy's joy matched her own. He became very protective, insisting she stay at home.

"You mustn't make this next film," he grumbled. "You have to take care of yourself. And the baby."

Crystal was amused, but shook her head. "I'm sorry, darling, but I am not going to walk out on this movie. I had to battle ten ferocious, nail-clawing bitches to get the role."

Jimmy laughed, even though he knew she was serious. Crystal was so intense about her acting that sometimes it frightened him. "I don't want you to do anything dangerous. Let the stunt people make their living. You have to be very careful."

"Don't worry. I will. Besides, the film will be over way before I'm ever showing. And I promise to drink lots of milk, go to bed by ten, and follow my doctor's orders."

"You must also take naps between scenes," Jimmy scolded her. "I'll get you a proper bed for your dressing room. You must have your rest."

"I feel so alive . . . and healthy," she said, clasping her hands behind her head.

"As long as you stay that way," Jimmy said, stretching out on the sofa, resting his head on Crystal's lap.

He glanced around the living room of Crystal's house. It was charmingly decorated with fine furniture and frilly curtains at the windows. Crystal liked collecting antiques and artwork, and the overall look was very feminine. He had few personal items in the house, as he went to his beach house to work on his screenplays. He felt uncomfortable in the Laurel Canyon house. It was too confining, and he liked to pace around when he was writing. It was time to make some changes.

"You know, we're going to have to sell one of the houses. We need something bigger now that the baby is on the way."

Crystal ran a hand through his hair. "I suppose so, though I hate to give up this place. I bought it after I won my Academy nomination. It's been my lucky charm."

"The Malibu property is worth twice as much as this one. I think we should hold on to it. Besides, it'll be fun to take the kids to the beach."

"Kids? As in plural?"

"Sure. Don't you want lots?"

"I'll be happy with just one if she or he is perfect and has your eyes."

"You'll be a swell mom. Your greatest role in life."

"I hope so. It'll be hard work being a mother and a superstar, too."

"You aren't thinking of working after the baby is born?" Jimmy said, a frown furrowing his forehead.

"Not right away, of course; I want to nurse the baby. But once the baby is on a bottle, I'll get back to my career," she said decisively. "I suppose I'll have to join an exercise class, but in a year I should be back in shape. I'll tell Moss I won't accept any roles until then."

"You're joking!" Jimmy sat up. "Who's going to take care of the baby while you're on the set?"

"We'll have a nurse. Or maybe an English nanny. I had a nanny when I was a child," she told him, smiling at the thought. "She always wore a uniform and a crisp white apron. After my parents died, I went to live with my grandmother. I think I missed my nanny most of all." Crystal paused. "Isn't that an awful thing to say."

"You were young and probably closer to your nanny than your mother and father," Jimmy said, surprised by Crystal's mention of her parents. She never talked about them or her life in England. "At any rate, that's what worries me. I don't want my children raised by . . . foreigners. You should take some time off."

"Now you're the one who's joking." Crystal stood up and began pacing the room, her arms flying in the air. "You know how fickle this industry is. If I'm away from the screen too long, I'll be forgotten. Movies are my life. I've never wanted anything more."

"Not even a husband or children?" Jimmy spat out angrily. "Is that it?"

"Of course not. I love you, and I love the baby that I'm carrying, but you surely must understand my feelings. I've only started my career. I want to be great—the best." Crystal stopped pacing and turned to Jimmy, a determined look on her face. "I want an Oscar, Jimmy, not just a nomination. I want the acclaim that goes with one, the recognition. I've worked too hard to stop now," she said, rushing from the room.

They bought a large house in Beverly Hills, and shortly thereafter Emily was born. Crystal enjoyed the first months of motherhood, but was relieved when she found the perfect nanny to take over. She knew she had to get on with her career before she was forgotten by producers and fans alike. Jimmy was accustomed to driving daily to the beach house to write, but once Crystal went back to the studio, he began working at home. Socorro kept the house functioning smoothly, and the nanny had come highly recommended, but Jimmy felt better being where he could keep an eye on Emily.

Crystal's career soared as the offers came pouring in. Jimmy finished the screenplay he had created for her, and Crystal won an Oscar for the role, proving she could play comedy as well as drama. They were Hollywood's golden couple—envied, talked about, invited to the A-list parties. Between films they went to the beach house, or sometimes they rented a cabin on Lake Tahoe where they could fish from the dock. These were happy times for them both. Crystal carried a camera everywhere, snapping photographs of her growing daughter. On occasion Crystal had to fly to exotic places to film on location, but Jimmy, Emily, and the nanny often accompanied her.

Jimmy stopped complaining about Crystal's quest for stardom. He learned to fill the hours while she was off filming. He bought a boat and became an avid sailor. He dreamed of sailing around the world, but Crystal only scoffed at his dream.

"That's ridiculous," she said, "and, anyway, I could never get away for that long."

The years passed, and Emily grew, becoming a charming little girl. Jimmy delighted in his daughter, devoting himself to her so much that his own work suffered. He grew restless, unable to write, the words eluding him.

The inevitable happened.

Crystal had been on location in New Zealand, and when she called Jimmy, she told him the film was draining all her energy. She was playing the widow of a wealthy sheep rancher. The story had been built around the widow's struggle to hold on to her ranch and her love for two men, her foreman and the handsome owner of a neighboring ranch.

Crystal learned how to ride horses, shear sheep, and birth sheep. "I never want to see a sheep or a horse again," she told Jimmy during one of their nightly phone calls. "I have bruises everywhere on my body."

At the completion of the movie, Jimmy and Emily joined her for a short vacation. They decided to visit the North Island, staying at the Huka Lodge on the bank of Lake Taupo. They went trout fishing daily and took long hikes, exploring the countryside, carting along picnic lunches.

The days passed quickly until their vacation came to an end; they were to return to Los Angeles the following morning. After dinner, Crystal and Jimmy played Old Maid with Emily until exhaustion finally won out. They carried Emily upstairs and put her to bed, then retired to their adjoining room.

Crystal took a shower, put on a new rose silk nightgown, and splashed herself lavishly with Opium before entering the bedroom. Jimmy was sitting in bed, reading his latest screenplay.

Crystal sat beside him. "Hey. This is our last night. No reading."

He threw the screenplay across the room. "I spent six months writing that, and my agent says it's a piece of shit," he groaned. "God, this business is driving me crazy."

"Then stop. Do something else," Crystal suggested, snuggling up to him.

"Like what?"

"Um, let's see. Maybe try your hand at directing. You've got a great eye for detail." She ran a hand down his thigh. "Or . . . I've been thinking we should start our own television production company."

"When did you decide to do that?" Jimmy asked, amazed by Crystal's revelation.

"Oh, I've been thinking about it a long time. Moss says it would be a good move, and we've got to think about our future."

"How come you never told me?" he said, his voice testy.

Crystal was startled. "Well, it just never came up before. Although I expect to go on acting in films forever, it might be better to give ourselves other options. I asked my business manager to work up some numbers for us."

Jimmy's face was taut with tension. "You know what I would like?"

"What?" Crystal purred, her hand toying with the hairs on his chest.

"I wish to hell you would consult with me before you make these decisions. I'm supposed to be your husband, but you'd hardly know it." He reached for his cigarettes and lit one. "It's one movie after another. When is it going to stop? I want a wife, and Emily needs a full-time mother."

Crystal sat up. "What brought this on? You haven't complained before, and I'm certainly not going to stop. I'm making more money now than ever, and this last film is going to get me an Oscar."

"You already have two Oscars."

"One of those was for supporting actress."

"That counts, too."

"Not for me. I want another for best actress. Katharine Hepburn has twelve nominations, and has won four. I want five."

"That's ridiculous. Besides, she earned three of those after she turned fifty."

"So. I've got plenty of time," Crystal said, cringing at the thought of growing older. The competition was increasing, with too many young faces popping up in recent films.

Jimmy got out of bed and walked to the dresser. He poured himself a brandy, then turned back to her. "I don't understand you. What makes you tick? What drives you?"

"I've worked damned hard to get where I am. I want to be the best. I want people to remember me."

"Next thing you'll want is a statue of yourself on Rodeo Drive."

"That's a dumb thing to say, Jimmy, and you know it."

Jimmy decided to change the subject. "When are we going to have another child? Don't you realize your biological clock is ticking down?"

Crystal reached across the bed and grabbed Jimmy's cigarettes. She lit one angrily before answering. "We've already discussed this. I can't give up another year of my life having a baby. Not now. We still have plenty of time. Maybe in a year or two," she said halfheartedly.

"There'll never be a right time, will there!" he said accusingly.

"You're being so unfair. If I was president of a large company that makes, oh, say tires, for instance, you wouldn't want me to stop making tires, right? So why should I quit my present career and set aside my goals? You have no idea how hard I've had to work to perfect my art."

"Art?" Jimmy said with a snicker.

Crystal was infuriated by his irritating manner. "Yes, art," she repeated. "Anyway, Moss has several new properties for me to read, and I'm doing the film in Rome next month. Who knows how long that'll take."

"That's what worries me."

"I thought you could fly over with me. We could do some sightseeing before I start filming."

Jimmy shook his head. "I'm not going to Rome, Crystal. I've had it. I can't chase around after you forever."

"What does that mean?" she asked nervously, watching as Jimmy hastily pulled on jeans and a shirt, slipping into his moccasins.

"It means I quit. When we get back to the States, I plan to move down to the beach house. Permanently! Since I seldom see my wife, except for these ever so brief periods between movies, I might as well live alone," he said bitterly, marching out the door.

Crystal was stunned. Jimmy had talked like he wanted a separation. Why? What had gone wrong? Why was he acting this way? She smoked several more cigarettes while waiting for Jimmy to return, her rage growing. She didn't believe he would really leave her. How could he even think of leaving her?

She smiled as she realized the solution. She would let him go. He would get over it. A few weeks at the beach house, and he would be clamoring to come back. All she had to do was wait patiently. She had nothing to fear. She had weathered worse storms. Worse situations.

"There's always a tomorrow," Crystal reminded herself, as she had done so many times in the past. She turned the light off, and when Jimmy came back to the bedroom, she pretended she was asleep.

XI

Lieutenant Wright reluctantly introduced Elizabeth Anderson to the FBI agents. They weren't pleased.

"You seem to forget that we're in charge," Agent Willis reminded him.

"I would think you'd be happy to get all the help you can," Wright said angrily.

They argued for another ten minutes until Wright was finally able to convince Willis that they should give Elizabeth a chance. The detective asked her to wait in the den, then walked out to the terrace. The sun was starting to set, and the garden was bathed in golden shadows. Jimmy and Crystal were alone.

"Is there any news?" Crystal asked expectantly.

"No, nothing yet," Wright answered, wishing he could give them some hope. He glanced around the garden. "Where's Simmons?" he asked sharply.

"He left shortly after you did," Jimmy said, surprised by Wright's tone.

Wright didn't like the news. There was something odd about Simmons constantly taking off in the middle of this crisis. "Did he say where he was going?"

"He probably went to the studio to pick up Crystal's fan mail. He said he would call later," Jimmy added. Wright knew he would have to do something about the secretary, but first he had to introduce the psychic.

"As I told you on the telephone, Mrs. Anderson thinks she can be of some help," Wright said. "I checked her out with the San Francisco department, and they vouch for her. I also talked to someone who used her on a couple of local

cases, and apparently she's one of the best psychic consult-
ants around."

"Is she here?" Jimmy asked.

"Inside."

"How much does she want?" Jimmy sneered.

"Money?" Wright asked. "As far as I know, she doesn't
expect to get paid. She volunteered her services."

Jimmy stood up. "Then let's get on with it."

They moved into the den, and Wright made the introductions. Socorro carried a tray into the room, poured coffee,
then shuffled back to the kitchen, mumbling to herself in
Spanish.

"Socorro is still blaming herself," Jimmy said, adding
cream to his coffee. He sat on the sofa next to Crystal.

Crystal shook her head. "I've assured her over and over
that it wasn't her fault. That it was . . . is . . . the act of
a madman."

"They usually are," Elizabeth said. "Mad, that is—at the
world, themselves, their parents."

Jimmy looked at the diminutive woman. "The Lieutenant
explained that you're a psychic and can see things. Did you
see the man who took Emily?"

Elizabeth turned from the bookcases, where she had been
studying photographs of Emily. She joined the others,
picked up a cup of coffee, then settled in a chair before
answering.

"No, I haven't seen him yet." Elizabeth noticed their
puzzled looks. "What I mean is, I'm sure he'll be revealed
to me soon. Or, hopefully, I'll be able to figure out where
he has taken your daughter."

"When?" Jimmy grunted.

Elizabeth sighed. It wasn't going to be easy convincing
them. "I assure you that I'm a very good psychic. I have
always had the power to see and feel things. Sometimes it's

something that has already occurred, at other times it's what will take place in the near future. I have no control over these events. I have to wait for it to happen. Do you understand?"

"Vaguely," Crystal answered. "My friend Peggy and I went to a psychic a few years ago, right after the news broke that Nancy Reagan consulted an astrologist. We figured if it was good enough for the President's wife, then we should investigate.

"I wore a disguise, so the woman we went to see had no idea who I was," Crystal continued. "Her predictions were, um . . . predictable and funny. At any rate, Peggy and I had a good laugh. Do you use tarot cards?"

Elizabeth smiled. "No. Nothing like that."

"How can you be so sure that you can help us?" Jimmy asked.

"Last week I had a premonition that something terrible was going to happen. Twice now, first on Saturday and again yesterday, I had the strangest feeling that a little girl was calling out to me."

Elizabeth dug into her purse and found her notebook. "I wrote down my thoughts. Let's see . . . yes, both times I heard a child's voice say, 'Mommy, mommy, where are you?' I believe she is in a dark, musty room painted red perhaps, though I can't be sure yet."

Jimmy set his coffee cup down on the table with a noisy clank. "That's it? How can you know it's Emily?"

"I don't," Elizabeth said, ignoring the sarcastic tone of his voice, "but I have this very strong feeling that it's her. It's difficult to explain." Elizabeth paused, gathering her thoughts. "When I saw your daughter's photograph in the newspapers and on television, and discovered that our birthdays are on the same day, I guessed that it had to be Emily. So I came here. I thought it important to be where the kidnapping took place. I'll need a lot of insight to find your daughter."

Wright noticed the skeptical look on Mitchelson's face. "I know this is a long shot, but if Mrs. Anderson can help us in any way, then why not take advantage of her, uh, psychic power."

Elizabeth inclined her head in a small gesture of thanks, grateful for Wright's words of endorsement. "The Lieutenant tells me that there's no physical evidence that your daughter has been kidnapped. That will make my job difficult, but not totally impossible." She sipped her coffee pensively before continuing. "As I told you, I've been receiving messages and images from your daughter."

"How do these images come to you?" Crystal asked.

"They usually come while I'm asleep. When I'm awake there are too many distractions. Unless of course, I have something from the actual kidnapping to guide me. Ideally that would be a piece of clothing that your daughter was wearing when she was taken." Elizabeth nodded. "I know that's far too much to hope for."

"Then what do you propose?" Crystal asked.

"I would like to see Emily's room. I rely on images and thoughts, which I piece together to form a larger picture." She slowly rose to her feet. "Perhaps I can get a reading off Emily's vibrations or even her imprint upon the room. That sometimes works."

Crystal stood. "I'm willing to try anything. Please come with me."

Jimmy waited until they left the room before turning angrily to the detective. "You've got to be joking. Do you really think that woman can find my daughter?"

Wright sipped the last of his coffee and set the cup and saucer down on the table. "I doubt it," he admitted.

"It's wrong to get Crystal's hope up, letting her think that woman is going to find Emily."

"Maybe so," Wright said, rising to his feet slowly. "But as it is, Mrs. Anderson is all we got at the moment."

"Why the hell hasn't the kidnapper called? Why hasn't there been a ransom note?"

Wright shook his head. "I don't know. I'm really puzzled about the case. If this is a kidnapping, we should have heard by now. I'm afraid we may be dealing with something worse."

Jimmy was appalled. "You think she's dead?"

Wright met Jimmy's look. "I hope not," he grunted. "I'll be at home if you hear anything."

Jimmy watched the detective's retreating back, then went to the bar and fixed himself a drink. God, he thought, where is she? Where is Emily?

Elizabeth followed Crystal up the curving steps, her hand trailing over the polished handrail. "Your daughter likes to slide down the banister," she observed, then stopped, a feeling of pain shooting up her arm. "Emily fell here and broke her arm."

Crystal turned, shock on her face. "That's right. How did you know?"

"An image. It's easy to see what has already taken place."

They continued up the stairs and entered Emily's bedroom. Elizabeth paused in the doorway and surveyed the room; it was charming, but the emptiness bounced off the walls. She closed her eyes, shutting out the pained look on Crystal's face. Images of Emily playing in the room flashed through her mind. She walked across the room and knelt before the huge Victorian dollhouse.

She peered inside, noting the detailed work. "This is incredible."

"Jimmy's father made it for Emily. He was a carpenter, and his hobby was making dollhouses."

Elizabeth sensed unhappiness related to the dollhouse. "Does he sell them?"

"He passed away last year."

Elizabeth shook her head. She should have known he was dead, but once again she was reminded that her energy to decipher the images was diminishing. So why was she so positive about Emily? Was it only her imagination? The need to prove that she still had her "psychic powers," as the Lieutenant called them?

"I'm sorry," she said. "It's often difficult for young ones to deal with death."

"Yes. It's sad. Emily liked him so very much, and now she has no grandparents. Just me and Jimmy." Crystal turned away and walked to the window. She pulled the curtains aside. Dusk was claiming the evening, and she noticed that the reporters had gone home, perhaps to children of their own, she thought. "Do you really think she's . . . alive?"

Elizabeth slowly stood up. "I know it," she said, walking to Crystal and laying a comforting hand on Crystal's arm. "We'll find her."

"When?"

"Soon," Elizabeth promised. "I need to think. Would you mind if I slept here in this room?"

Crystal turned to her. "Will that help?"

"I think so. I like to touch and feel things that belong to the, uh, missing person."

"I'll ask Socorro to change the sheets."

"No. Leave them. It'll help," Elizabeth said. "I use all my senses, and I want to pick up on Emily's smell."

Elizabeth glanced around the room. "There are so many dolls. Is Emily's favorite here?"

"Her Barbie doll is missing, but the teddy bear on her bed is the one she's had since she was a baby. She always sleeps with it."

Elizabeth walked to the bed and picked up the bear. She lifted it to her nose; it smelled vaguely of talcum powder. Emily's smell, she decided. "Does it have a name?"

"Just Teddy."

"When I was a child I had a rag doll I was fond of. I still have it tucked away in a trunk." She set the bear down on the pillow. "Emily and I probably have a lot in common. Our personalities are similar, since we were born on the same day."

"Is that why you want to help?"

"I really do believe that Emily and I are ruled by the same cosmic influences. Our lives are on parallel planes that are converging at this time, in this place. It's my destiny to be here."

"I don't understand entirely, but if you can, please help me find her," Crystal pleaded, her eyes brimming.

Elizabeth held her arms open, welcoming Crystal into their comforting warmth. "I will," she promised. "I will."

XII

Kandy glanced up at Richard Cummings as he walked into the apartment. "Look," she said, pressing the volume button of the remote control. "They still haven't found Crystal Smythe's daughter."

Richard sat on the sofa. He wasn't surprised by the newscaster's lack of information. "I'm tired of that crap," he said. "Change the channel."

Kandy pressed the forward button until she found her

favorite music channel. "Too bad about the kid. I saw they mentioned her ex-husband, the polo player. Too bad *you* didn't marry her, huh?"

Kandy's voice was a squeaky rasp. She was a cheap imitation Marilyn Monroe, and her little girl, dumb blonde act was more irritating than amusing. She'd come to Hollywood hoping to win a look-alike contest, but a transvestite did a better job of emulating the late sex symbol and won the prize. Kandy tried to break into the movies, but her look was a dime a dozen. Like so many other hopefuls, she wound up on the streets—broke. A grease monkey pimp jumped on her and used her until he dumped her for a younger girl. Kandy still turned tricks though, making enough to pay the bills and buy drugs. It suited Richard fine.

He didn't like her teasing him about Crystal. It had been a mistake telling her, but he couldn't help bragging about having had an affair with the number one actress in tinsel town. Too bad Kandy didn't have some of Crystal's talent. Or sophistication. As it was, Kandy got on his nerves, but he had to put up with her for a little while longer. But not too much longer.

"So how come you're not working?" he asked.

"Gimme a break. I turned three tricks this afternoon," Kandy said, digging into her deep cleavage. "Look what I bought. A little piece of heaven."

Richard eyed the crack. Normally he'd be pleased to ride the roller coaster, but he had a lot to do in the morning.

"You got any smoke?"

"The finest Jamaican in town," Kandy replied, tossing him a joint. "You sure you don't want some of this?"

Richard dragged heavily on the joint and began to relax. It'd been a long day, and he was tired. He'd been on the fringe of success for most of his life, and now his luck was finally changing. He'd hit rock bottom more than once, but always managed to claw his way out of the hole.

The first time his luck went sour was when Crystal abandoned him. He closed his eyes, but his mind whirled with gloomy memories, spinning garishly colored pictures of a past life filled with grief and evil.

tuesday

I

Jimmy awoke at five. Crystal was sound asleep, exhausted after three days of constant worrying and waiting for news. There had been no hesitation about his sleeping in their bed. Their separation was a forgotten thing in the face of their shared crisis. He slipped his arm out from under her and got out of bed. He went to the bathroom, splashed water on his face, and returned to the bedroom. He sat on the chaise lounge, smoking a cigarette, studying Crystal. She looked so vulnerable when she was asleep, when her defenses were down. Like the woman he had fallen in love with. He remembered when he first met her.

He had been impressed. So many actors and actresses never stopped acting. They were always posing, flirting, filled with themselves and their supposed importance. Their egos were inflated, their confidence easily shattered by the merest bit of gossip. Crystal wasn't like that. He found her to be both shy and unpretentious. She seemed more worried about her acting skills than her public image.

After they were married, he discovered a different side of Crystal—one he hadn't counted on. He learned that her career took precedence over everything, including their marriage. Something from her past drove Crystal, but he didn't know what. He thought he knew why, and once he had attempted to ask Crystal about her marriage to Goldman, but she refused to discuss it.

177

"It's past history," she told him.

He had heard those words often enough. As soon as she completed one film, she was eager to start the next.

"You're only as good as your next film. Anything else is past history," Crystal said.

His resentment grew. He was convinced that her compulsion was driving them apart. He wanted a wife, and although he was happy with Emily, he had always expected to have more children. Crystal's inability to settle down to a normal life was aggravating. Too late, Jimmy realized that Crystal's only concern in life was getting her next role. Not that she didn't love her daughter. In fact, Crystal claimed that everything she did was for Emily's benefit. Jimmy gave up trying to persuade Crystal that the best security she could give Emily was herself. To be there when the child needed her, not in bits and pieces. But Crystal was stubborn and would never change. She was too busy being a star, too busy adding Oscars to her collection.

There were other things that bothered him, that put wedges into their shaky marriage. Everyone knew who Crystal was, but he felt he had become a nonentity in her life. Like walking into restaurants and being called Mr. Smythe. That really annoyed him. So did having Neil around all the time. Crystal consulted him about everything, often shutting Jimmy out.

Jimmy firmly believed Simmons was using Crystal, attaching himself to her so he could write an unflattering book, a biography that would reveal all the intimate details of Crystal's life. Why else would he hang around as a gofer? Jimmy wondered. He had tried discussing it with Crystal, but she had laughed, saying Neil was her best friend and she couldn't survive without him. Maybe Jimmy should have insisted.

Agonizing thoughts flowed through his mind. Poor

Emily. She had suffered the most, not understanding why
her parents didn't love each other anymore. Was it too late
to be a family? If only they had compromised; if only
Crystal had spent more time with Emily; if only he had been
tolerant of Crystal's need to act. If only one of them had
been home, then Emily wouldn't be . . .

Crystal stirred, opened her eyes, and saw Jimmy sitting
across the room. "Hi," she said, still groggy from the
sleeping pill she had taken the night before. She sat up,
glancing at the clock to check the time. "Have they found
Emily?"

Jimmy crossed the room and sat on the bed beside her.
"No. Not yet." He brushed the hair from Crystal's forehead. "I forgot how beautiful you are when you sleep. I've
missed being in bed with you, feeling you in my arms."

Crystal sighed deeply, his touch rekindling pleasant
memories. In the early years of their marriage, Crystal
would come home from the studio exhausted, and Jimmy
always insisted that she stretch out on the sofa to relax. He
would have a drink ready, then massage her back while he
told her about his day. The ritual released the tension
she felt after being on the set. Socorro would then bring
Emily in, fresh from her bath, and the next half hour was
spent playing with their daughter before they had dinner. As
Emily grew, her need for attention increased, and the ritual
with Jimmy was soon a memory.

"I was dreaming about Emily. Remember that time we
were up at Lake Tahoe and Emily was lost. She was only
three then."

Jimmy laughed. "We woke up and she wasn't in her
bed."

"We finally found her stark naked on the dock, feeding
bread to the ducks. I was so afraid."

"So was I. She could have fallen in the lake. We were very lucky."

Crystal felt a twinge of guilt; the demands of her career had not only spoiled her marriage, but had also affected Emily. First there was the film in Dallas; Emily had chicken pox, and Jimmy had to stay home to take care of her. Then she accepted the role in the Russian epic. For three months she had been alone in Moscow, since Jimmy refused to bring Emily to that frigid climate.

When Crystal returned, she was surprised by Emily's reluctance to come into her arms.

"Why shouldn't she be wary of you?" Jimmy said sarcastically. "You're always going away. She's not sure if you're her mother or not."

Crystal resolved to spend more time with her daughter. For the next few months she stayed at home, being the dutiful mother and wife. Although she received countless scripts to consider, she found none that she really wanted. She kept busy answering fan mail, studying investments, and even began painting, but she became bored easily.

Things changed when Neil was injured, and Crystal found something new to occupy her time.

It was Neil who sensed how restless Crystal had become and convinced her that she needed to work. Moss had sent her the New Zealand script, and she was excited about the part she was being offered. She wanted the role, but she had promised Jimmy. She moped around the house for days.

Jimmy finally confronted her. "Face it. You're not happy if you're not working."

"That's ridiculous," she told him.

"Sweetheart, I know you better than you know yourself. Sitting here at home has lost its charm."

"That's not true. I love being here with you and Emily."

"But there's something else you love. You need to be in

front of those cameras," he said, "being a part of the fantasy. Go ahead. Call Moss and tell him you'll accept the role."

Crystal had been surprised by his understanding. She didn't need to be told twice. She did the movie—and the result was the fight that led to their separation.

She had been unfair to both Jimmy and Emily. And now, because she had given such priority to her acting career, her daughter had been taken away from her. Why had she been so stupid? It was all her fault. If only I had been home, she admonished herself once again.

"Will we find Emily?" Crystal whispered, looking up at Jimmy.

He saw the fear in her eyes. Unrelenting fear that matched his own. He slipped under the covers and pulled Crystal into his arms. "I know we will," he said, his voice cracking with emotion.

They held each other, their closeness the only assurance that they would find Emily. They made love wordlessly, giving each other comfort, pretending for a moment that everything was normal.

II

Emily stood at the bedroom window, angry that she had been kept in the tiny room for so long. She had watched the television news and knew they were looking for her, but she was worried that they would never find her. She knew she was far away from home, since they had driven on the freeway for a long time. Then they took another road through a narrow canyon and entered the town.

They had driven past a beach, then up a street called Bluebird Canyon Drive, way up into the mountains, past the house with the cats painted on the front porch. From the window she could still see part of the ocean, but trees obstructed most of her view. If only she could get out of the room, she thought. Then maybe she could get help from a neighbor. Or maybe she could find her way back down the mountain. Then she would look for a policeman to help her.

There was only one problem. He kept the door locked. Maybe she could get out the window. Maybe she could get away.

She tried to lift the window, then banged it with her fists, but it wouldn't budge. She felt the edges again and realized it was painted shut. She would need something sharp to loosen the paint. Somehow she was going to have to get a knife. Somehow she was going to escape.

III

Elizabeth awoke in Emily's bed and reached for her note pad. The images had come while she slept, her head resting on Emily's pillow, the sweet smell of talcum still lingering on the pillowcase.

She wrote quickly, then leaned back against the pillows and studied the list. She was dismayed that there wasn't more. It was like a jigsaw puzzle, still incomplete, lacking the pieces to make it a whole picture. That nice Lieutenant Wright is going to be unhappy, she thought. He wants facts, figures, specific details, not vague feelings. Elizabeth knew she'd have to come up with more to satisfy him. She needed the missing piece that tied it all together.

"Hmnph! Just old age," she mumbled to herself.

She had helped the police solve cases with even less to go on, but she wasn't as confident as she had been in those earlier years. The images were no longer sharp. There were blank holes in her psyche—but still she felt compelled to continue to help in whatever way she could.

"Old age?" she scolded herself. "I'm in the prime of my life."

She got out of bed. A shower would help clear her head and ease the ache out of her bones.

IV

Anna Jefferies sat up in bed. She was thirsty, undoubtedly from the salted peanuts she had eaten the night before. She knew she shouldn't have eaten them, but she had been nervous. She had waited up for John, finally falling asleep while watching a late-night movie.

She went into the bathroom and drank some water, then opened the connecting door to John's bedroom. His bed was unmade, but he wasn't in it. She entered the room, noting how he had thrown his clothes about haphazardly when he undressed. Always in a hurry, always running off somewhere.

Anna heard the distant whirr of the garage door and walked to the window. It was John, backing out of the garage in his blue Jaguar. She had bought him that car as a birthday present, but he had never given her a ride in it. He was so ungrateful.

She wondered where he was going so early in the morning. He usually slept late if he didn't have to go to the studio. Why the rush? Something was happening, something mysterious, something he wanted to hide, and she meant to find out what. She would call her father. He had helped her before. He would know how to handle John and get to the bottom of the mystery.

V

When Elizabeth went downstairs she found that Lieutenant Wright had arrived and was having coffee with Jimmy and Crystal in the dining room.

She accepted scrambled eggs from Socorro, then turned her attention to what the detective was saying.

"It's my fault," Wright said. "I should have told him not to discuss the case with anyone."

Elizabeth didn't understand. "Did something happen?"

"The gardener spoke to a reporter, and what little information we have is now on page one of the *L.A. Times*," Wright replied, holding the newspaper up for Elizabeth to see.

"It's too late to complain about it now," Jimmy said.

"What about the list of names we gave you?" Crystal asked.

"We're working on it. We were able to question the man who drives the van to day camp. He says that after he dropped off Emily, he had two other stops. Then he went home to his wife."

"What about the camp counselors?" Jimmy asked.

"Checked them out, too, and they all have air-tight alibis," Wright said. "And the movie director, Victorio Marsala, was at the Polo Lounge Friday afternoon."

"It was just a wild guess," Jimmy said.

"Have you thought of anyone else we should question?"

Jimmy shook his head. "Crystal and I have racked our brains, but it's difficult. Most of the people we know are in the movie business, and they're also friends. How could we ever suspect them?"

"Stranger things have happened," Wright said, pushing his coffee cup aside. "You never use babysitters?"

"No. Socorro takes care of Emily," Crystal said.

"Well, that's that. I've run out of ideas, and to tell you the truth, the FBI guys aren't much happier. We thought for sure this is a kidnapping, but since there's been no word, no demand for money, we think you'd better prepare your-selves for the, uh, possibility that your daughter has been, uh, murdered."

Wright said the words softly, but they echoed harshly in the room. The pain, and realization of what he'd said, was revealed in the facial expressions of Jimmy and Crystal. They turned to each other, grasping hands.

Elizabeth set her coffee cup down with a noisy clatter. She had hoped to be able to give the Mitchelsons more information, but she would have to go with what she had. It wasn't much, but at least it would give them hope. "I think you're wrong, Lieutenant. Emily is very much alive."

"What? How do you know? Has your sixth sense told you where to find our daughter?" Jimmy spat out. "Personally, I think you're off your rocker. Why don't you leave us alone and get out of here."

"Jimmy!" Crystal cried, embarrassed by his outburst.

Elizabeth was momentarily stunned by his viciousness, but recovered, realizing that Jimmy was suffering deeply, afraid that he would never find his daughter. Jimmy needed something tangible to believe in, not the abstract promises of an old woman.

"I think I've come across some clues to where Emily is being held," she said patiently.

"Oh yeah?" Jimmy said, staring at her with eyes that were hard and filled with contempt. "How?"

Elizabeth refused to be deterred. "There are two different psychometry techniques that I use in psychic investigations of missing persons. The first is the gathering of information by holding an object that the person used or touched. Ideally I would use something the victim was wearing."

"Which we don't have, of course," Wright said.

"No, but I tried something else. I was hoping I could form some impressions by sleeping in Emily's bed last night. I thought if I concentrated on Emily's aura, I would get a reading."

"Her aura?" Wright asked, not understanding, yet hoping that maybe she knew something, anything, that would help.

"Emily is undergoing a great deal of emotional stress, and I thought her aura—or spirit—might be transferred to familiar surroundings or a favorite item. Like her teddy bear."

"Why the bear?" Wright asked.

"She's used to sleeping with it as a source of comfort," Elizabeth explained. "But that didn't work."

Elizabeth spread her toast with apricot preserves before continuing. "Then I tried using the second psychometry technique. That's where you study a photograph of the missing person. It's preferable to use one in which that person is looking directly at the camera. The eyes are very important, as they reveal the soul."

Wright watched as Elizabeth munched on her toast, seemingly lost in her own thoughts. "What did that achieve?"

"Before I went to sleep, I concentrated on Emily's photograph. I tried to project myself into her awareness."

"What were you able to learn?" Crystal asked, leaning forward, elbows on the table. She refused to give up hope. She wasn't quite sure if she understood what Elizabeth was doing, but she trusted the woman and prayed she was right about Emily being alive.

Elizabeth finished her egg and the last bite of toast before answering.

"I think we're getting somewhere," she finally replied. "Let me explain: In astral projection, a psychic's aura, or spirit, if you prefer, leaves the body and travels to other places."

"Astral projection!" Jimmy threw his napkin on the table and stood up. "This is getting us nowhere."

Elizabeth calmly reached for the coffeepot and refilled her cup. "I know it sounds strange, but it's working."

"What's working?" Jimmy growled. "You're wasting our time, sitting here talking about spirits when we should be out looking for Emily."

Crystal turned in her seat. "Please be quiet, Jimmy. I want to hear what Elizabeth has to say."

Elizabeth smiled at Crystal. "I *know* I'm in communication with Emily. I can feel it." She raised her hand to deter more questions. "Sleeping in her bed, holding her teddy bear, studying her photograph, have all enabled me to project myself into Emily's presence."

"Then where is she?" Jimmy snapped. "What do you see in your crystal ball?"

"I don't know where—yet," Elizabeth answered truthfully. She reached under her chair and picked up her notebook. "The images I am receiving were part of the dream I had last night. When I awoke this morning, I wrote down what I could remember. And now I need your help."

"What kind of help?" Wright asked.

Elizabeth opened her note pad. "Since I projected my spirit into Emily's subconscious, you must understand that the images I received are those of a nine-year-old."

Jimmy lit a cigarette and snapped the lighter shut. "So what does your spirit tell you?"

Elizabeth sighed. He wasn't going to let up. He was facing an unknown. His daughter was missing, and there was nothing he could do, so he was striking out at what he didn't understand.

"The first images I received in San Francisco were of a dark, musty-smelling room. I believe this means that Emily is being held prisoner in a house or building that hasn't been used for some time. The color red seems to be associated with the house, but why or how it's connected is still vague."

Elizabeth paused to sip some coffee. "When I heard her voice, her words were, 'Mommy, mommy, where are you?' I assumed she was waiting for you to join her, Crystal."

"Was?" Crystal said. "Does that mean she's no longer waiting?"

"I haven't heard her voice these past twenty-four hours. There are a couple of possible reasons for this. Once I left San Francisco, I probably moved out of range of her communications."

"Why is that?" Crystal asked.

"The easiest way to explain it is to picture me as a radio. In San Francisco, my house is on a bluff overlooking the ocean, so there's no static interference. Here in Los Angeles, I am surrounded by tall buildings, thousands of cars and trucks, countless television sets, you name it."

"Yes, I understand now," Crystal said. "What's the other reason?"

"I hate to say this, but I think Emily has given up hope. She's disappointed and afraid, and may think you're not coming to get her," Elizabeth said, her tone gentle and motherly.

"If we can believe the gardener, Emily waved at the driver of the car and got in willingly. She had to know him," Wright interjected, thinking that at least Elizabeth was on the right track. "She must have thought she was going to meet her mother."

"A good theory, Lieutenant," Jimmy observed, "except we need facts."

Elizabeth ignored the interruption. "I believe I am receiving vital images which will tell us where Emily is. They're disjointed, but they will soon form part of the puzzle."

She referred to her notebook. "What I have written may not make sense, but I'm sure I'm on the right track."

Jimmy returned to his chair, clumping down in the seat. "This is ridiculous. Isn't it conceivable that you may be wrong?"

"Please have patience with me," Elizabeth implored. "I would like each of you to concentrate and try to make a picture in your mind. You may know the place where Emily is being held.

"I am sure the kidnapper took your daughter down a busy highway from which Emily could see the ocean, tall trees, and mountains. There are two signs involved: one with the word 'bluebird,' the other has something to do with shrimp."

"Is that it?" Jimmy asked.

"She is probably near a beach or lagoon. And . . ." She paused, considering. ". . . For some reason, a cat is involved. I'm not sure if it's alive or stuffed or made of glass, but it seems important to Emily."

Jimmy laughed, his tone bitter. "Are we supposed to use your so-called clues to find Emily?"

"As I told you, this is what Emily saw and a child looks at things differently than an adult. I know they don't seem like much now," Elizabeth said defensively, "but they *are* clues."

"How do you know that?" Wright asked, sorry that there was so little to go on. He had secretly hoped the psychic would come up with something positive. An address, a name, anything that would help.

"I'm sure these are the things Emily saw, what she thinks about," Elizabeth insisted. "It's what happened to her before she was locked up in the room."

"What kind of room?" prompted Wright.

"I'm not sure. I believe Emily can see out a window. I think I told you the color red was involved. I'm sure of it now," Elizabeth said stubbornly. "Now it's up to us to piece everything together."

Wright shook his head. "You've described just about all of California, not to mention the entire United States. Mountains, beaches, trees; where the hell do we start?"

Crystal frowned heavily. "Nothing makes sense."

Elizabeth shook her head. "Since Emily knows who the kidnapper is, you also must know this person," Elizabeth told Crystal. "In which case, you might be able to identify the clues. You have to help me find where he has taken her."

Jimmy couldn't believe what he was hearing. "This is really stupid. It's common knowledge that we have a beach house. And it's even near mountains and tall trees." Jimmy pushed his chair back and stood up. "What are you trying to pull, Mrs. Anderson? An exclusive story for the *National Enquirer*?"

Agent Willis entered the room and dumped a pile of mail in the middle of the table. "Want to sort through this?" he asked.

It was Crystal who noticed the special delivery envelope. "My God! The handwriting is Emily's."

"Yes. It's from her," Jimmy said, reaching for it.

"No. Stop. It's got to be from the kidnapper," Wright said excitedly. "This is the break we've been waiting for. He's finally made contact."

He reached for the envelope and split it with his breakfast knife; he carefully removed a folded piece of paper, then spread it open slowly, using another knife. "Don't anyone touch it; it might have fingerprints."

Jimmy leaned over Wright's shoulder. The letters were of different sizes, but it wasn't difficult to read the chilling note. He read out loud: "IF YOU WANT EMILY, GET ONE MILLION DOLLARS READY. DON'T TELL POLICE. I WILL CONTACT YOU."

"That's Emily's signature," Crystal cried. "Why did he make her sign it?"

"So you'll know it's authentic," Willis explained, excited by the sudden turn of events. He'd been ready to pull out, and now they finally had something to go on.

Wright studied the sheet of paper. "It isn't much to go on. The paper is cheap bond, and the letters were probably cut from a magazine," he said.

Elizabeth stretched across the table and reached for the paper. She placed her napkin over Emily's signature.

"You shouldn't touch that," Willis admonished her. "There might be fingerprints."

Elizabeth ignored him. "The kidnapper is smarter than that. He never touched the letters; he used gloves. However, I might be able to get a reading on him."

They watched as Elizabeth slowly ran her hands above the letters, then closed her eyes, standing silently as she absorbed the images that flowed through her mind. As she began to speak, her voice was strangely hollow.

"He is a weak man. Indecisive. He thinks about money and revenge. He's an evil man."

"Damn it! Any idiot could figure that out," Jimmy shouted.

Elizabeth winced at his harsh words. "There is something more. I see death. Someone is going to die."

"Is it Emily? Has he hurt her?" Crystal cried, wiping at the tears which ran down her face.

"No," Elizabeth assured her. "For the present, she's all right."

"Don't you worry, Miss Smythe. I mean, Mrs. Mitchelson," Willis corrected himself. "Now that the kidnapper has contacted us, we'll be able to find her. I'll take the ransom note to headquarters. Mrs. Anderson could be wrong. There might be fingerprints."

"There won't be any," Elizabeth asserted. "I'm sure of it. He used gloves."

"What about the post office?" Wright asked. "The envelope has a Hollywood postmark."

"Right," Willis said, peeved that the policeman was always butting in. "I'll have one of my men question the postal employees. It's a long shot, but maybe someone can remember who sent it," he said crisply. "I'll see you later."

Elizabeth was glad Willis was leaving. He had been quite verbal about his opinion of psychics, undermining her efforts to convince the Mitchelsons she could find their daughter. She was used to skepticism, but Willis had been downright rude, and his attitude was influencing James Mitchelson. No wonder she was having such a hard time getting a true picture. There was too much opposition to her techniques. Too much animosity in the air.

"The note says not to tell the police," Jimmy reminded them. "Doesn't that creep read the newspapers? Doesn't he watch television? It's general knowledge that the police have no clues. Doesn't he know that?"

"He's probably worried about the FBI," Wright said. "Maybe he thinks they'll foul up the delivery of the ransom money."

"If that's the case, I want those FBI fellows to clear out,"

Jimmy said decisively. "We've got to do what the kidnapper says. Otherwise, Emily might wind up getting . . ."

"Killed?" Wright asked bluntly. "That's exactly what we want to prevent."

"You're forgetting one thing. Emily willingly got into the car with him. She knows her kidnapper. He has to kill her," Elizabeth reminded them, studying each face as her chilling words penetrated their confused minds. "He has no choice."

Wright nodded. "Mrs. Anderson is right. He'll never let her go. We have to find Emily before anything happens to her."

"How long do we have?" Jimmy asked, gritting his teeth.

"Depends upon how long it takes for him to figure out how to collect the money," Wright answered. "I suggest you start getting it together. A million dollars is a lot of money. Once you have it, the FBI will want to mark the bills."

Jimmy shook his head, knowing he couldn't fight both Wright and the FBI. "I'll call our bank immediately."

"I can't stand this," Crystal sobbed. "When will it ever end?"

Jimmy held Crystal in his arms, wishing he could do something, feeling powerless. "Don't worry, darling," he whispered, stroking her hair. "We're going to find her."

VI

It was late when Neil arrived at the house. The crowd was back, spurred on by the article in the *Times*. He was immediately besieged by five reporters. One of them stuck a television camera in his face. They began shouting at him, tossing questions at him.

"Have the police found Emily?"

"What do the police have to say about the kidnapping?"

"Were they able to trace the blue car?"

"How is Crystal holding up?"

Neil pushed aside the microphones. "No comment."

"Just a simple statement for the press," insisted the red-haired reporter.

Neil remembered her: Selma Siegel. She was the troublemaker. "I see you scored big."

"You mean about the gardener?" she said sweetly. "Just lucky. Something to keep the story alive."

"I also read your piece about Crystal's former husband," Neil said. "You've certainly been busy. I didn't know Mr. Goldman was back in Los Angeles."

"Is he a suspect?"

"You'll have to ask the police that," Neil said.

"According to Mr. Goldman, he was in Santa Barbara over the weekend. He played in a polo match on Sunday and didn't return to Los Angeles until yesterday morning. He was quite gracious to consent to the interview."

"Yeah, I bet he was," Neil laughed. Crystal had sworn him to secrecy when she told him the details of her disastrous honeymoon night with the Argentinian. He wondered why Julio had suddenly decided to speak to the press. What was his game?

He turned and stared at the street. A van was parked at the curb, a MAP OF THE STAR'S HOMES sign painted gaudily on its side panel. Three cars were parked behind it, the occupants standing on the sidewalk, having their photographs taken with Crystal's house in the background. Another car slowed as it passed, the passengers gaping and pointing. It was a carnival, and the spectators expected to be entertained.

"You want a story?" he asked Siegel. He pointed at the

sightseers. "There's your story. They don't give a damn about Emily. All they want is a show," he said gruffly and hurried inside.

VII

Charlie Fischer saw the White BMW approaching the gate. He knew the car was leased, but the driver, Pierre Montbleau, liked to pretend it was his own. Filming on his picture had been suspended—maybe permanently, if you listened to the studio gossip. If Crystal Smythe didn't come back on the set, Melvin Schuller might shut down production. Charlie stepped out of the guardhouse, timing his movements to make sure the director would have to stop.

"How you doing, Mr. Montbleau?" asked Charlie. "Any word on Ms. Smythe's daughter?"

"No. Nothing. This is very stressful for me. I had wished to finish this film so I could spend some time on the Riviera this summer. Now it seems this will be impossible."

"Too bad," Charlie said. "So what's happening with the movie?"

"Who knows? It is very difficult to make the film without the star," he said, shrugging his shoulders. "For me, I am going home. I will get into my jacuzzi with a very cold martini and think about other things."

With that pronouncement, the director lapsed into French. Charlie didn't understand, but he didn't mind. He was used to the eccentricities of the people who went in and out of the studio. Movie people! Hmmph! Charlie raised the gate. "Take care, Mr. Montbleau."

He watched the director speed out into the street with no regard for oncoming traffic. "Foreigners," he muttered. "Don't know how to drive in this country."

Charlie checked his watch. It was almost time to call it a

day; the night watchman would be coming on soon. Charlie wished he could stay, but the studio said he couldn't work any overtime. He would have done it for free, just to have something to do. The prospect of going home to an empty house was unappealing.

He stepped inside the guardhouse and gathered up his thermos and newspaper. And then he noticed the manila envelope—the one from the fan with the T-shirt in it. Charlie had forgotten about it, though he had intended to give it to Crystal's secretary.

"Looks like he ain't going to come in today," Charlie said, talking to himself once again, a habit he'd acquired after his wife died.

Charlie decided he would take the envelope to Crystal's dressing room. It would give him something to do and delay his having to go home.

VIII

He walked into the house and set the tape recorder on the kitchen table. He had worked hard on the plan, and now it was perfect. First he would make the recording, then drive back to the city. He would have to find a way of delivering it without getting caught, but that shouldn't be too difficult. He would have to avoid the post office now, just in case the cops thought he would use that method again. They had probably alerted the postal clerks to be on guard for anyone mailing something to Crystal. He would have to figure out something else. There was so much to think about, so much to take care of. Like where to make the pickup. It had bothered him, but he had finally worked out a plan. He would iron out the details later.

He went to the bedroom and unlocked the door. "I want you to do something."

Emily looked up at him. "What?" she asked listlessly.

"Come out to the kitchen," he said.

Emily followed him, curious, happy to be out of the room which had become her prison. She glanced at the kitchen door. Was it locked? she wondered.

He caught her glance and raised a hand menacingly toward her. "Don't even think of trying to leave here."

"I wasn't."

"Sit," he commanded, reaching for a spiral notebook. "I want you to make a tape recording for your mother."

"Why?" she said warily.

"You want to see your mother, don't you?"

Emily stared up at him. Her cheeks were tearstained, and the days of fear were etched in her eyes. "Yes," she mumbled.

"Then, I want you to read something for me. Read it out loud and slowly."

"Yes," she answered, too tired to resist.

"You must read the whole thing without stopping," he cautioned her, "even if it confuses you. Do you understand?"

"I have to read it without stopping?"

"That's right. Now, when I nod my head, you begin to talk." He opened the notebook, pointed to the page, and nodded as he pushed the record button.

Emily began to speak, reading the words slowly. "Put the money into a . . . a . . . briefcase. You must go alone. They will be watching you. If you do not obey, something will happen to me." Emily paused, tears welling in her eyes, her lower lip trembling. She looked up at him, afraid, hating him.

He pushed the stop button. "I told you to read it without stopping," he said, his face red with anger. "If you don't, you'll be sorry."

Emily wiped her eyes on her sleeve and gulped noisily. She wondered if he would hit her. She looked up at him; his eyes were narrow slits warning her to obey. When he pushed the record button, she began reading.

"You will wear a two-piece swimsuit and a loose blouse. Do not wear any jew . . . jewelry. You will drive to the Santa Monica Pier on Friday. You must be at the phone booths near the steps by eleven A.M. Wait there. Take the blouse off. When the telephone rings, answer it. You'll get more in . . . structions then."

He pressed the stop button, then rewound the tape. "You did good, Emily," he said, patting her hand.

Emily toyed with the salt and pepper shakers on the table. He seemed happy now.

"If you get the money on Friday, will I be able to go home?"

"Sure, kid," he said as he removed the cassette from the machine.

"What will you do with the money?"

He had thought about that a lot. He'd be a millionaire—and he knew just what he was going to do. First he planned to go to the French Riviera. He would buy some new clothes and then a car. Next he would visit the casino in Monte Carlo. If he got bored, he would travel to the Italian Riviera. Maybe he would meet some movie people. He would offer his services as a consultant on films. They made a lot of movies in Italy, and he would lend them his expertise.

He looked down at Emily. "I'm going to spend it," he said, laughing as he opened the refrigerator. He carried eggs and ham to the stove and started preparing dinner. He would feed her and go, since he still had a lot to do. His plan was simple, but he had to time the route.

He had chosen the Santa Monica Pier because he could

watch it easily. Once he saw Crystal arrive at the phone booths, he would call and give her more instructions. He was no fool; he knew the FBI would be watching, and they would have the telephone bugged, too, but he was sure he could outfox them.

He laughed. He had learned all the tricks about kidnapping from the movies. What worked, and what failed. Of course he still hadn't figured out the rest of the details, but he had plenty of time.

He dished the ham and eggs on a plate and handed her a knife and fork. "Take this back to your room," he told her. "I've got things to do."

Emily couldn't believe her good luck. He had actually handed her a knife. It was just what she needed. Now she would be able to escape.

"When will you be back?" she asked him.

"When I get here," he said gruffly. "Now get into that bedroom."

IX

The noise from the construction next door drifted in through the window. Wright closed the window and turned on the air conditioner. He'd be happy when the new city hall was completed and he could move into a larger office. Wright swiveled around, leaned back in his chair, and put his feet up on the desk. He was tired. He felt like he was banging his head against a brick wall. There weren't enough clues to solve the case, not enough information. What was the motive? Was it the money? Revenge? He tossed the folder on his desk and looked at the detective who was slouched down in the only other chair in his crowded office.

"You're sure?" he asked.

Detective John Francis yawned. He had been trailing Neil Simmons for the past two days, a tiring and boring job.

"Sure, I'm sure. Sunday night he went to a gay bar called Rafters. He was there about two hours and left around midnight in his own car. He followed a gray Mercedes to the address in Beverly Hills. He stayed there all night, and I called the license plate in to the Department of Motor Vehicles. They confirmed that the car belongs to the District Attorney, Joe Vitale."

Francis lit a cigar before continuing. "Monday morning Simmons went home, changed clothes, drove to the bank, and then was at Crystal Smythe's home most of the day. He left at four-thirty, went to the grocery store, and returned to his own house. At six the gray Mercedes arrived at Simmons' place, and the D.A. entered the house. He stayed until midnight, then I saw him and Simmons kiss when they parted."

"Son of a bitch!"

Francis grinned wickedly. "I didn't think Simmons was planning on going out again, so I went home to sleep. I picked up surveillance at seven this morning."

"Yeah, go on."

"Simmons went jogging, then had breakfast at Ships on La Cienega, where he just happened to run into the D.A.," Francis said. "Isn't that cozy?"

"Shit! There goes my theory that Simmons is the kidnapper."

"I never guessed the D.A. would be involved."

"We might be able to use this piece of information someday."

"How?"

"I don't know, but it's sure nice to have a hold over that asshole. Let's not mention this to anyone."

Francis ran a hand through his thick red hair. "I'm certainly not going to tell."

"Well, at least I know about Simmons. I thought he was hiding something. Obviously it's his romance with Vitale."

"The guys at the DMV wanted to know why I was calling in Vitale's license plate." •

"What'd you tell them?"

"I said he was parked in a no-parking zone."

"Good thinking."

"So what's happening on the case?"

"We got a ransom note today. The FBI took it down to their lab."

"You're out of it?"

Wright thought that over. He had a stack of folders on his desk, all pertaining to cases he was working on, but none was as intriguing as the Emily Mitchelson kidnapping.

"Not if I can help it. This is still my territory, and I want to help Ms. Smythe and her husband find their daughter."

"Well, if there's anything I can do."

Wright shrugged. "It's all a waiting game."

X

Kandy stumbled into the apartment and headed for the bedroom. It had been a long day, and she had worked her butt off. Literally, she thought, grinning to herself. Now all she wanted to do was lay back and get high.

"Hey, Ricky. Are you here?" she called, her speech slurred.

Richard sat up and flicked on the nightstand lamp. He watched as Kandy made her way to the foot of the bed. He sensed that she was bombed out of her mind.

"So where were you, hot shot? I waited for you all day long. I thought you were going to take me to dinner."

"I got busy. I had a lot to do."

"You left me without the car. I had a trick out in the valley, and I had to take a taxi," she said in her squeaky voice. "It's my car. My pretty little blue car."

Richard grabbed her purse and opened it. His suspicions were right. The crack was there. And something else, a hypodermic needle and an envelope filled with enough heroin to kill a horse.

"Where'd you get this?" he asked angrily.

"Paulie gave it to me to hold."

Richard knew Paulie, a Sunset Boulevard pimp who supplemented his income by dealing dope. Richard suspected she was lying and planned to keep some of the heroin for herself.

"I thought I told you to stop working for Paulie. He's bad news."

"My, my. Aren't we touchy, Mr. Big Shot," she said, undaunted by his tirade since he was always shouting about something. "Did you see in the newspaper that the man who kidnapped your ex-girl friend's kid was driving a blue car?"

"What about it?" Richard said, suddenly alert, his attention riveted on what she was saying.

"Didn't you tell me that you were going to pay Crystal back? Didn't you say you were going to get a lot of money from her? Didn't you say that?" Kandy insisted.

Richard realized that Kandy wasn't as doped up as he thought. "Don't give me a hard time."

Kandy picked up a bourbon bottle and poured a glass full. She drank hard, then refilled her glass. "Did you take that little girl? Is that why you needed my car? My *blue* car?"

"Shut up," Richard shouted at her. "You don't know what the hell you're talking about."

"You think I can't put two and two together?" Kandy sat on the side of the bed and undid the straps of her four-inch heels. She kicked the shoes into opposite corners and peeled off her nylons. "I'll bet you took that girl, and I'll bet you're holding her for ransom."

"I told you to shut up!" Richard stormed at her as he reached across the bed and viciously slapped her face.

Kandy gasped and fell back against the headboard. "I didn't mean anything," she whimpered, knowing she had gone too far. "I'm sorry."

Richard towered over her, glaring at her, hating her, knowing that the time had come. Kandy knew too much; she had outlived her usefulness.

wednesday

Jimmy had insisted she take a sleeping pill the night before, but it had been a restless night, filled with terrifying dreams. Crystal awoke with a pounding headache. She slid out of bed, careful not to disturb Jimmy. She went downstairs, stopping in the kitchen for a glass of orange juice to wash down some aspirin, then went out to the garden.

It was early, but the sun was shimmering brightly, and the day promised to be a hot one. Crystal dove into the pool and swam its length twenty times. Exhausted, she wrapped a large towel around herself and collapsed on a chaise lounge. She accepted the cup of coffee Socorro brought to her.

"I went to church early this morning and lit a candle to the Virgin Mary. She will help us find Emily."

Crystal smiled weakly at the maid. "Thank you. I appreciate your prayers."

"I feel so bad. I wish I could do something to help," Socorro said, tears springing to her eyes as she retreated back into the house.

At least she can cry, Crystal thought. Her own tears had stopped as she realized that crying wouldn't bring Emily back. She felt drained of all emotion, steeling herself for the worst news. The FBI investigators had taken over her life. Their electronic equipment was spread out in the living room, and they were intercepting every phone call that came to the house. She thought it was foolish for them to believe that the kidnapper would call. He had to be smarter than that.

Crystal shuddered. The chances of finding Emily were a thousand to one. Maybe a million to one. And once they paid the ransom, what were the odds that the kidnapper would release Emily? The percentages weren't good. She had overheard the FBI agents talking; they were doubtful that Emily would be alive.

Crystal realized that their only hope was Elizabeth. "She *must* find Emily before it's too late," Crystal said out loud, then glanced around the empty garden, surprised that she was alone. "Before it's too late," she repeated slowly, closing her eyes, blotting out the painful thoughts, wondering if there was enough time.

Melvin Schuller entered the den and sat heavily on one of the leather chairs. He crossed one leg over the other, smoothing the seams of his Armani silk suit. "Has there been any news?"

"No. Nothing," Jimmy said, studying the rotund man.

"How's Crystal holding up?"

Jimmy shook his head. "It's wearing her down."

Melvin nodded. "This is a terrible thing. Terrible."

Crystal entered the room. She had showered and washed her hair, but hadn't applied make-up. Her face was drawn, the lips compressed.

"Hello, Melvin," she said softly, bending to kiss him on the cheek.

"How're you doing, sweetheart?"

"I'm tired, Melvin." Crystal sat on the sofa, tucking her legs up. She was wearing a lightweight jumpsuit, the rose color a bold contrast against her pallid skin. "I'm sorry about the movie," she apologized.

"Not to worry," Melvin assured her. "I'm going to recast the male lead anyhow. We'll have to redo all the scenes you did with Jefferies."

"Why? What happened?" Crystal asked, puzzled.

Melvin studied his manicured hands, avoiding Crystal's eyes. "Jefferies went on a binge, got drunk as a skunk, and wrapped his car around a tree last night. I'm surprised you didn't hear about it. It was on the morning news."

"We haven't turned the television on or read the newspapers this morning," Jimmy explained. "All this focus on our lives is very upsetting. The television people are the worst. They went out to Emily's summer camp and interviewed several of the other children."

Melvin nodded. "I saw that, but you've got to understand they're just doing their job."

"Not when it's happening to you," Jimmy said. "So how is John?"

Melvin removed a Havana cigar from his pocket, unwrapped it and snipped the end, then lit it, puffing happily. Though many people thought of him as a tight wad, it wasn't true. He enjoyed many luxuries, and a good cigar was a must on his list. Another thing that was important to him was loyalty, which he repaid handsomely, except Jefferies had failed in that department.

Anna's phone call hadn't been surprising. Melvin had also been suspicious of his son-in-law, and for over a week his private investigator had been following Jefferies. John was a creature of habit and could usually be found at Nicky Blair's posh Sunset Boulevard restaurant. The investigator's report was thorough, complete with photographs that were practically pornographic. Jefferies was having an affair with a tall Eurasian girl.

John hadn't been loyal to Anna, so he had to be punished. It didn't take long to figure out how. The accident had been planned; Melvin had one of his men fix the brakes on Jefferies' car. Unfortunately, Jefferies had survived the accident. Perhaps it was just as well. Anna would still have her husband.

"Jefferies is paralyzed. His spinal cord was severed," Melvin said evenly, without a trace of pity.

"That's just awful," Crystal said, even though she hated Jefferies.

"Yeah, it's a shame," Melvin agreed. "Of course this means his movie career is over."

"Poor Anna," Crystal said, still able to feel compassion for another.

"Best thing that could happen to her," Melvin said, a smug smile spreading from ear to ear. "At least she'll know where he is, and the baby will have a father who's around."

"Wouldn't it be better to write off the movie?" Jimmy asked. "The insurance will surely cover the loss."

Melvin's face registered shock at the suggestion. "Are you kidding?"

"With Jefferies out and Crystal unable to continue, it seems you don't have much of a movie left."

"We'll wait," Melvin interrupted, "and reshoot all of Crystal's scenes with Jefferies. We're already looking for a replacement. I'm thinking we might be able to get . . ."

"This isn't the time or place to be talking about this," Jimmy growled, "and it might be a hell of a long time before Crystal is ready to resume acting."

"It'll be worth waiting for. With all this brouhaha about Crystal, we're getting a free ride on the publicity train."

"Is that all that interests you?" Crystal asked, infuriated by Melvin's insensitivity.

Melvin flicked ashes into a large ceramic ashtray on the coffee table. "It's not like that, sweetheart, but what we got here is an unusual situation. Everyone's following the kidnapping on television and in the newspapers. Your public loves you, Crystal, and they want to see you get your daughter back."

"I don't give a damn about what the public wants," Crystal spat out.

"The television networks are negotiating for your old films. A Crystal Smythe week," Melvin said enthusiastically. "That'll mean big earnings for the studio. And for you, too. You gouged me plenty for your starring role and percentage share of 'The Kiss of . . .'"

"Stop it!" Crystal shouted, leaping to her feet. "My daughter has been kidnapped by some maniac, and all you can think of is how much money I can earn for you! I won't listen to this madness."

Melvin stared after her, his mouth parted in surprise, as she ran from the room. "Gee. I'm sorry. I didn't mean to upset Crystal. I just wanted to distract her."

"I know," Jimmy said, fully aware that Melvin never did anything without having a motive. He stood and accompanied Melvin to the front door.

"You'll call me as soon as you hear something?"

Jimmy wondered if Melvin's concern was about Emily or his investment in Crystal. "As soon as possible," he promised, firmly closing the door behind him.

II

Elizabeth stretched out on the bed, pressing Emily's photograph to her forehead. "Come on, honey. Speak to me. Where are you? Open your mind to me. Let me read your thoughts. Don't lose patience. We'll find you."

She rested quietly, waiting for the images, but none came. Why? What was wrong?

Crystal knocked on the door and entered Emily's bedroom. "Are you okay?"

"Yes, I'm fine," Elizabeth answered, sitting up.

Crystal crossed to the dollhouse and knelt before it. She began moving the tiny living room furniture around, then picked up two miniature dolls: a woman and a child.

"Emily and I like to play house together. She pretends she's the mommy and I'm her little girl."

Crystal began humming a tune, rocking back and forth on her heels. Elizabeth felt alarmed. She had seen it happen to other parents whose children had been kidnapped. Crystal was giving up hope. She was beginning to mourn.

"Tell me about Emily," she urged Crystal, leaning back against the pillows.

Crystal was silent, thinking, then slowly began speaking. "She was such a pretty little thing when she was born. When we brought her home from the hospital, she weighed seven pounds, ten ounces. She had the curliest mop of dark hair . . . just like Jimmy's. I was hoping it would stay that way, but it became lighter as she grew older. I remember . . ."

Elizabeth listened to Crystal's memories. Talking was the best therapy and would give her less time to brood. Occasionally Elizabeth nodded or made a comment, but her own thoughts were elsewhere. She had to figure out where Emily was being held—*before* the ransom money was paid. After that it would be too late.

III

Peggy joined them for lunch. They ate outside on the terrace, sitting in the shade of a huge pepper tree. Socorro had served them cold salmon with a dill sauce, then retreated back to the kitchen.

"The hardest part is the waiting," Jimmy said, lighting a cigarette.

Peggy reached for the pitcher and refilled her glass, then squeezed some lemon into her iced tea. "What kind of person would do this?" Peggy asked Wright.

He wiped his mouth, then neatly folded his napkin and placed it on the table. "The FBI guys are making up a psychological profile of the kidnapper. They think we're dealing with a psychopath who kidnapped Emily to get back at Crystal. The theory makes sense to me."

Peggy's eyes grew large with surprise. "Why?"

"Because he waited so long to send the ransom note," Wright said, reaching into his jacket for a cigarette. He searched his pockets for matches, then accepted a light from Jimmy. "We think the kidnapper's initial intention was something other than money."

"Like what?" Jimmy asked.

Wright shrugged his shoulders. "Who knows? I don't think he has a written plan. It was probably a spur of the moment thing."

Crystal stood, walked away, then spun around angrily. "What difference does it make? He has Emily," she said, her face cruelly contorted, "and no one's doing anything to get her back. The FBI just sit around waiting for the phone to ring. What if he doesn't call? Maybe he's raped her; maybe she's dead."

Jimmy jumped to his feet and grabbed Crystal, shaking her. "Emily's alive!" he shouted. "You have to believe that!"

Crystal looked up at him, her body trembling. "I can't. Not anymore. I've lost her. I'll never see my baby again," she screamed, losing all control of her emotions. "It's all my fault. I did this to her. I killed her. Oh, Emily, baby. Forgive me. Forgive me. Oh, God. Help me. Help me."

Peggy's voice penetrated Crystal's thoughts, bringing her back to reality. "Stop that," she commanded. "We are going to find Emily," she said, enunciating each word slowly and clearly as she came around the table and gently took Crystal's arm. "Come on, honey. Perhaps you should lie down."

"I don't want to lie down. I want a drink," Crystal said, pushing Peggy aside. "Anyone want to join me?"

"That's not a solution," Peggy told her.

"No, but it damn well helps," Crystal mumbled, walking into the house.

Elizabeth had remained silent during Crystal's outburst, recognizing her pain. "Let me go to her. I understand."

Wright stubbed out his cigarette and excused himself. "I have to call my office."

Peggy waited until they were alone and then turned to Jimmy. "I wish there was something I could do for Crystal."

"She's slowly coming apart," he said miserably.

Peggy patted his hand. "She's strong, Jimmy. That's what I liked about her when we first met. She was so full of confidence." Peggy paused, remembering. "Crystal positively glowed. You may find this hard to believe, but I knew it then that she was going to be a star."

"And she did it."

"Yes, but she had a few setbacks. Like Richard. He was such a bastard, and Crystal was really devastated by him."

"Richard? Crystal never told me about him."

"Best forgotten," Peggy said, realizing she had said too much. "All I can tell you is that he was a real scum-bag. Anyhow, Crystal bounced back. She's a fighter, you know."

"Yes. I know."

"She didn't let that jerk get her down. Once she had an

opportunity to prove she was an actress, there was no stopping Crystal." Peggy shook her head. "It was too bad that her marriage to Julio turned out to be a farce. I suppose she told you about that."

"No. Crystal has never told me," Jimmy said, embarrassed that he knew so little about his wife's past.

"It's just as well," Peggy drawled. "She was convinced that she would never meet the right man. And then you came into her life. It seemed like the perfect marriage. I'm really sorry things went rotten between you two."

"We had a long talk last night, and we've decided that if . . . I mean, *when* we get Emily back, we're going to live together again. Be a real family."

Peggy beamed brightly, pleased that her best friends had resolved their differences. "I'm glad. I know Crystal has missed you. She's just had her priorities all mixed up."

"Like being the world's greatest actress?" Jimmy asked. "I guess I was jealous of her fame," he admitted. "Since we've been living apart, I've had plenty of time to rethink our relationship. I know Crystal can't stop acting, but I'm learning to accept that. Crystal is strong and very independent, and nothing will ever change her."

"Would you really be happy if she were any different?"

"No. Probably not. I love her just the way she is."

"Good!" Peggy exclaimed.

"You've been a good friend," Jimmy said. "The best."

Peggy glanced at her watch. "I'm sorry, but I have to leave now. We're driving up to Santa Barbara this evening. We have that damn housewarming on Saturday, and everyone's invited. It's too late to cancel."

"I understand," Jimmy said.

"I feel like I'm deserting you, but we'll be back Sunday evening," Peggy promised. "You'll let us know if you hear from the kidnapper? Or as soon as you get Emily back?"

"We'll call you if there's any news."

Peggy grasped Jimmy's hands, searching his face. "Do you think this Mrs. Anderson can help?"

Jimmy shrugged. "I don't know a heck a lot about psychics, and to tell you the truth, I don't believe she can actually help us find Emily. However, Lieutenant Wright informs me that she's been quite successful in similar cases."

A small frown wrinkled Peggy's forehead. "You know, everyone worries about Crystal and how she's holding up," she said, "but what about you? Are you okay?"

"I'm angry. I feel so damn helpless," Jimmy admitted. "What's strange is that it took something like this to get Crystal and me back together."

"You were never really apart," Peggy said, kissing him on the cheek. "She loves you very much—and she needs you. She always has."

IV

"I questioned the gardener thoroughly," Wright said brusquely. "He doesn't remember anything else. I'm sure if he did, he would have told the newspaper reporters."

Elizabeth followed the detective out the front door. "Yes, you're probably right, but I thought I might get a reading from him."

"Does that work?"

Elizabeth stooped to pluck a geranium bud, sniffing the woody smell, thinking there was no other scent like it in the world. It always reminded her of her childhood home and the pots on the front porch which her mother so carefully tended. Until her death. She wondered if the present owners of the house still kept geraniums. Maybe she would go back for a visit, to see how things had changed. Yes. She would do that. But first she had to find Emily. She turned her attention back to the detective. He deserved an honest answer.

"Sometimes it works. Not often, mind you; maybe once in a hundred cases. Since the gardener was the last person to see Emily, it's certainly worth a try." She glanced around. "I see the reporters and gawkers have gone."

"They probably went to lunch, but they'll be back," Wright said wryly. "Tragedy is so damn exciting. This is real life drama. It fuels their imagination. It stimulates their souls. They think they're a part of it."

They found the gardener edging the grass along the side of the house next door. Wright tapped him on the shoulder.

"Mr. Morales, may we talk to you?"

Morales stood up, removing his hat. "I'm sorry about the newspaper. I didn't mean to do anything wrong."

"Yes, yes, I know," Wright said impatiently. "Look. This is Mrs. Anderson. She's trying to help us find Emily."

"*Pobrecita*," Morales said, shaking his head back and forth, obviously upset by the kidnapping. "I see her all the time waiting for her *madre* to come home from the movie making. She is such a nice little girl."

Elizabeth nodded in agreement. "Could you tell me what you saw when the man took Emily. Everything, just the way it happened."

"I 'ready tole the policeman. And the reporter. I don't know nothing else," he said, seemingly distressed by his part in the drama.

"Yes, but *this* time I would like you to tell me. Just close your eyes and slowly try to remember. Make a picture in your mind of everything that happened."

Morales gave Elizabeth a strange look, as if she were crazy, then shrugged. He'd do anything to make up for his mistake. The reporter had tricked him. It wasn't right, but now it was too late. If the lady wanted him to tell the story, he would do it, even if it wasn't a whole lot. He closed his eyes, frowning.

"What do I do now?" he asked.

Elizabeth put a hand on his arm. "Pretend you're watching television, and tell me what you see. You were gardening and you saw Emily. What was she doing?"

"She walk down the street . . . then goes to the Miller house. From there she come back and say hello to me." He paused, remembering. "Then she see the . . . the blue car and she say, 'Hi, Richard' and then she get into the car and then they drive away." Morales opened his eyes. "That's all."

Wright stared at him. "Did you say Richard?" he asked, his voice gratingly sharp.

"What?" the gardener asked nervously.

Wright poked a finger in the Mexican's chest. "You said she called out to someone named Richard."

"Oh! Yes, that's right! I tole you that."

"No, Goddamn it," Wright exploded. "You never said Richard."

"*Ay chihuahua*!" the gardener said, slapping his head. "I forget."

"You son of a bitch," Wright shouted, grabbing Morales' shirt front. "How the hell could you forget?"

Elizabeth stepped between them, pushing Wright back. "Stop it," she told him, then turned her attention to the trembling gardener. "It's all right, Mr. Morales. Thank you for your help."

Wright glared at him. "Don't speak to the Goddamn reporters. You understand? I don't want them to know anything about this. *Comprende, amigo*? If you do . . ."

"I'm sure Mr. Morales won't say anything," Elizabeth told the detective.

"I'm going to have one of my men keep an eye on you," Wright shouted over his shoulder as Elizabeth steered him back into the house.

"He'll keep quiet this time," Elizabeth told Wright. "You frightened him."

"So who the hell is this Richard? Obviously Emily knew him, which means the Mitchelsons have to know him, too. It's time for answers."

"Who is Richard?" Wright demanded as he entered the den.

Crystal looked up, startled. "Who?"

"Who is Richard?" Elizabeth repeated. "The gardener remembered today that Emily called out his name before getting into the car."

"I don't know anyone named Richard," she said hastily.

Wright noticed how tightly her hands were clenched and saw that her lower lip was trembling. The name Richard obviously had unpleasant memories associated with it. What was Crystal hiding?

"I believe you must be mistaken," he said. "I'm sure if you'll just take a minute, you'll remember someone in your life named Richard. Someone who would want to cause you harm or injury. Or get revenge?"

Neil had just entered the den and moved swiftly to Crystal's side. "Do you think it's Richard Cummings?" he said in a low voice.

Crystal grasped Neil's hands. "My God! It can't be possible," she whispered to him. "He wouldn't do something so foolish."

"I knew he would be trouble," Neil said under his breath. "When you told me that you and Emily had run into him, I had a feeling that we hadn't heard the last of Richard."

Wright sat down, removing his notebook from his pocket.

The FBI investigators had joined them, and all eyes were on Crystal. Unfriendly eyes, hostile eyes. She felt that they were accusing her.

Jimmy was startled as well. Peggy had mentioned someone named Richard. A man who had something to do with Crystal's past. It was Jimmy who asked the third time. "Who is Richard?"

Crystal turned and looked at Jimmy. She had never told him about Richard; it was part of her life that she wanted to forget. Of course Peggy knew most of the story, but it had been Neil to whom she confessed her shame. Neil, who had listened to her story, had passed her the box of tissue to wipe her eyes and then fixed her a cup of tea.

She remembered his words. "He was using you, and you're damn well lucky to find out before it's too late. It's all in the past," Neil had told her. "It's done with. Now you must concentrate on the future. If you want to be a movie star, then you must work. Work hard to be the best."

Crystal had forced herself to forget the man, to never look back, and now Richard had returned to haunt her. To get what he wanted. There had never been any real escape from him. She had always known that someday he would make demands on her. But she hadn't expected this.

Wright could see that she was debating with herself. It was time for secrets to be told. "What are you hiding, Mrs. Mitchelson?" He waited for her to reply. There was no doubt she was embarrassed, but it was too late to hold back. "Are you trying to protect him?" he asked, hoping the blunt accusation would force an answer.

"No, of course not," Crystal said hastily, her eyes downcast. She knew there was no way she could avoid it now. The story had to be told; Emily's life depended on it.

"When I first came to Los Angeles I met Peggy Ballwin. She was Peggy Mason then, and we were both struggling actresses. We were roommates until Peggy got married. After she moved out of the apartment, I met Richard."

"Last name?" Wright prompted.

"Cummings," Crystal replied, her voice shaky. "He had an apartment in the same building, and, um, we became friends. He helped me get some modeling jobs, and um, some other things."

"Were you lovers?" one of the FBI agents asked.

Crystal looked up at him, startled by his rude tone. She remembered his name. Willis. She didn't like him, or the way he was staring at her.

"Yes," she murmured, "for a while. Maybe six months."

Crystal glanced at Jimmy. How could she tell him about that period of degradation. Days when she was doped up, satiated by Richard's lovemaking, willing to do anything for him. There was no way she could avoid it. She had to tell them something.

"Richard sold grass, as we always had a supply in the house, and occasionally he would bring home some cocaine. There were pills, too, and booze. I was having trouble getting work, but I don't think that I really cared—not as long as I had Richard. Then one day he told me he had landed a movie role for me." Crystal laughed bitterly. "I was very excited; it had finally come true. I thought I was going to be a movie star."

"Then what happened?" Willis asked.

Crystal cleared her throat. "He took me to a motel and introduced me to this . . . this pornographer. It finally dawned on me that Richard was only using me—that he didn't love me. I ran from that room—and kept on running."

Neil stood and walked to the bar in the corner. "That's when Crystal and I became friends." He poured brandy into a glass and carried it back to Crystal. "She turned her life around, devoting herself to her acting. When she landed her first supporting role, we were both elated by her success. Richard saw the film and then tracked Crystal down to my place."

"He was dreadful, threatening me, demanding money. He said he would tell everyone about our affair," Crystal explained, shuddering as she remembered. "I was ready to pay him off, but Neil wouldn't let me."

Neil sat on the armrest of the sofa. "I figured that none of the scandal sheets would take the risk of running the story without proof, so I kicked him out and told him I'd have him arrested for harassment if he ever came around again. After that, we didn't hear from him. We thought he had crawled back into his hole."

Crystal sipped the brandy, then picked up the story. "I didn't see him again until a few weeks ago. Emily and I were out shopping, and we stopped at the Hamburger Hamlet for lunch. Richard saw us there and came to our table."

"What did he want?" Wright prompted her.

"I was afraid he would say something nasty, but he seemed quite cordial. He mentioned reading about my separation from Jimmy in one of the supermarket newspapers—the *National Enquirer*, I think."

"He's a little behind the times, don't you think," Jimmy said. "That's certainly old news."

"He said he had been living in Las Vegas and had just returned to Los Angeles," Crystal explained. "We talked about my last film, and, I don't know, um . . . just chit-chat. Nothing of importance."

"What happened next?" Wright asked patiently.

"He asked me if I could help get him a job at the studio. I said yes, and he gave me his phone number." Crystal sighed heavily, leaning back against the sofa cushions. "I only said yes because I wanted to get out of there and away from him."

"That was it?"

"Yes," Crystal mumbled, "But I remember how he patted Emily on the head. He asked her how she was spending her summer vacation. I didn't like him questioning her, but I didn't want to make a scene. I finally promised to call him in a few days."

Wright leaned forward in his seat. "Do you still have the phone number?"

"I threw it out when we got home," she said, biting her lower lip. "I never really intended to help him."

Willis threw his hands in the air. "We've got the name of the kidnapper, and no way to find him. He could be anywhere in the city." He thought a moment. "Do you know if he was ever arrested?"

"I don't know."

"What about a middle name?" Willis asked.

"I believe it was Alexander, and if I remember correctly, he was born on June 14, 1945. Flag Day."

"Would you happen to have a photograph of this Richard? Perhaps I could psychometrize him," Elizabeth said.

Crystal shook her head. "I didn't keep anything that would remind me of him."

"What about his friends?" Wright asked. "Or his old hangouts?"

"His favorite place was Barney's Beanery. We often went there to meet friends."

"Give me names," Wright insisted.

"I don't remember. It's been so long ago." She paused as ugly memories crowded her mind. "There was one man. A black man, except he was an albino. They called him Bunny."

"That's a start," Willis said. "We'll get our men working on it."

"I'll see if Cummings has a driver's license or an arrest record. If he does, we'll at least have a photograph of him, and maybe even an address," Wright said, standing. "I'll see you later."

Crystal closed her eyes, thinking. Was it only money that Richard wanted? He was such a vile person. Had he touched Emily? Would he harm her? Crystal hugged herself, wondering when the nightmare would end.

V

In a few hours Lieutenant Wright had returned with a photograph. "Your former boyfriend was arrested twice, both times for selling drugs. Suspended sentence on the first count for fingering his supplier, and a year in a Nevada jail on the second."

Neil studied the photograph, then nodded. "Yes, that's him."

"Did you get an address on the bastard?" Jimmy asked.

"An abandoned building in North Hollywood."

"May I see the photograph please?" Elizabeth requested. "Perhaps I can get a reading."

The minutes ticked away as Elizabeth concentrated. She finally came out of her trance. "It's no use; I'm not getting anything."

She stood and paced around the room, then spun around to Wright. "Is the gardener still around?" Elizabeth asked. "This is a long shot, but perhaps if he saw the photo it might trigger his memory."

"You're the psychic," Wright said, "so you ought to know."

"Do I note some doubt in your voice?"

Wright shrugged. "Christopher Swatt says you're one of the best, and your case history record is interesting."

"You've been doing your homework," Elizabeth remarked.

"Just trying to figure out how you do it."

"By piecing the puzzle together," Elizabeth said edgily, growing impatient with him. "By using any bit of information I can dig up. Isn't that what you would do?"

Wright held up his hands, amazed by her tenacity. "Okay, truce. I admit it's worth a try. I'll go look for him."

He returned shortly with the gardener. "Look at this picture. Is this the man you saw?"

Morales studied the photograph, squinting. "Yes. This is the man. He smile and wave, and he say 'Hello, Emily.' I don't think nothing of this," Morales explained, "because all the time people come to pick up the little girl."

"What about the car?" asked Wright. "Can you remember what kind of car it was?"

Morales shrugged. "No. Only what I tole you."

Wright turned to Elizabeth. "Satisfied?"

"It was worth a try," she said, then thanked the gardener for his cooperation.

Jimmy waited until Morales left the room. "What happens now?" he asked Wright.

Agent Willis picked up the photograph. "We'll have copies of this sent to all the departments. I'll also have someone go back to Barney's Beanery with a copy. When my man went over there earlier, he hit a brick wall; no one knew Cummings or the albino. Now that we have a photograph of Cummings, we might get lucky."

"If you don't mind, I'll go to Barney's myself," Wright said.

"That's a West Hollywood locale," Willis noted, "and out of your jurisdiction."

Wright stopped himself from laughing. Willis was a royal pain in the ass, but there was nothing he could do about it. "True, but even Beverly Hills residents like to go slumming."

Melvin's bodyguard entered the den. "There's a boy outside on a bicycle. He brought this package."

Wright pulled the brown paper wrapping off, being careful to handle it gingerly. "It's a cassette." He glanced at Jimmy. "May we use your tape recorder?"

"Yes, of course," Jimmy answered. "Do you think it's from him? I mean Cummings."

"Probably." He turned to the bodyguard. "Hold the boy. I'll want to question him."

Willis stood up, his tall, gangling body towering over Wright. "*I'll* question the boy," he said pointedly.

His attitude didn't bother Wright; he knew how to handle his type. "How 'bout we both question him. You FBI guys have a way of intimidating people," he said sarcastically. "And this is still my case."

"May we hear the tape, please?" Crystal asked in a choked voice.

They waited impatiently while Jimmy turned the recorder on, then listened to the tape in silence. It was Crystal who spoke first.

"She's still alive," she whispered, her face ashen. "Thank God."

Willis asked Jimmy to play the tape again. "Did you hear that?" he asked when the short message was over. "Emily said *they*. Looks like Cummings has some help."

Wright shook his head. "I don't think so. If he had help, he wouldn't have waited this long. Let's talk to the boy who delivered the tape."

Willis readily agreed. "Yeah. Let's see what the kid knows."

Melvin's bodyguard escorted the boy into the room. He was young, perhaps twelve or thirteen, wearing tennis clothes.

"What's your name, son?" Willis asked.

"Craig Christina."

Willis smiled at him. "Do you live around here?"

"Yes, sir. A couple blocks over," he said nervously. "I'm going to be late for dinner."

"Just a few more questions," Wright promised. "Where did you get the package?"

The boy looked at the anxious faces of the adults, then stared in amazement as he realized he was in the same room as Crystal Smythe. He reluctantly turned his attention back to the policeman. "A man gave it to me. He said if I delivered it here, someone would give me twenty bucks."

Willis showed him the photograph of Cummings. "Was this the man?"

Craig studied it, then shrugged his shoulders. "Maybe. The man was wearing sunglasses, and he had a hat on. A gray cowboy hat."

"What else was he wearing?" Willis asked.

"Blue jeans and a white and blue striped shirt." He glanced down at his wristwatch. "Can I call my mom? She's going to be angry."

"Don't worry about your mom, Craig. We just got a couple more questions," Wright said. "Did he have a car?"

"He was kinda sitting on the hood of a car. A blue Ford. I think it's a couple years old, and, oh yeah, there was a dent in the back fender. On the right-hand side."

"You're very observant," Wright said. "Was he alone?"

"Yeah," Craig answered, his eyes drawn back to Crystal. "Listen. I gotta go. Can I have my money?"

Jimmy pulled bills from his pocket and gave the boy a twenty.

"Thanks, mister."

Willis followed Wright and the boy out of the room. "We'll need your phone number and address for our records," he told the boy. "I think you've probably figured out what this is all about, so you know you can't speak to anyone regarding what you saw or what happened."

Craig looked up at him. "Does this have something to do with the kidnapping of Miss Smythe's daughter?"

"That's right; it's a police matter. You can help us by not telling anyone about this. That means no one," Willis said, his voice menacing. "I don't want you speaking to any reporters. And don't talk to your friends, either. It's important that no one know, not even your mother. The little girl's life is at stake. Do you think you can keep this a secret and help us?"

"Wow! Sure. I won't say anything," Craig promised.

Wright hoped the boy would keep his promise. He reached into his pocket and handed the boy his card. "If you can remember anything else, be sure to call me."

VI

It didn't take long to track down Cummings. Kevin Brown, the burly nighttime bartender at Barney's Beanery, identified him from the photograph.

"Not a very good photo, but, sure, I know him," he told Lieutenant Wright.

"Has he been in here recently?"

"Not on my shift. Not in the past week," Kevin said as he busily dipped dirty glasses into soapy water, then rinse water, before putting them in a rack to dry. "I've seen him in here with Kandy."

Wright flipped open his notebook. "Who's Kandy?" he asked, raising his voice over the din of the bar.

"Don't know her last name. She's a hooker, an independent, though she does turn a lot of tricks for Pete Rizzo. She's a Marilyn Monroe look-alike, so she gets pretty steady work."

Wright nodded, glad he had found a talkative bar man. "What else do you know?"

Kevin started slicing lemons. "She's different. She does a lot of other stuff. Supermarket openings, the Long Beach drag races. You know, that kind of thing. She's usually in demand."

Wright sipped his Coke and ate a handful of peanuts, thinking it wasn't much of a dinner. "So how come Kandy turns tricks if she's doing so good as a look-alike."

Kevin shrugged and picked up a rag to wipe down his already spotless bar. "Doesn't. Not enough money to cover all her needs," he said. He pressed a finger to his crooked nose. "She likes nose candy. Lots of it. Know what I mean? That's why her name is Kandy. But with a K."

"You got any idea how I can find her?"

"She lives over in Hollywood. On Vista del Mar at the top of the hill. A pink Mexican bungalow that was chopped up into apartments."

"How come you know where she lives?"

"I used to date a girl in the same building," Kevin said. "You want another Coke?"

"No, thanks. What do you know about Richard Cummings?"

"He's Kandy's boyfriend." Kevin leaned across the bar. "There's something wrong with that guy. He acts real mean. Isn't nice to her. I think he's just using her. You know. Like I seen him take money from her. And he drives her car."

"What kind of car?"

"Ford, I think. Blue. He's not a very good driver. He backed into another car on the parking lot. Kandy had to cough up the money for the damage." Kevin shook his head. "I don't know why she puts up with him."

Wright asked a few more questions, then excused himself. Kevin was a good talker, but Wright had a man to catch.

It took Wright less than twenty minutes to arrive at Kandy's building. There was no blue Ford in the garage. But he found Kandy's name written on a pink card stuck under the doorbell. Kandace Metropolis. Strange name, he thought, as he rang the bell several times. There was no answer, so he knocked on the manager's door. Wright showed his badge and stated his business. The manager was reluctant, but finally obliged and opened the apartment door.

Wright was angered by what he found. Kandy Metropolis, alias Marilyn Monroe, was dead, a hypodermic needle still stuck in her arm. He figured she'd been dead at least twenty hours. He put a call through to Willis.

He quickly explained the situation. "Looks like a heroin overdose," he said, then hung up and looked down at the body. There was something wrong.

He knelt beside Kandy and pushed her hair back. There were ugly bruises on the girl's neck. Wright guessed that she had been choked and the heroin injected afterward to look like an overdose. There was something else that interested him. The newspaper with Crystal's photograph was crumpled in Kandy's left hand. Wright couldn't be sure, but he had a hunch she'd been silenced because she knew too much.

He did a hurried search of the apartment and struck gold. He found a suitcase on the top shelf of the bedroom closet, and inside were several pornographic photos of Cummings with different girls. Some of them didn't look like they were over eighteen. He would have Francis contact the known pornographers, and maybe he'd get a lead on one of the girls in the photos.

Wright glanced back at Kandy's abused body. It made him ill to know how vile a man he was dealing with. And now it appeared that kidnapping wasn't enough; Cummings had added murder to his crimes. Would Emily be next?

VII

It was after ten when Wright walked into the den. "I've got some bad news for you."

"Is it Emily?" Crystal asked anxiously.

"No, nothing like that, but it still isn't pleasant news," he said. "I don't want to upset you, but you should know everything connected to the case."

"What is it?" asked Jimmy.

"Cummings has been living with a girl called Kandy," he said. "I've just come from her apartment."

Jimmy grasped Crystal's hand, expecting the worst. "Did you find Cummings? What about Emily?"

Wright shook his head. "I don't think Emily was ever there. Kandy was dead and Cummings nowhere in sight."

Crystal gasped. "How horrible."

"Of course we don't know for sure, but Cummings probably killed Kandy."

"Isn't there some way of finding him?" Jimmy asked.

"We believe the car he's using was Kandy's so we're trying to track down the license plate number. As soon as we get it, we'll have every law enforcement agency in the city on the lookout for the car," Wright said. "There's only one problem."

"What's that?" Jimmy prompted the detective.

"He must suspect that we're on his trail. Kandy might

have known something important—like where Emily is—so Cummings had to silence her."

Jimmy lit a cigarette and studied the policeman. "What are our chances of finding our daughter, Lieutenant? Please be honest."

Wright sighed. "Do you mind if I pour myself a drink?"

Neil jumped to his feet, happy to have something to do. "We all need one," he said. "What would you like, Lieutenant?"

"Scotch-on-the-rocks, please." Wright fell into one of the leather chairs. He was feeling tired, but he had to go on. He wouldn't be able to rest properly until Emily was found—dead or alive—and Cummings was behind bars.

"The lab boys will be going over Kandy's apartment with a fine-tooth comb, so we hope to turn up something that will lead us to Cummings," Wright said as he accepted his drink.

"What if they don't find anything," Jimmy asked.

"Truthfully, I don't know," Wright answered, then took a grateful sip of his drink before continuing. "The problem is that Cummings could be hiding Emily just about any-where in the city, or the state, as far as that goes."

"That's not true, Lieutenant. We have the clues I've received through mental communication with Emily," Elizabeth said. "I think we can narrow the search down a bit. All we need is a map."

"You've got to be kidding," Jimmy scoffed. "Just how the hell do you think you're going to be able to find Emily if the police can't?"

"I don't know, Mr. Mitchelson," Elizabeth said patiently. "All I can do is try. Don't you think you owe as much to your daughter?"

Jimmy pounded the wall. "What are you implying? That I don't care what happens to Emily?"

Elizabeth regretted her words immediately. She hadn't wanted to offend him, but James Mitchelson attitude was getting to her.

"I'm sorry," she said, "but you must understand that I need everyone's cooperation if this is going to work. I've been doing psychic investigative work for a long time, and trust me, even though it seems confusing, I firmly believe that the images I am receiving come directly from Emily. Please let me help you find her."

Jimmy slumped on the sofa. "Oh, God," he cried, "where's my daughter? Where's my Emily?"

Crystal put an arm around him, torn by his pain. "We'll find her darling. Elizabeth will help us."

"I love her so," he sobbed.

"I know, darling," Crystal said, comforting him. "So do I."

Elizabeth turned to Neil. "Could you find me a map of California?"

"Sure," he said. "I've got one in my car, and a AAA Travel Guide." Neil returned with the map and spread it out on the coffee table.

Elizabeth reached into the deep pocket of her dress, producing her notebook. "Let's try piecing together the puzzle."

Crystal sat on the floor, and Wright pulled his chair closer to the coffee table. Though Jimmy was embarrassed by his outbreak, he swallowed his pride and faced Elizabeth. "All right. How do we begin?"

Elizabeth pointed at the map. "If I'm reading Emily's thoughts correctly, she's being held somewhere near the ocean or a lagoon. She can also see mountains, which mean's she's somewhere west of the Sierra Madres."

"I don't know of any lagoons in California," Neil said.

"I believe Emily also saw two signs: one with the word

'bluebird,' and on the other, the word 'shrimp,' " said Elizabeth.

"Maybe they were names of towns," Crystal suggested. "Look at the city and town index, Jimmy, and see if there's a listing for either one of them."

Jimmy ran a finger down the list. "There's no town by the name of Shrimp, but there's a Blue Jay in section P–17. And there's a town called Blue Lake in section B–33."

They eagerly consulted the map. It was Neil who found the first town. "Blue Jay is up near Lake Arrowhead. That's in the mountains."

"But not near a beach," Jimmy pointed out.

"A lake has beaches," Neil reminded him.

Wright shook his head. "But there's no lagoon near by."

"Well, it's one possibility," Neil said. "Where's Blue Lake? Did you say B–33?"

"Wait a minute," Crystal said. "According to Elizabeth, the clue is bluebird, not blue lake."

"We should check out all the possibilities," Elizabeth told them. "Sometimes the words get mixed up in thought transference, or the words get transposed."

"Blue Lake is a small town on Humboldt Bay in northern California," Neil read from the Travel Guide. "The nearest big town is Eureka. Shrimp fishing is the major industry."

"Shrimp! That must be the town," Crystal said. "What do you think, Lieutenant?"

Wright shook his head. "Blue Lake is too far north. It's a long day's drive, and I'll bet Cummings has Emily somewhere a lot closer."

"Wait," Elizabeth interrupted, trembling with excitement. It was suddenly clear to her. "Look at this," she said, pointing on the map to a town south of Los Angeles. "Laguna Beach! Laguna means lagoon. I'm sure of it now.

That's where Emily is being held. I thought the word was 'lagoon,' but it was my mistake."

"Mrs. Anderson could be right," Neil said. enthusiastically. "And, see, there's a Laguna Nigel and a Laguna Heights. I haven't been in that area in years, but they're all near the ocean, and surrounded by mountains."

Crystal pointed at the map. "There's also a South Laguna."

"Emily is definitely in the Laguna area," Elizabeth said. "Somewhere in the hills. If I was there, I'm sure I could find her."

"Then that's what we must do," Crystal said decisively. "We can drive down tomorrow and start searching."

"Wait a minute," Wright said. "This is police work. The FBI guys won't like you wandering off without them."

Crystal stood up. "We only have tomorrow. I say we go and look. If it doesn't work, then I'm going to deliver the money on Friday."

"What do you think you're going to look for?" Wright asked.

Crystal shrugged her shoulders. "I don't know. The car, maybe."

"I don't like the idea," Wright said, frowning.

Crystal moved to the bar and poured brandy into her glass. "I can't stand this waiting. Sitting here and doing nothing. Elizabeth will find Emily. I know it."

"What if Cummings should call?" Wright said. "You have to be here."

"Neil can wait here with the FBI guys," Crystal said evenly. After all the days of worrying, she felt that there might be a chance of finding Emily. She knew Elizabeth had to be right. "We can call him to see if there are any new messages."

Elizabeth sat back on the sofa, her own confidence

reinforced by their enthusiasm. "Once we're in the area, I'm sure I'll get a reading. Don't forget, we have the other clues. The color red is important, and a cat and a bluebird have some significance."

Jimmy lit a cigarette, dropping his match in the brimming ashtray. Maybe he had been wrong. He was still skeptical about the psychic, but wondered if there might be something to her theory. It sounded crazy, but for the moment it was all they had. The change in Crystal was miraculous. She was acting more decisively, showing hope where there had only been despair.

"I agree with my wife, Lieutenant. I know that your men and the FBI are doing their best, but that's not enough. I'm not sure if I want to believe in psychic power, but right now Elizabeth seems to be our only chance of finding our daughter."

Wright cleared his throat noisily. "Willis isn't going to like this."

Jimmy looked at the policeman, their eyes locking. "Don't tell him," he said firmly.

Wright stood and began to pace around the room. It was a long shot, but maybe some of Elizabeth's clues were valid. If he didn't agree, they would go without him, and that could be dangerous. He looked at the distraught couple and realized that he couldn't say no. He made up his mind, hoping it was the right decision.

"This isn't right, but since I can't stop you, I guess I'll have to tag along."

"Thank you," Crystal said gratefully. "I know we'll find Emily."

Wright stared at Crystal. Even in grief she was beautiful. She seemed so convinced that they would find her daughter. Personally, he thought it would be a wild goose chase, but he would go along with the pretense, if only for their own protection. Just in case they should somehow stumble into Cummings' hideout.

"I'm going home to get some sleep," he said, "and I suggest you also get some rest. Tomorrow is going to be a long day."

VIII

Neil followed Crystal out to the patio. The night had cooled considerably, and the smog had lifted. Stars glimmered, their twinkling light a good omen for the day to come.

"It's been so busy around here that we haven't had a chance to talk," he said, sinking onto a chaise lounge next to Crystal.

"I know," Crystal said. "What did you want to discuss?"

"You have no idea how upset I am about Emily. Maybe if I had come back here Friday afternoon instead of going to my place . . ."

"It's not your fault, Neil," she assured him.

"I wish there was something I could do."

"Just being here is all I need."

"I haven't been very helpful," he admitted. "I've had a lot on my mind."

"I did notice that you seemed preoccupied," Crystal said. "Is there something you're not telling me?"

"It's a small problem, but I think I have it worked out."

"What?" Crystal asked.

"It's nothing, really."

"Come on. I know you better than that," she said. "We've been friends for such a long time. You should know you can tell me anything."

"You have no idea how much I value our friendship," he replied.

"You're not ill?" she asked anxiously.

Neil shook his head. "No, it's not that."

Crystal sighed with relief. "Thank heavens! I worry about you."

Neil patted her hand. "I know."

"But there *is* something wrong," Crystal insisted. "You've been acting so strange lately."

"I'm sorry. I wanted to tell you, but it's something I had to work out on my own."

"Tell me what?" Crystal asked, puzzled by his attitude.

"It's not that I don't enjoy working for you, but it's time I stop sponging off you."

"You earn every penny of your salary."

"But it's not enough," Neil said. "The job is fun, but I need something more in my life."

"What did you have in mind?"

Neil knew an explanation was in order. He briefly told Crystal about the club he wanted to open. "I think I've finally come up with the money I need," said Neil. "A friend is interested and promised to lend it to me."

"Why didn't you ask me? I would have loaned you the money."

"I know how you are about money," he said, his tone softened by her care. "I didn't want you to think I was taking advantage of our friendship."

"That's the dumbest thing I ever heard," Crystal said, scolding him. "Besides, you're more than just a friend. You're the brother I never had."

Neil smiled warmly at her. "Thanks."

"I mean it," she said, standing up. "After we find Emily, I want to see this project of yours."

Neil couldn't get over the change in Crystal. The past few days had been so draining emotionally, and yet, here she was, filled with hope, acting more like her old self. He walked back into the house with her.

"Do you really think Mrs. Anderson will find Emily?" he asked.

"Yes. Yes I do," Crystal said, her voice confident. "Tomorrow we'll find her."

thursday

I

Emily awoke with a start. "Mommy?" she called out. She was answered by a hollow silence, a silence which reminded her that she was still his prisoner.

She had chipped at the dried paint that sealed the window until she heard Richard arrive. She then had jumped into bed, and when he entered the room she held her breath, pretending to be asleep. He hadn't noticed, and after using the bathroom, he left the room, locking the door behind him. Afraid to make noise, not daring to continue working on the window, Emily slept.

When she awoke, she realized it was almost dawn. She got out of bed and walked to the window. The stars had faded, but the sun still hadn't crested the mountains. She wondered why her mother hadn't tried to find her. Did her father know she was kidnapped? Richard had said he would let her go on Saturday, but she didn't trust him. He had lied about taking her to see her mother, so he was probably lying about letting her go. The newspeople on the television said the police had no clues to her disappearance. If the police couldn't find her, then she would just have to find a way to escape.

Emily went to the door and pressed her ear against the wood. Was he there? She couldn't hear any sounds. Maybe he had gone back out while she was sleeping. She decided she would have to chance it.

She picked up the dinner knife and began chipping at the paint, slowly making progress. Emily smiled to herself; it was really working, and soon she would be able to get out of the room. She didn't hear the door open.

"What are you doing?" he shouted at her.

Emily turned, hiding the knife behind her. "N . . . nothing," she stammered. "I was just looking out the window."

"What's that behind your back?"

Emily shook, her eyes large with fear. "I wasn't doing anything."

"The hell you say," Richard growled, stomping across the room. He jerked her arm, and Emily dropped the knife.

Richard bent and picked it up. He glared at her, and then his eyes followed hers downward to the paint chips strewn across the dusty wooden floor.

"What were you doing? Trying to escape?" he asked, his voice heavy with sarcasm. "You're just like your mother, except for one difference. She got away from me, but you won't, chicken face."

Emily rubbed her arm, frightened by him. She wondered what he meant about her mother getting away. "What are you going to do?"

Richard ignored her and left the room, locking the door behind him. Emily crawled onto the bed and began to cry. He was really angry now. He would never let her go. She heard a noise outside and returned to the window.

Richard was standing on a ladder. He lifted a board to the window and began to hammer it, pounding furiously on the nails.

Emily shook her head. "No, no," she pleaded, watching in horror as her view of the mountains and sea slowly disappeared.

She slumped down on the floor, sobbing. Now they

would never find her. He had sealed her into the room; she was really a prisoner now.

II

Agent Willis had spent the night dozing on the living room sofa and awoke with an ache in his neck. He studied himself in a mirror. His suit was rumpled, and he needed a shave and shower. "But first a cup of coffee," he said out loud as he walked into the kitchen. He was surprised to find Howard Wright following the Mitchelsons and the psychic lady out the back door.

"Where are you going?" he demanded.

Wright shrugged his shoulders indifferently. "All the reporters and cars stopping here make them nervous. A few hours at Mitchelson's beach house will do them good. Simmons will stay here to answer the telephone."

Willis didn't like it. There was something the policeman wasn't telling him. Had the plan changed? Could they possibly be going to make a drop of the ransom money? But that didn't make sense, since the kidnapper hadn't called, nor had any other packages arrived. Maybe Wright was telling the truth—that the Mitchelsons just wanted to get away. But why take the psychic with them? What hocus-pocus was she trying to pull?

"It doesn't seem right to me," Willis finally said. "I think they should stay pat."

"We can't hold them here," Wright reminded him. He knew he should tell someone what they were planning to do, but it was so farfetched that no one would believe it. "I'll be with them, so don't worry."

"Yeah, well I guess it'll be okay," Willis said grudgingly. Wright breathed a sigh of relief as they drove away.

"Good. No reporters on the scene yet. But keep your eyes open for any cars that might be following us."

Wright zipped over Sunset Boulevard to the San Diego Freeway and headed south. Early morning traffic into town was heavy, but they were headed in the opposite direction. Within the hour they reached the Laguna Beach turn-off and sped down the curving canyon road. Wright slowed to a snail's pace as they entered town, eyes alert for the blue Ford. As the road dead-ended at the Pacific Coast Highway, he turned to Elizabeth.

"Which way?" Wright asked.

Elizabeth was startled by an image flashing through her mind. She pointed out the window. "That beach. It's the one Emily saw."

Crystal leaned forward. "You're sure?"

"Yes. She was here. She saw the people playing volley-ball and asked if they could stop to watch." Elizabeth smiled secretly to herself. She had been afraid she wasn't getting a true reading, but now that she was here and could see the beach, she knew she was on the right track. "I think they turned south here."

Wright made a left turn, and Elizabeth took out Emily's photograph. She concentrated on the eyes, willing Emily to speak to her. They drove slowly, silent, searching, waiting for a sign. When they arrived in South Laguna, Elizabeth finally spoke.

"I've lost contact. We must return to Laguna Beach. I don't think they came this far."

Wright made a U-turn and drove back to the town's busiest intersection, then parked the car at Tomasito's, a small restaurant across from the main beach. Crystal tied a scarf over her head, added a floppy straw hat, then donned dark glasses to complete her disguise.

"Ready," she said.

They chose a large booth against the window and ordered breakfast. They ate in disappointed silence, watching the beach activity. Sun worshipers arrived, staking out an area on the sand, spreading towels, unfolding beach chairs. A more energetic group of young men were playing a fast game of basketball. Though no one said it, they all had the same thought: Was Cummings out there?

Elizabeth sipped her coffee pensively. "Emily is here somewhere; I can feel it. However, there's been a change in the thought transference. I think he has moved her, or she might be locked in a dark room."

"What do we do now?" Jimmy asked.

"Keep looking," Wright replied.

III

Richard drove northeast to Disneyland. He was going to need some money, and maybe a credit card or two, which was why he was going to the land of Mickey Mouse. All he had to do was find someone who looked more or less like himself. Then he would pick the sucker's pocket. He'd been doing it for years, and Disneyland was a prime hunting ground. Find a guy with three or four kids in tow. Someone who would carelessly put his wallet in a back pants pocket. It was so easy to bump into or trip over a kid, pat him on the head, brush up against daddy. Bingo! Lift the wallet, and you got instant cash, credit cards, identification.

It was too bad about Kandy, but she had become a liability—and had to be silenced. Even if the police found her, he had fixed it to look like an overdose. There was nothing to tie him to her. He had made sure to take all his personal items with him. Not that there had been a whole lot, since it was best to travel light. Besides, once he had the money, he'd be buying a whole new wardrobe.

He grimaced. He had almost blown it. When he gave the tape recording to the kid, he had worn a disguise. Unfortunately, he hadn't taken the same care with the car. He didn't think the kid had noticed the license plates, but to be on the safe side, he had driven to a dark airport parking lot and lifted a set of plates. Even if the cops knew what kind of car he was driving, the plates wouldn't match up.

He was still angry about Emily's trying to escape. She wouldn't get out now; he had seen to that. He wished he could get rid of her, but he had to keep her alive until he had the money. He knew a thousand things could go wrong, especially when he went for the money. Not that he didn't think his plan was foolproof.

It was so simple it was perfect. He would have Crystal wait at the Santa Monica Pier phone booth for instructions. Then he'd tell her to drive to another phone booth. It was important to keep her moving, and to switch cars, since the one she would be driving when she left her house would undoubtedly have some extra equipment that hadn't been factory-installed.

He wasn't stupid. That was why he wanted her in the two-piece swim suit—so he could check to see if she'd been wired. Of course they would try hiding a bug in the briefcase with the money, but he planned to have her switch the money to a red satchel.

He slowed his speed. Better not get a speeding ticket now, he warned himself. One thing for sure, he thought, the FBI guys would be following her, but he'd be watching, too. If it looked like it wasn't going to work, then he'd abort and wait for another chance. As long as he had the girl, he was in command.

He smiled, feeling very clever. He had thought of everything. Well, maybe not everything. There was still Emily. He would have to kill her. That would be the hardest part. He had done everything else in his life, but never killed a kid. It had to be done, though, since she could identify him.

He knew how to get rid of the body. He would bury her outside in the garden. All he had to do was kill her. He wanted to use the gun, a .38. It was easy to handle, but noisy; someone might hear a gunshot. He would have to get rid of her somehow. Maybe he would choke the little brat.

He laughed. It was a great plan, and everything was going smoothly. He whistled as he drove; by tomorrow evening he would be a very rich man.

IV

"Go slower this time," Elizabeth cautioned. "We might see something."

Once again they drove past the landmark Hotel Laguna at the end of the beach. Its white facade with red trim was featured in several oil paintings being hawked by street artists. A few blocks farther on, they spotted the Pottery Shack; its front yard was crammed with table displays of colorful pottery and glazed animal statues.

Crystal leaned forward, grasping Jimmy's shoulder. "Maybe they sell cats. We could stop to ask."

Wright slowed at the next corner. "This traffic is something else," he said. Finally finding an opportunity to make a left turn onto Cress Avenue, he parked the car next to a fire hydrant.

The Pottery Shack was crowded with tourists roaming the aisles, choosing brightly painted dishes and pottery. Jimmy spotted a cat bank.

"What do you think?" he asked Elizabeth, holding it up for her perusal.

She shook her head. "No. It's all wrong. Emily wasn't here," she said.

"Now what?" Jimmy asked as they returned to the street, then stopped abruptly, staring in disbelief. He pointed at a small gray building on the down side of Cress Avenue.

"Look," he said, awed by his discovery. "The sign on that bar says Little Shrimp."

Elizabeth clapped her hands. "That's it. The sign Emily saw. This is where they turned."

"Then we're on the right track," Wright said as they trudged back up the hill to where he had parked the car.

They stood on the corner, undecided, not sure which way to go, surrounded by green lawns which fronted neat little houses, the flowerbeds carefully tended.

Elizabeth shaded her eyes and looked beyond the trees to the mountains that rose steeply behind the burgeoning subdivision homes. She could see splotches of white mixed in with stands of tall pine trees, evidence that the mountain tops were accessible and populated.

"Emily is up there," she said, her voice full of conviction. "I know it."

"How will we ever find her?" Crystal sighed.

"What clues do we have left?" Jimmy asked.

"The bluebird?" Elizabeth suggested.

"Could be a street," Wright replied. "Let's ask." He spotted an elderly man walking a German shepherd. "I'll bet that fellow is a local," he said and called to the man.

The old gentleman turned to them. "What's your problem?" he growled.

"Not very friendly," Elizabeth whispered.

Wright pulled out his police badge and approached the man, stopping short of the dog, which was straining at his leash, ready to attack.

"I'm Lieutenant Wright of the Beverly Hills Police

Department," he said, his eyes on the dog. "Would you happen to know where Bluebird Street is?"

"Ain't no Bluebird Street around here," the man said gruffly, pulling the dog.

"Thanks," Wright said, backing away.

"Course there's a Bluebird Canyon Drive."

"There is?"

The man nodded. "A couple blocks that-a-way," he said, pointing south as he walked off, the snarling dog's eyes menacingly fixed on the policeman.

Wright took his hat off and wiped his brow with a handkerchief. Was it only a coincidence? If Mrs. Anderson was correct, they were on the right trail. He turned to the others. "Shall we check it out?"

"Yes," Jimmy said, his voice infused with growing enthusiasm. "We've come this far, and Elizabeth's been right, and . . . maybe . . . there's something in this psychic stuff."

Crystal grasped his hand. "We're going to find Emily," she said. "I know it."

They returned to the car and began their search. They drove three blocks before Jimmy spotted the green street sign with white letters. "Look, Elizabeth," he said excitedly. "Bluebird Canyon Drive. This must be the sign you say Emily saw."

Elizabeth nodded, her sense of awareness rekindled. "Yes. Emily was driven past this point. I can feel it."

They proceeded up the mountain, passing small cottages and bungalows, then larger homes with carefully manicured gardens. They crossed several intersections, but Elizabeth urged Wright to continue climbing higher in the mountains. The road narrowed, twisting and curving, the houses more scattered, the vegetation changing to clumps of weeds.

They came to yet another turn in the sinuous road, and

Elizabeth shouted, "Stop! There's the red," she said, pointing to a house partially hidden from the street by tall bushes of red bougainvillea.

Wright parked the car. "Do you think she's in there, Mrs. Anderson?"

Elizabeth studied the house. "No. Not here, but I'm sure Emily is somewhere nearby."

Wright glanced over at Crystal. Her face showed the strain of hope. "Let's walk," he suggested.

The road became even narrower, the houses shabbier, lost relics shadowed by pine trees. They continued past a little white house, its front gate falling off its hinges. Red bougainvillea trailed over the side wall. An old man, well over eighty years of age, stared at them impassively as he watered his pots of flowers.

"Now I'm sure of it," Elizabeth said. "The red is definitely the bougainvillea. But how can we find the right house? It grows everywhere."

"Look," Jimmy said excitedly as he leaned against a picket fence, pointing at a small Cape Cod house which had been painted with cats of all sizes and colors.

Crystal quickened her pace, hurrying to Jimmy's side. "The cats," she cried, tears springing to her eyes. "We found the cats!"

Elizabeth puffed to a halt. "Yes. This is the place."

"Emily?" Jimmy shouted. "Can you hear me? Emily?" He was answered by an eerie silence, the birds' chattering interrupted by his outburst.

Wright shook his head. "You're making too much noise. What if Cummings is in there?"

"All I care about is my daughter. I have to know if she's here." He began banging on the front door, but there was no answer.

"Maybe we should just go in," Crystal said, turning to Wright.

"We can't do that," Wright told her. "We don't have a search warrant, and besides, we don't know that she's in there."

"Well, maybe you can't do it, but I don't give a damn. I'm going to find my daughter," Jimmy said angrily. He rattled the doorknob, but the deadbolt was in place. "I'll see if there's a back door."

"Howdy," said the old man from the house next door. "Can I help you folks?"

"Possibly," Wright answered. "Do you know who lives here?"

"Sure I do," he replied. "Who are you?"

"I'm a policeman. Lieutenant Wright. I'd like to question the people who live here."

"Got any identification?" the old man asked.

Wright produced his badge, and the man studied it before handing it back, satisfied.

"I'm George Edgar," he told them, "but most people around here call me Ace. You see, I was in the air force during the war . . . the big one, you know . . . I got shot down over . . ."

"I'm sure it's a fascinating story," Wright said, interrupting the man, "but right now I'm more interested in finding out if you know the names of the occupants of this house."

"Only one person lives there. The cat lady."

"Does she have a name?"

Edgar nodded. "Janice Beatty. But everybody up here just calls her 'the cat lady.'"

"Do you have any idea where we can find her?"

"She's probably down at the Sawdust Festival. Got a booth there. She's had one there every year for as far back that I can remember. Talented little lady; coming up with those ideas for them critters. I've bought a couple myself for my friends. You see, she . . ."

"Thanks for your help," Wright once again interrupted the talkative neighbor.

"Why you looking for her?" asked Edgar, not ready to be dismissed.

"Just wanted to ask some questions," Wright said over his shoulder, leading the others back down the road to his car.

V

Elizabeth read aloud from a brochure. "The Sawdust Festival is an annual exhibition of work done by local artists and craftspeople. Held in a eucalyptus grove, the meandering footpaths, paved in sawdust, weave in and out of cleverly decorated stalls and booths. Over two hundred artisans, glass blowers, artists, potters, and metal workers demonstrate their skills. Strolling minstrels, jugglers, and clowns offer a variety of entertainment."

"Okay. Let's find the cat lady," Wright said.

Children darted about excitedly, bumping carelessly into adults, their voices raised in infectious laughter as they discovered new delights. Crystal was saddened that their parents were ignoring them, their interest riveted on snatching up souvenirs.

"All those kids running around loose," Crystal mumbled to Jimmy. "Don't their parents care what happens to them? They could get hurt or lost, or even kidnapped. Don't they know how dangerous it is?"

Jimmy held her hand. "No one ever expects that it could happen to them."

They made their way through the crowd, searching every booth. One was shaped like a Grecian temple and featured hammered jewelry. Another was a tent hung with colorful paper kites. Hand-carved cuckoo clocks filled a miniature Swiss chalet; swirling weather vanes adorned a gaily painted gazebo.

They circled a small bubbling fountain, the water cascading over river rocks into a man-made pond, and spotted the blue wooden structure. Hanging over the entrance was a sign painted on a weather-worn piece of wood: The Cat House.

Wright cautioned the others to wait as he glanced inside the booth. The shelves were crammed with metallic cats of every size and color. A short woman, her hair a curly mop framing a kewpie doll face, was showing one of the cat creations to a customer. Wright guessed her to be forty, but she was dressed more like a girl of twenty. She wore a red knit top, black and white polka dot flared miniskirt, and neon-green tennis shoes and socks.

He waited patiently until the customer had paid, then stepped inside. "Miss Beatty?"

"Yes. What can I do for you?" she asked, a bright smile lighting up her face.

"My name is Howard Wright," he said. "I would like to speak to you in private, if that's possible."

Janice was surprised, but turned to the teen-aged girl behind the desk. "Watch the store for me, Kelly."

She led Wright to a wooden bench that was bathed by a patch of sun. "So, what would you like to talk about?" she asked.

"Emily," he said loudly, hoping for a reaction.

Janice's face was a blank. "Who is Emily?" she asked, totally puzzled. She had thought the man wanted a cat made to his own specifications.

Elizabeth couldn't wait. Like Lieutenant Wright, she knew the element of surprise was important. She walked up to them, unable to resist asking her own questions. "Where is she? What have you done with her?"

Janice was confused. "What are you talking about? I wish someone would explain."

Elizabeth sensed it at once. There was no fear in Janice Beatty's thoughts. "She doesn't know anything," she told Wright.

Janice stood, shaking out her skirt flounces. "What is this about?" she asked indignantly. "Who is this lady?"

Wright ignored Beatty's question. "She's our only connection, Mrs. Anderson."

Elizabeth smiled at the charming young woman. "I am a psychic, and this gentleman is a police officer. I'm helping him investigate the kidnapping of Emily Mitchelson, the daughter of Crystal Smythe."

"For goodness sake," Janice exclaimed. "I heard about it on the television news. Why do you think I would know anything about that little girl's disappearance?"

"It's a little hard to explain," Elizabeth volunteered, "but for some reason, I think your house holds the key to our search. Would it be possible for us to go there with you?"

Janice was intrigued by their request. "I don't know what you expect to find, but I'll be happy to be of assistance," she said, thinking there had to be a mistake. "If you'll wait a moment, I'll get my purse, then we can go to the house. I assure you that I have nothing to hide."

VI

They entered the living room of the small house. Cats cluttered every available space: table tops, the mantelpiece, a desk. Lace curtains, fluttering at the floor-to-ceiling windows at either end of the dusty room, filtered the late afternoon sun. Old paintings hung on the walls. A Tiffany lamp stood sentinel to an arrangement of wild flowers. An art deco statue of dancing nymphs vied for attention. A collection of crystal cats were hidden behind a profusion of potted plants, adding to the charm.

"It's like an antique shop," Crystal whispered to Jimmy as they sat on an ancient sofa.

Janice entered the living room carrying a large tray with a coffeepot and an assortment of mugs painted with cat faces. She poured and handed a mug to Crystal.

"I used to make these, but they didn't sell very well. Then I got into metal sculpting. I make more money now," she said. "Would you like sugar?"

"No, thank you," Crystal said. "I like your house. You have so many treasures."

"It's small, but just right for me," Janice said, serving the others their coffee. She sat in an old rocker. "I wish I could help you find your daughter, but I don't know how, Miss Smythe."

Crystal pointed to a photograph of Janice in an ornate frame. "Were you in the theater?"

"Kind of. Amateur stuff. I thought I could make it in Hollywood, but I got pregnant instead." Janice picked up a photograph. "This is my daughter. She's twenty-five."

Crystal was surprised. "You don't look that old."

Janice laughed. "No stress. I live a relatively quiet life, work at home, make the rounds of art festivals and street shows."

"May I look around?" Elizabeth asked. She moved into the bedroom, which was as uniquely decorated as the living room. Hats and scarves, a basket of letters, and ornate perfume bottles filled the dresser top.

She walked down the hallway and entered the narrow studio. Shelves were filled with cats, and the scarred workbench was cluttered with metal clippers, a blow torch, hammers, and pliers.

Elizabeth stared out the window. In the distance, beyond the tree tops, she could see the ocean. This was what Emily saw. Or *had seen*, she thought. Emily no longer stared at the view. Why?

Elizabeth couldn't understand it. She had been sure that they would find her here. She had felt the vibrations when they stood outside, but now that she was in the house, it was as if Emily had disappeared without a trace. She leaned forward and noticed a small garden below the house.

She returned to the living room. "What's downstairs?"

"A studio apartment I sometimes rent out, and next to it is a storage room," Janice replied. "If you'd like, I'll show you."

The search below proved to be fruitless. They found nothing and returned to the living room.

"I'll make some more coffee," Janice suggested.

"No. We should be leaving," Wright said. "The traffic will be heavy now. It'll take a couple of hours to get back to the city."

Once back in the car, Elizabeth shook her head, sighing heavily. "I thought for sure we would find Emily here, but the trail has gone cold. I'm not receiving anything new from Emily. It is a very strange feeling. Almost as if she has shut a door so that I can no longer read her mind."

"So what do we do now? Wait for more clues?" Wright asked, frustrated by the dead end.

"It's so sad," Elizabeth mumbled. "The child must be weary, disillusioned, fearful. I believe she is very tired and sleeping now, which is why I can't get a reading."

Jimmy was disappointed, too. For a few tense hours he

had believed Elizabeth was on the right track. Had all her clues been simply coincidence? It certainly didn't make sense.

"We're all tired," Jimmy told her. "Dinner and some rest will help, and who knows, perhaps later on you'll be able to pick up on Emily's thoughts."

"Yes. You're right. I am tired," she admitted. "I will get some sleep, and tomorrow we will find Emily," she said, hoping she sounded convincing, wondering if she still had the power to do so.

VII

Elizabeth half-listened to Jimmy as he told Neil about their search in Laguna Beach. She still couldn't believe that they hadn't found Emily. She had been so positive they were on the right path. What had she done wrong? What had she overlooked? Would they ever find Emily? She finally excused herself.

"I'm going to my room. Or rather, to Emily's room. I still don't understand why we didn't find her. Maybe if I sleep, the answer will come to me."

Neil waited until she had gone upstairs. "The old lady obviously isn't as sharp as Lieutenant Wright thought."

"Maybe not," Jimmy said as he accompanied Neil to the front door, "but for a while there she had me believing that we'd find Emily. Let's just pray that the FBI can do it."

"They will," Neil said, though he had his doubts. Time was running out fast, and they were no closer to finding Emily than they had been a week earlier. "If you need me, I'll be at home."

Jimmy watched Neil drive off, then joined Crystal in the

den. "This waiting is driving me crazy," he said, handing Crystal a large snifter of brandy.

Crystal leaned back against the sofa cushions. She was tired, and the strain of the past few days was taking its toll. She had lost weight, and there were heavy shadows under her eyes. "I was so sure we would find Emily today."

"It was just a wild goose chase. What more could you expect."

"That's not what you said earlier," Crystal said, angered by his reversal. "You were very enthusiastic when we first found the house and discovered the cat lady."

"But Emily wasn't there," Jimmy argued, "and Elizabeth admits that she's lost contact. Maybe she never did have a reading on Emily. Maybe her wires got crossed."

"Her clues were valid," Crystal insisted. "Laguna Beach, the shrimp sign . . . and the bluebird that led us to the cat lady."

"And it could have been coincidence. There's nothing to tie those so-called clues to Emily," he snarled. "Nothing at all. I think it was just the over-active imagination of an aging woman."

Crystal recognized the anger in his voice. They had disagreed so often, but now wasn't the time for arguing. They had to work on this together. She needed his strength.

"That's a mean thing to say."

"But true."

Crystal sipped her brandy. She had tried not to think of what Richard might do to Emily, but she knew he was capable of every vile act. If they paid the money, would Richard release Emily? Deep down, she knew he wouldn't.

As if he had read her mind, Jimmy reached out and grasped Crystal's hand. "What type of man is he?"

She didn't answer right away. It was part of her life she had wanted to forget. "I was fascinated by him," she began, speaking hesitantly. "He was so different from the boys I had known back in Cape Mary. I was lonely and thought I was in love with him. He kept me drugged up. I was flying, happy to be with him, until he tried to put me in that porno film. I don't know why it took me so long to come to my senses."

"It could have been worse."

"It took me months to rebuild my self-esteem. Oh, Jimmy," she sobbed. "I can't stand it. Knowing he has our daughter."

"We'll find her."

"Yes," Crystal gulped. "But will she be alive?" she asked bitterly.

"You mustn't think like that."

Crystal stood, defeated, no longer able to ignore the bitter reality. "Kidnapped children are seldom found, you know."

Jimmy jumped up and pulled Crystal into his arms. "You mustn't think that way, darling." He stroked her hair. "What was it that you used to say? Something about tomorrow?"

Crystal rested her head on his shoulder, remembering. "There's always a tomorrow," she said.

"Then you've got to keep believing that tomorrow we'll find Emily."

"I'm afraid, Jimmy," Crystal whispered.

"So am I," he said, rocking her gently. "So am I."

VIII

It was after ten when Richard returned to the house. He carried a bag into Emily's room. "I bought you a hamburger and fries, and there's a chocolate shake, too."

"I'm not hungry."

"Suit yourself."

"When are you going to let me out of here?" she asked angrily.

"After your mother pays the ransom. You know that."

Emily glared at him. "What if she doesn't have the money?"

"She'll get it. Your mom is a very rich lady. You live in a fancy house, have fancy cars, and she earns big bucks on every film she makes. She'll pay, if she wants you back," he said, laughing cruelly, his voice sending chills down Emily's spine as he closed and locked the door.

Emily opened the bag. The hamburger and fries were still warm, and the aroma reminded her that she hadn't eaten since early morning. She sat on the bed while she ate, watching a news program on television.

A photograph of herself and another of her mother flashed on the screen. ". . . Though there have been no new developments in the Emily Mitchelson kidnapping, our reporter spotted her mother, Crystal Smythe, Hollywood's leading actress, leaving the house early this morning in the company of her husband and a police officer who has been working on the case. A fourth, unidentified woman was with them. Meanwhile, the reward of $50,000 for any information that will help the police find Emily has been increased to $100,000 by Melvin Schuller, owner of Beechwood Studios. On the national scene . . ."

Emily turned the television off. She wondered where mommy and daddy had gone. Maybe they were trying to find her.

She went into the bathroom and brushed her teeth with the old toothbrush she had found. Her mother always made her brush her teeth after meals. She used the toilet and

returned to the bed, crawling under the covers. She closed
her eyes, saying her prayers like Socorro had taught her, but
she couldn't remember the words. She huddled in the dark,
shivering despite the heat, and began crying. "Mommy,
daddy, please hurry up and find me."

IX

Elizabeth sat up, clutching the bedclothes to her chest. She
was sweating, but felt chilled to the bone. She had heard the
voice again, this time more clearly. Emily was crying,
calling out for help.

She turned the lamp on and reached for Emily's photograph. "Speak to me, Emily. Tell me where you are," she
said, concentrating on the child's eyes. "I'm here, sweetheart. So are mommy and daddy. We want to find you."

Elizabeth waited, hoping Emily would reveal something
new, something that would help them find the child. She
fought off sleep, knowing she had to be alert to intercept
any new message. She started nodding, and slipped into a
semiconscious state, projecting herself into Emily's mind
and awareness, their auras floating and merging, becoming
one. She sensed that Emily was dreaming fitfully, reliving
the nightmare of the past few days.

Elizabeth envisioned the journey to Laguna Beach, experiencing the long drive as Emily had seen it. The curving
road up the mountain, the red bushes, the house with the
cats. She could see Emily standing at a window, looking at
the mountains and trees, the ocean . . . and . . . and
then nothing . . . except fear.

Something had happened to change things. Richard had
done something which frightened Emily. Emily was locked
in darkness, a darkness Elizabeth couldn't penetrate.

Elizabeth was confused by the dream. They had found the road, the house, the cat lady, and then suddenly the trail had gone cold, mysteriously coming to a halt. What was she missing? Where had Richard taken Emily?

friday

I

Richard waited until after midnight to begin digging. He had to be sure no one would drive by and see the beam of his flashlight. He chose a spot on the south side of the house which was partially concealed from the road by sturdy juniper berry bushes. The ground was hard, and it took over two hours to dig the hole. Emily was small, so it didn't have to be big—but he had dug it deep, just in case dogs or wild animals came sniffing around. There were plenty of raccoons and possums in the Laguna foothills, foraging around trash bins, their presence often encouraged by residents who thought of them as pets.

He heard a car approaching and quickly turned off the flashlight. The car continued up the road, and Richard breathed easier. The driver hadn't noticed. Good. It was risky selecting a spot so close to the house and road, but he didn't have much choice. Luckily, Wayne wasn't a gardener; by the time he returned from the oil fields, the weeds would cover the makeshift grave.

Richard carried his pick and shovel back into the house and dumped them in the kitchen closet. He walked into the bedroom, locking the door behind him. He stared down at Emily; she was mumbling in her sleep. He entered the bathroom and showered, washing away the sweat and dirt, letting the water beat down on his stiff muscles. He was unaccustomed to doing hard work. He dried and checked his face. He was too vain to shave off the mustache, so he had decided to grow a beard as a disguise. Still scruffy-looking, it would be weeks before it was full, but it would serve his purpose later in the day. Not that he thought anyone was looking for him, but he couldn't risk being recognized.

He checked Emily again, saw that she was still sleeping, and relocked the bedroom door. He went into the kitchen, put some ice in a glass, and poured some scotch. He gulped it down, then refilled his glass, adding some water this time. He carried his drink into the living room and sat on the sofa.

Richard dismantled the gun and began to clean it. He had had a great day, and everything was planned to perfection. He had picked the sucker's pocket and got his wallet and credit cards. Then he went to different agencies and rented the automobiles he needed, driving them to the desired locations. Next he visited the various telephone booths and wrote down the numbers, and finally he had timed the driving distances.

Everything was falling into place. He had listened to the news reports, but the police still didn't have a clue. Now it was all up to him. He checked the gun and loaded it. He didn't think he would need it, but any number of things could go wrong. It was his insurance that there would be no hitches.

Richard began to feel drowsy and drained the rest of his scotch. It was almost four in the morning. He would sleep a few hours, then drive to Santa Monica. The countdown had started—and he was on the road to riches.

II

Elizabeth awoke with a start. She checked her watch; it was almost nine o'clock. She showered and dressed quickly, fumbling with the buttons of her blouse. She found Jimmy and Crystal in the dining room talking to Lieutenant Wright. She sat at the table and accepted coffee, orange juice, and a sweet roll from Socorro.

"I'm really sorry I wasn't able to help," Elizabeth pronounced after savoring her first cup of coffee. "The only thing I'm sure of is that Emily is alive. I thought I had made contact with her last night, but she was only dreaming. She must be terribly exhausted from the fear and tension."

Crystal crumbled her sweet roll, not eating. "How can you be so sure she's all right?"

Elizabeth reached for the coffeepot and refilled her cup. "We know that Richard will keep her . . . um . . . alive until he collects the ransom money. He might even hold on to her for another day or two as a safety measure."

"There's no guarantee of that," Wright said.

Elizabeth shrugged her shoulders. "I confess I've been confused about this case. As I mentioned previously, since I've . . . ahem . . . gotten older, I seem to have some difficulty in seeing the whole picture." She paused pensively. "I've been thinking of calling a psychic lady that I know."

"Another one? What good will that do?" asked Jimmy.

"I assumed that your daughter was taken to the house of the cat lady because Emily had been thinking about her. Of course we now know that Miss Beatty is not involved, but I'm *sure* Cummings must have driven past her home at some time, which is why the house is part of Emily's thoughts. I've been hoping there would be some new insight to your daughter's location, but I haven't received any new images," she admitted.

"Yes, yes, go on," Wright urged. "Get to the point." He had had a sleepless night, thinking himself foolish to have gone off with them. His captain was angry about his taking off on a wild goose chase. *"Let the FBI handle things,"* had been his blunt advice. Wright had pleaded for one more day, feeling he owed that much to the Mitchelsons.

Elizabeth noted the edge to the Lieutenant's voice. He was tired and obviously upset about not finding Emily and her kidnapper. "I still believe Emily is in Laguna Beach," she said with quiet determination.

"If she is, then why didn't we find her yesterday?" Jimmy asked angrily.

Elizabeth sighed, feeling Jimmy's pain. "I don't know," she said truthfully. "That's why I think I should call this friend of mine. Sometimes we work together on difficult cases. She might be able to get a different reading on Emily than I have, and supply the missing pieces of the puzzle."

"We're just going around in circles," Wright said. He looked up as Neil entered the room.

"They want you in the den, Crystal."

"Yes. I'm coming." Crystal rose slowly to her feet. She patted Elizabeth's hand, sensing the older woman's dismay at her failure. "I'm sure you'll figure it out."

Elizabeth looked up at Crystal. "She's there, I tell you. I've never been surer of anything in my life."

"I want to believe you," Crystal whispered, then turned and walked out the door.

Gerald Willis had been an employee of the Federal Bureau of Investigation for over twenty years. He had been involved in several kidnapping cases, and they were never easy. This one was no different. The odds were stacked against them, and it was highly unlikely that they would find Emily alive. The best they could hope for was to find Cummings and put him behind bars for the rest of his life. The meet was set for busy Santa Monica Pier, which would be filled with tourists and local Los Angelenos seeking the sun. How the hell would they be able to spot the kidnapper, much less hope to follow him to wherever he was hiding the child.

He stood by the bookcases and faced the distraught parents. "As I've explained before, the best chance we have to finding your daughter is to proceed with the payment of the ransom money."

"I still don't see why I can't go in Crystal's place," Neil said. "It could be dangerous."

"We appreciate the offer," Jimmy assured him, "but as Agent Willis pointed out, Richard is expecting Crystal to show up. Any change in the plan could put Emily in jeopardy."

"That's right," Willis said. "As to Mrs. Mitchelson's safety, we think we can provide her all the protection she'll need."

"What's your plan?" Wright asked.

"This Cummings character obviously guessed that we would try to wire her, which is why Mrs. Mitchelson was instructed to wear a two-piece swimsuit and no jewelry. We have a transmitter that's so small we could easily hide it in an earring, but Cummings must have figured that out," Willis explained. "However, we've installed a transmitter in the briefcase handle, and another in the car. No matter where she goes, my men will be following."

At that moment another FBI agent named Jackson entered the room. He was dressed in torn blue jeans and a loose-fitting sweat shirt. He toyed with the volume control of what appeared to be a cassette player, which hung from his neck, then tapped the headphones clamped to his ears.

"This will pick up on the transmitter signal in the briefcase. I'll be keeping track of Mrs. Mitchelson," he said, "and there'll be other men in the area with similar devices."

"What about a tap on the telephones at the pier?" Wright asked.

"We've already thought of that, but it probably won't do much good. Cummings will undoubtedly tell her to go to another telephone booth for further instructions, and it's unlikely he'll stay on the line long enough for us to find him," Jackson said. He had only been with the FBI for five years, but he wasn't lacking in experience; he had previously done intelligence work for the navy.

Jimmy studied Jackson and Willis. He hadn't asked, but he assumed that they were both armed. "It doesn't seem like enough."

"In addition to ourselves, there'll be an unmarked car parked near the pier and other men on foot in that area," Jackson assured him. "Now that we have a photograph of Cummings, we're hoping we'll be able to spot him."

"Everyone is wired, so we'll be in constant touch with each other," Willis said confidently.

"The next part is a little tricky, Mrs. Mitchelson. When you speak to Cummings, you must pretend that you don't know it's him. We're fairly sure that he'll be watching you, and he could even have an accomplice."

"Yes, I know," Crystal said.

"After he gives you your instructions, do what he says immediately. Don't look around for us," Willis warned.

Neil leaned across the table to light a cigarette for Crystal. "Do you think Cummings will have Emily with him?"

"That's very doubtful," Willis said. "His goal is to get

the money. His holding card is Emily, so he'll keep her secure until he gets paid."

"After you drop the money, you should come back home, Mrs. Mitchelson. We'll be switching our attention to whoever picks up the briefcase."

"He won't suspect?"

"We hope not. As I said, the transmitter is in the handle of the briefcase," Jackson assured him. "If we're lucky, we'll be able to follow whoever takes the money, and hopefully he'll lead us to wherever Emily is being held."

"If you're lucky," Jimmy repeated sarcastically.

Willis frowned, feeling the blood rush to his face. "That was a poor choice of words," he admitted. "We assume that there'll be no hitches."

"You're quite sure Crystal won't be in danger?"

"Like I said, Cummings' goal is the money. He'll avoid any personal contact with Mrs. Mitchelson. There's no reason for him to suspect that we know his identity. He was careful about making contact with you, knowing it would be difficult for us to identify him."

Jackson cracked his knuckles noisily. "On the other hand, we may get lucky and be able to spot Cummings at the pier. If we do, we nab him. Once we get him down to headquarters, we have ways of making him talk. I learned some really neat tricks when I was in navy intelligence."

"That's enough of that kind of talk," Willis warned his boastful partner.

Crystal stood. "If you don't mind, I think I'll go upstairs now to change into my swimsuit."

Jackson checked his watch. "Yes, that would be a good idea. I'll see about the car."

Jimmy accompanied Crystal to the car. He tossed the briefcase on the seat. "Are you okay?"

"I'm afraid," she admitted. "What if something goes wrong?"

"We have to believe that everything will be all right."

"There are no guarantees," she mumbled.

Jimmy pulled her into his arms. "I wish I could go with you."

"Me, too."

"Do everything just the way Cummings tells you. Don't take any chances."

"I won't."

"The FBI will be there with you. They'll catch Cummings—and find Emily."

Crystal looked at him with tear-filled eyes. "This is all my fault. If only I had been here to protect her."

"Stop blaming yourself," Jimmy said as his lips closed on hers. "I love you very much."

Crystal touched his cheek. He was so gaunt, and she knew he hadn't slept the night before. "I love you, too."

She reluctantly got into the car and closed the door. She buckled her seat belt, inserted the key, and started the motor. "This is it," she said, breathing deeply.

Jimmy managed a pained smile. "Drive carefully. I'll see you soon."

"Yes," Crystal said, putting on her sunglasses. "Soon."

III

Richard parked the car and began walking toward the pier. He was wearing a fishing cap, dark sunglasses, cut-off blue jeans, and a Dodgers T-shirt. He carried a fishing pole and tackle box. A half-smoked cigar was clamped between his teeth.

It was an exceptionally warm day, and the beach and pier

were crowded. He smiled to himself. It was a perfect setup, and there was no way the cops could spot him.

And one thing for sure—they were there. Waiting. Maybe the guy leaning against the blue van, he thought. Or the two guys eating ice cream cones. They had hard-sole shoes on and sports jackets. It was too hot for a jacket, but these guys didn't seem to mind. How else could you hide a walkie-talkie or a shoulder holster?

Richard boldly walked past the telephone booths. It was a great day, he thought. A million dollar day, to be exact. He stopped near a souvenir stand and glanced at his watch. It was five minutes to eleven. Would she be on time? He flipped through the postcards, deliberated over several, then finally paid the concessionaire. He looked back at the phone booths while he waited for his change. He spotted a woman holding a briefcase. Yes. She had come.

He walked back the way he had come, glancing briefly in her direction. Good. No jewelry. A scarf and hat on her head and sunglasses, which he hadn't bargained for, but they were obviously a disguise. It wouldn't do to have any of her fans suddenly recognizing her. She still had the blouse on, but no, she had started to remove it.

Good. No concealed mikes, but just to be sure, he'd have her get rid of the scarf and hat. It was time to put the next step into motion. He walked away from the pier, past the cops, strolling, taking his time.

Crystal waited impatiently. It was eleven, and still no phone call. She felt conspicuous, standing on the pier with a briefcase in her hand, wearing a swimsuit.

She studied the people that walked by, worried that someone would recognize her. No one noticed; they were too busy talking and laughing, making plans. Children squealed noisily, teenagers with blaring radios pressed to their ears roller-skated by, and tourists with cameras posed friends under the Santa Monica Pier sign. A panhandler approached her and asked for some change. She shook her head no and moved closer to the telephone booths. She wondered how long she would have to wait.

He walked two more blocks, then crossed the busy intersection and stopped near a bank of telephones. He dialed the number and slipped the cotton in his mouth. She answered right away.

"Yes?"

"You have the money?" he asked her.

"Yes."

"Listen carefully. Drive to Newport Beach. Take the Newport Beach Boulevard exit to the Coast Highway. Cross the bridge over the Coast Highway to Balboa Peninsula. Drive to the ferry landing. There's a Winchell's Donut Shop nearby. Take the briefcase with you and wait outside the donut shop. And take off the scarf and hat."

He hung up and slowly walked away. The cops would follow her, but he knew what to do.

Crystal put her blouse back on and returned to her car. She started the engine and pulled out into the traffic. She glanced into the rearview mirror, but couldn't spot Willis. Was he following her? She reached for a cigarette as she eased into the traffic on the Santa Monica Freeway.

She would follow Richard's instructions without fail—and hope that nothing went wrong. She pulled onto the San Diego Freeway, easing into the flowing traffic headed south. It was about a forty-minute drive, she calculated, if the traffic wasn't too congested. The only problem area would be near the South Bay curve.

Forty minutes of agony, and then what? Would the FBI

agents be able to keep track of her? What would happen at Newport? Only time would tell.

She checked her speedometer. Ever since the speed limit had been increased to 65 mph, Californians had taken it upon themselves to drive like demons. She was in the fast lane, and the car behind her was practically on her bumper, edging her own speed well past seventy. She signaled and pulled into the lane on her right, slowing down. She was in a hurry to get to Newport, but wanted to be alive when she arrived.

IV

Wright slammed the telephone down. "She's on the move again. Headed south to Newport Beach."

"Why do you think he's making her go so far?" Neil asked.

"Cummings is smart. It's the tourist season, so he's probably planning on getting lost in the crowds after he picks up the money."

"Yeah," Jimmy said, "but he was careful that Crystal wouldn't be wired. Don't you think Cummings will guess there's a transmitter in the car to enable the FBI to follow Crystal anywhere?"

Wright nodded. "I'll bet he plans to have her leave the car in Newport. There are hundreds of souvenir stands and tourist shops there—and boats. Lots of places where she could leave a briefcase. That's why he's making her go south. The FBI won't have time to properly set up surveillance."

"I should have gone with her," Jimmy said angrily. "If I could just get my hands on this Cummings."

Elizabeth listened to them, only half-aware of what they were saying. There was something bothering her; something she was missing. She stood and walked outside. Under any other circumstances it would be a perfect day—the sky cloudless, the temperature hovering in the eighties, a soft breeze rustling the palm trees.

On a day like this, Elizabeth sometimes went to a park near her home, where she would lay on a blanket under the protective arms of a favorite redwood tree, a book opened on her chest.

Unfortunately, this was not a day for relaxation. There were too many disturbing thoughts crowding her mind. Such as why she hadn't been able to locate Emily. She was positive the readings were right, but what was the link? What had she overlooked?

Elizabeth had placed a call to her psychic friend, but she wasn't home; hopefully she would return the call soon. She knew Emily was in Laguna Beach somewhere, but she had gotten her "wires" crossed. That happened sometimes. If she could just get her friend to go there, perhaps the two of them could figure it out.

Elizabeth sank to her knees at the edge of the swimming pool and stared into its aquamarine depths. She dipped her hand into the water, watching it ripple as she drew small circles. She blocked out the rest of her pleasant surroundings and thought of Emily, projecting herself into the girl's thoughts and memories.

Elizabeth could see Bluebird Canyon Drive as it wound up the mountain through its tunnel of overlapping pine and eucalyptus trees. She pictured the bright red bougainvillea down the road from the house with the cat faces which Emily had spotted. And then Emily had stood at a window, studying the mountains on either side of the deep canyon and the ocean in the distance, until . . .

Elizabeth shuddered. She could sense Emily's fear.

"Oh, Emily," Elizabeth sighed. "I know you're there, but I don't know how to find you."

She began to reverse the pattern of the circles she was drawing in the water. There was something else bothering her. Crystal! She's in danger, too. Elizabeth suddenly gasped in fear. What had Lieutenant Wright said? Crystal was headed south.

She struggled to her feet, thinking once again that she was getting too old for this work. She must tell the others. Laguna Beach was south, and that's where Crystal was driving, right into the trap—and the danger.

V

Emily flipped the television dial to the noonday news, hoping there would be something about her. She turned up the volume when the "Hollywood Reporter" segment came on and her photograph flashed on the screen.

"There is still no news regarding the kidnapping of Emily Mitchelson, daughter of Crystal Smythe, Hollywood's premier movie star. Our reporter on the scene spotted Miss Smythe leaving her home this morning under a police escort, presumably to deliver the ransom money personally to the kidnapper. We will keep you updated on this real life drama. Meanwhile, television and movie idol Tom Selleck has signed . . ."

Emily turned the television off. Was it true? Was her mother going to pay the money? She hoped so. She hated the room she was in; it was hot and stuffy. And she wanted to go home. She wanted her mother and her father.

VI

Crystal turned off the freeway at the Newport Beach exit as she had been instructed. Newport Beach Boulevard was jammed with traffic. It had been a long time since she had driven this way, and she was unsure of where to go. She breathed easier when she finally saw the sign BRIDGE TO BALBOA ISLAND.

The road narrowed, and traffic slowed to an agonizing pace. Crystal spotted another sign, its arrow indicating that the Balboa Island Ferry was straight ahead. She gripped the steering wheel tighter, tensing as she approached the end of the peninsula. She followed the signs to the ferry, glancing once again in the rearview mirror. She hadn't spotted the FBI agents who were tailing her, but then, she hadn't expected to. They were professionals and knew their job. She came to a stop at the corner of Palm Street and looked to her right. She could see the ferry landing at the end of the street. She glanced up ahead and saw the Winchell Donut sign.

She parked in a red zone; for once she didn't have to worry about getting a parking ticket, since the FBI had plastered Official Police Business decals on both the front and back windows.

Crystal grabbed the briefcase and got out of the car. She stood undecided; had he said to wait outside or to enter the donut shop? There were some telephone booths nearby. She walked to them and waited, hoping he would soon call and tell her where to deliver the money, and then, maybe . . .

She shuddered; there was no longer room in her vocabulary for the word "maybe." There was no doubt in her mind that Richard was not going to return Emily to her. She would have to rely on the FBI to do that job.

Where was he? Why didn't he call? She studied the cars passing by. Was Cummings in one of them? Was he checking to be sure she was alone?

She began to feel nauseated as the smell of frying donuts

filled her nostrils. It reminded her of the food served on location. When she was pregnant with Emily, she had been constantly ill, and her morning sickness had slowed production.

She remembered that it was a suspense movie. She had been chased by a maniac and almost killed. But that was make-believe, and this was real life. Cummings was the maniac in her present nightmare.

She leaned back against the wall, wondering how long she would have to wait for the nightmare to end.

VII

"We must leave immediately!" Elizabeth exclaimed as she rushed back into the den. "Crystal is in great danger."

Jimmy stared up at her. "What?"

"I feel so stupid," she said, shaking her head. She began pacing back and forth, her arms flailing. "It's all falling into place now. I just didn't see the whole picture. That often happens, you know, but I should have been more alert. I remember a murder case in Chicago. The same thing happened. I had directed the police to the right spot, but we couldn't find the body. I knew it had to be there, and of course it was, but we couldn't see it." Elizabeth gasped for a breath, then continued. "I should have remembered, but the police bungled everything. You see . . ."

"Calm down, Mrs. Anderson," Neil cautioned her. "You'll make yourself ill."

"What? Oh, yes," she said, "how foolish of me. That was all so long ago."

"You said Crystal is in danger," Jimmy reminded her.

"Yes, yes, of course." Elizabeth sat on the sofa next to Jimmy. "May I have a glass of water, please?"

Wright walked to the bar in the corner, poured water into

a glass, added ice, and carried it back to her. She sipped her water gratefully, then picked up her story.

"You know, it was actually something you said, Lieutenant."

Wright looked at her quizzically. "I don't understand."

"When the FBI called earlier they told you Crystal was headed south to Newport."

"That's right."

"And, as I recall, Laguna Beach is just ten miles or so south of Newport."

Neil's mouth dropped. "She's right."

"Well, I'll be damned," Wright said. "Cummings is moving Crystal south to an area we visited yesterday at Mrs. Anderson's insistence. That can't be coincidence."

Jimmy grasped Elizabeth's hands. "You said Crystal is in danger."

"I can't explain it, but I have this feeling that something is going to go wrong with Cummings' plan. We must drive to Laguna Beach and try to prevent it."

"But we don't know where to look," Jimmy argued.

"Then we'll have to go back to Miss Beatty's house. Somehow I still have the feeling that the answer is there," she said, her voice full of conviction.

Neil gaped at her. "You can't be serious! We have to wait here for Crystal to come back."

"What if she doesn't?" Jimmy asked harshly. "What if Cummings has some other plans for her? We have no way of knowing what he intends to do."

Wright nodded. "Mr. Mitchelson . . . Jimmy . . . is right. We don't know what Cummings is planning, but he *is* luring Crystal south. Say it's sixth sense, or whatever you want, but I'll bet anything that the next stop is Laguna Beach. I think I would like to be there when they arrive."

Jimmy noticed that the Lieutenant had switched to first

names. He smiled at the policeman and stuck his hand out. "Thanks, Howard."

"Then I'll go, too," Neil said grudgingly.

"It's better that you stay here," Wright told him. "Someone has to be here by the telephone. We'll call you when we get there."

Elizabeth rose heavily to her feet. "We'd better get started."

"It could be dangerous," Jimmy warned her.

"And I could be wrong—but I'm going with you," she said decisively. "I'm sure that once we get there, I can be of some help."

"Then it's settled. Let's get moving," Wright said. "Cummings has at least an hour's jump on us."

VIII

Richard was on the opposite side of the street. He casually glanced over at Crystal. Good. She had figured it out; she was waiting by the phone booths. It was unlikely that the FBI guys had been able to tap the lines, but even so, he had his bases covered.

He turned the corner, walking slowly, then stopped at a marine supply store and peered at the window display. He studied his reflection. He had changed clothes, choosing white shorts and a lightweight navy-blue knit pullover. He had even changed into white canvas shoes, and a yachting hat covered his hair. He looked like any of the boat owners in the area. He smiled to himself. The disguise might not be necessary, but there was no point in taking a chance on being spotted.

He saw a plain green sedan roll past Crystal. There were two men in the car, and this was the second time they had driven around the block. There had to be others, but he hadn't been able to pick them out. There were a few cars in the line for the ferry, but since there were two ferries making the short hop to Balboa Island, the pace was quick. He decided it was time to put the next phase into action.

He continued around the block, then crossed the street and walked back to the ferry landing. Tourists thronged the boardwalk, laughing and pointing at the myriad of luxury sailboats docked in the bay. Music blared from every souvenir stand and fast-food restaurant. The ferris wheel at the landing was moving, and the shrill screams of young girls filled the air.

Richard stepped into the noisy video games arcade. He went directly to the telephone in the back and dialed one of the numbers he had written on the back of a book of matches. He quickly stuffed the cotton into his mouth. Crystal answered on the first ring.

"Listen carefully if you want to see Emily. I will not repeat," he said slowly. "There's a white Datsun with a red rose attached to the antenna parked next door at the Bal Harbour liquor store. The car keys are under the floor mat. A red nylon satchel is on the car seat. Put the money into the bag, then throw the briefcase into the trash barrel.

"Get into line for the ferry," he continued. "The exact change is in the car's ashtray. Speak to no one. Take the ferry to Balboa Island. Drive straight ahead and cross the bridge to the mainland. When you arrive at the Pacific Coast Highway, turn south toward Laguna.

"After a couple miles you will see a stoplight. There are three different gasoline stations on the corner. The Hamilton House Motor Lodge is on the other corner. Stop at the telephone booths there and wait for your next phone call." He paused, sweating profusely. "Did you understand?"

Her hesitant yes was music in his ears. He hung up and took a handkerchief from his pocket to dab his brow, then wiped the phone clean. He quickly backtracked to Palm Street, where he could watch what was happening. There was the risk she might get back into her own car, or try to leave a written message for the cops. Hopefully she believed that there were other people watching her and wouldn't do anything dumb.

He crossed the street to the opposite corner. He could see her standing by the white Datsun. He had used it to drive to Santa Monica and back to Newport, parking it at the liquor store. He had also been careful about wiping his fingerprints off everything he had touched.

He saw her carry the briefcase to the trash barrel, then return to the car. Good. He had worried that the damn thing was wired. He watched as she backed cautiously out of the parking lot and pulled into the line for the ferry. He waited, then smiled as a camper pulled in behind her. The passengers were a couple with two kids. The next car to get into line was a convertible with two young couples.

He breathed a sigh of relief, and then he spotted the green sedan pull in line. It had to be the FBI guys. Too late, he laughed to himself. The ferry only took three cars at a time. He walked to the corner and bought a Coke, then returned. A ferry had come in, and the cars advanced, but the green sedan had stayed in line.

He counted the cars. Crystal was number six in line. There was no way the police would be able to drive onto the ferry without being spotted. And he had to assume they would know he'd be watching.

Everything was going smoothly, he thought, as he strolled casually down to the landing and joined the group of tourists walking aboard the next ferry. He would wait on the opposite side—in his own car.

Yes. Everything was going according to plan.

IX

"Damn it!" Wright exploded. "A flat tire, and the spare is flat, too."

They had pulled over into the emergency parking strip and now stood staring in dismay at the tire. The San Diego Freeway was at its busiest time of the day, and cars hurtled by, whipping at the dust.

"We passed an emergency call box," Jimmy said. "I'll walk back and call for help."

Wright shook his head. "No need. I'll get help quicker than you. There *are* some advantages of being an officer of the law." He got back into his car and turned the emergency flashers on, then called in his request to the dispatcher.

Elizabeth stood by the fence, watching the cars race by. There was something bothering her. She was getting that feeling again. Cold tendrils of fear grasped her heart. Something bad was going to happen. Something she couldn't stop.

X

Crystal was frightened. Was he watching her? There were so many people walking along the boardwalk that it would be difficult to spot him. She wished there was some way to communicate with the FBI agents, but what if he saw her. She had to hope they would find a way to follow her.

The line began to move forward, and she put the car into gear. He had outsmarted them, but maybe there was a way she could let someone know what was happening.

She could try telling the person who collected the toll money on the ferry, but what if Richard had an accomplice watching? With a million dollars in ransom forthcoming,

Cummings could afford to pay someone for helping. Suppose others were involved; there were plenty of greedy
people in the world.

No. She couldn't do it, she thought. It was too risky.
There were too many unknowns; what if someone really
was watching her? Was it the man in the red T-shirt and blue
jeans? He had looked in her direction twice. She watched as
he sauntered down to the landing. He would be boarding the
ferry when she drove onto it. Was he the one?

XI

Willis was furious. He had advised Ramsey and Morawski
in the green sedan to keep their place in line to see if Crystal
actually drove onto the ferry.

"God only knows what Cummings told her. I wish we
could ask her, but it's too damn dangerous. There's still the
possibility that Cummings has someone helping him."

"Son of a bitch," Jackson cursed as he came to a grinding
stop at a crosswalk. He watched sullenly as several people
poked their way across the street. "It'll take us forever to
drive around the peninsula to the mainland and the other
side of the ferry."

"Turn the siren on and cut around those turkeys," Willis
said, pointing at the slow-moving cars ahead of them. "We
should have known Cummings would do something like
this."

"So he guessed about the car. How the hell did he know
the briefcase would be wired?"

"He's a smart cookie," Willis admitted. "What about
patching through to the local police?"

"You think they can help? By the looks of traffic around
here, they're probably up to their ears in problems of their
own. You ever see so many Goddamn tourists?"

"They may still be able to spot the white Datsun for us."

"Yeah, sure," Jackson said irritably. "Call in the license plate number, and tell them no lights or sirens and not to approach her."

Willis glared at him. He didn't like the young upstart giving him orders. "I know what I'm doing," he growled, wishing he had more men to back them up, and wondering how he was going to find Crystal and her daughter.

XII

Crystal pulled to a stop in front of the motel. She wondered how long it would take the FBI to find her. She glanced around. There were cars pulling in and out of the three gasoline stations, going about their business. She looked at the gasoline gauge of the Datsun. It showed less than a quarter tank. Obviously he wasn't planning on her driving much farther.

She sighed, picked up the red satchel, and got out of the car. She waited by the telephones, feeling the heat. There was no air-conditioning in the rental car, and her blouse was sticking to her back.

Was he watching her now? Waiting to see if she had been followed? Her heart thumped wildly. She was very close to Laguna Beach, and the significance wasn't lost to her.

Elizabeth had been right all along. Cummings must have hidden Emily somewhere nearby; otherwise, why would he lead her here? It couldn't be coincidence, Crystal said to herself, but if Emily was in Laguna, why hadn't they found her?

One of the telephones rang, startling Crystal. She hesitated, then raised the receiver to her ear. "Yes?"

"Listen carefully," he said slowly. "Walk across the

street to the Circle-K grocery store. There's a red Ford parked there. The keys are under the floor mat.

"Drive south, past Laguna Beach, approximately five miles. After Crown Valley Parkway there's another stoplight, where you'll see a blue sign. It says Monarch Plaza Shopping Center. Turn left and park near the Safeway supermarket. Understand?"

"Yes," she replied, realizing how carefully he had planned everything. Constantly changing cars would keep anyone from following her.

"Leave the car unlocked, and put the money satchel on the floor of the car. There's a couple of dollars in the ashtray of the car. Enter the grocery store, buy a carton of milk, then wait by the telephones outside. You will receive a phone call instructing you where you can find Emily. Understand?"

"Is she all right?" Crystal shouted. "Please don't hurt her . . ."

She was answered by a dial tone.

Crystal hung up and leaned back against the wall of the telephone booth. He's totally mad, she thought, but she would have to follow his instructions. If only she had a pencil and could leave a message, but what if he was watching? She had no choice; she would have to do as he commanded. He was running the show—holding the reins of her destiny in his hands.

Richard dropped some change into the cigarette machine, selected his brand, then lit up. He stood at the window of the Shell gasoline station, watching.

Good! She was doing as he had instructed her. He smiled to himself, stopped for a drink of water at the fountain, then sauntered outside to his car.

It was a beautiful plan, and everything was proceeding on

schedule. In a very short while he would be holding a
million dollars in his hands. He sat in his car and waited,
watching as Crystal pulled out of the parking lot and headed
south on the Coast Highway. He studied the other cars
passing by. None had slowed down, none had stopped,
none had noticed.

He started whistling as he put the car into gear. He was
going to get away with it after all.

XIII

Elizabeth was leaning against the wire fence which divided
the noisy freeway, watching the mechanic change the flat
tire. She glanced at her watch. It was getting late, and
Richard was steering Crystal toward Laguna Beach.

Would they arrive in time? she wondered. They had
waited what seemed an eternity for the mechanic to arrive.
She studied the faces of her distraught companions. Wright
stood hovering over the mechanic, trying to rush him along.
Jimmy's face was creased with worry, his hands shoved in
his pockets as he paced back and forth.

She wondered if they would be able to find Emily before
Richard picked up the ransom money. After that it would be
too late . . .   There would be no reason to keep her alive.
If only she could figure out what she was missing. Terror
gripped her; she had the clue, so why couldn't she solve the
puzzle.

Once again her thoughts went back to what little she
knew, seeing it the way it had appeared to Emily. They had
arrived in Laguna Beach, and Emily was excited when she
spotted the ocean. He had driven down the highway, turned
at the Little Shrimp sign, then up into the mountains, over
the curving road, past the red bougainvillea. They had
driven past the house with the cat faces . . . and . . .

Elizabeth gasped. "My God! That's it." She rushed to Jimmy's side. "She's right there. All the time, she was right there. I didn't see it, or rather, I saw it, but didn't realize what I was seeing."

Jimmy grasped Elizabeth's arms, worried that the elderly woman would have a heart attack. "Please calm down, Elizabeth."

She turned to Lieutenant Wright. "We must go there now. Emily is there. I know she's in terrible danger. We must get there before him."

Wright pushed his hat back on his forehead. "What is it?"

"We were so close, you see, but we didn't look in the right place," Elizabeth said, trembling with excitement.

Jimmy's face was a blank, confused by Elizabeth's agitated manner. "We don't understand what you're trying to tell us."

Elizabeth took a deep breath. "I've realized my mistake. Everything happened as I saw it—or rather, as I interpreted what Emily was experiencing. Emily *did* see Miss Beatty's house, but then she was taken somewhere up above. She's being held up on that mountain road in a house which *overlooks* Miss Beatty's."

"You're sure?" Wright asked.

"Yes. I'm sure. I had a feeling the other day that Emily had been taken away, because the images had stopped coming, but maybe Cummings moved her to another room. Or," she paused, closing her eyes. "No. He put something over the window, or else he closed some shutters. I'm not sure, but I do know that both Crystal and Emily are in great danger. I can feel it. We must hurry."

The mechanic slammed the trunk shut. "All done."

"Let's get moving," Wright said, hoping that they could

find the house before anything happened to the girl. Or to Crystal, if Mrs. Anderson was correct.

XIV

Crystal drove into the parking lot of the Monarch Bay shopping plaza. Lush foliage and sprawling trees lined the meticulously trimmed lawns and walkways of the complex. The stores and boutiques were set back from the parking lot, shaded by a broad veranda. She spotted the Safeway at the far end and pulled into a parking spot. She got out of the car and quickly walked into the supermarket. She raced to the dairy section, picked up the milk, then hurried to the front of the store.

"Please. It's an emergency," she pleaded, pushing ahead of an elderly woman in the check-out line and tossing the money on the counter.

"You should wait your turn," the young girl behind the cash register said, shaking her head back and forth in disapproval, her blonde ponytail swishing the air.

"Please hurry," Crystal said angrily to the girl, then turned to the woman she had shoved aside. "Sorry," she murmured guiltily, shrugging her shoulders.

The girl rang up the sale, mumbling to herself, then handed Crystal her change. She reached for a bag, but Crystal snatched the milk from her and ran off without a thank you.

The girl stared after Crystal. "Well, it takes all kinds," she told her patiently waiting customer. "Would you look at that! All that rush, and all she's doing is standing outside by the telephones. There ought to be a law against her type."

"It's really a disgrace," declared the elderly woman as she removed items from her shopping cart.

Crystal paced back and forth, mindless of the disturbance

she had created. She glanced around. Was he watching her? Why was he waiting? Ring, damn it, she beseeched the telephone. Ring.

She heard a dog barking somewhere nearby. She turned around and looked down the row of cars. A man was running, clutching a red satchel in his hand.

With a start, Crystal realized it had to be Cummings. She dropped the milk carton and dashed across the parking lot to the median and its protective covering of bushes. She crouched down, moving stealthily toward the far end.

She heard a car door slam and a motor start. She dared to peek through the bushes; a blue Ford was backing out of a parking space. She waited as it pulled past her. Although he was wearing sunglasses and some sort of mariner's cap, she was sure it was Cummings.

She slipped across the driveway and ran up the grassy knoll behind the First Interstate Bank. She crouched behind a low hedge and spotted Cummings making a right turn onto the Pacific Coast Highway. He was going north. Back to Laguna Beach. Back to . . .

Crystal shuddered. She didn't know why, but for some reason she believed he was going to Janice Beatty's house, back to Bluebird Canyon Drive.

She turned on her heel and went racing back to the supermarket. She stumbled inside to the check-out stand. The elderly woman whom she had rudely pushed aside was still talking to the girl, writing out a check.

"Excuse me," she said breathlessly, pulling off her sunglasses. "I'm Crystal Smythe." She snatched the pen from the woman and wrote her telephone number on the check book. "Please call this number and tell my husband I delivered the money and I'm going to the cat lady's house. He'll understand. Tell him it's Cummings."

The elderly woman's eyes bulged with indignant shock as

Crystal ran out the door. "Good heavens! I've never seen anyone so rude. I want to speak to the manager."

The girl gasped her astonishment as she watched Crystal's hasty departure. "My God! That really *was* her!"

"Whatever am I going to do with this?" the woman asked, rattled by the scribbled handwriting across her check.

"Don't you know who that was? It was Crystal Smythe," the girl said, snatching the checkbook from the woman. "She's that movie star whose daughter was kidnapped," she cried over her shoulder as she raced to the manager's desk.

Crystal was oblivious of the people who watched her frantically run from the store back to the red Ford. She sighed with relief as she got into the car; Cummings hadn't taken the car keys. She gunned the motor, backed out recklessly, smashing into a brand new Cadillac, and careened out of the parking lot.

XV

Jackson looked inside the white Datsun. The keys were still in the ignition. He slammed the door shut. "Shit," he exploded. "I thought sure we had her after the highway patrol spotted the car."

"Any suggestions as to what we do now?" Willis asked.

"Shit," he said again, drawing the word out. "This bastard Cummings has outfoxed us."

The green sedan pulled alongside. "No sign of her?" the driver asked.

"Disappeared. We don't know if she's on foot or if she got into another car," Willis admitted grudgingly. He looked around, hands on his hips, then nodded his head. "Okay, someone must have seen her. Maybe an attendant at one of those gasoline stations can tell us something. Let's spread out and see if we can find a witness."

XVI

Richard walked into the house, singing to himself. He dropped the satchel on the kitchen table, then opened the refrigerator. He had chilled a bottle of champagne—Dom Perignon, the expensive stuff—provided by Ralph Dobson, the sucker whose credit cards and money he had lifted at Disneyland.

He popped the cork and poured the wine in a tall goblet, then sat at the table and raised his glass in a toast. "To the perfect crime," he laughed, "and to the future."

He drained the champagne, belched, then refilled his glass. He opened the satchel and began removing the bundled stacks of money. He began counting, his eyes glistening as he set the money in neat little piles.

The plan had worked beautifully. Not one hitch—except for that damn dog in the parking lot at the Safeway. It had scared the shit out of him. He had gotten the money and was returning to his car, trying to stay low and keep an eye out for any cops. He had brushed up against the pick-up, and all of a sudden a dog leaped up from the back and lurched at him. He had almost been bitten by the German shepherd. Luckily, the dog had been tethered, or otherwise he might not be sitting here now. He was sure it was curtains, but no one had seemed to notice. He had watched his rearview mirror, but couldn't spot any cars following him.

It had gone off so Goddamn smoothly that he was almost in shock. Of course he had planned everything carefully, but there had been moments when he thought he might not get away with it. Too bad he couldn't tell anyone.

He lit a cigarette and reached for his note pad. He had

made a list of all the things he had to do, and now he scratched off the top items with a flourish. Done; done; and done. He stared at the next item. Emily. After he took care of her he would be free. He glanced at his watch. It was too early to deal with her. He would have to wait for the protective cover of darkness. Around ten or eleven would be good. There wouldn't be too much traffic on the road then, but he would still have to be careful.

He decided he had time for a nap before dealing with Emily. He carried his glass and the bottle of champagne into the living room and stretched out on the sofa. In a few hours he would be on his way.

Emily heard him arrive, singing. He was happy, which could mean only one thing: He had collected the ransom money. Now maybe he would let her go. She hated the darkened bedroom that she considered her prison and would be happy to go home and sleep in her own bed.

She waited impatiently, wondering how long it would be before he took her back to her mother, then frowned. Emily realized that she had caused all this trouble. She never should have trusted him. Her father had made her promise never to get into a stranger's car, but she had thought Richard was mommy's friend. He had seemed so nice, but he had lied to her. Why had she done it? Would she be punished for having disobeyed?

She huddled on the bed, grasping her knees. She had another terrifying thought. What if he had been lying to her about going home. What if he never let her go. Would she ever see her mother and father again?

"Mommy, mommy, where are you?" she sobbed. "Please, mommy. I want to go home. I promise I'll be good. Please, mommy," she repeated over and over, hoping somehow someone would come to rescue her.

XVII

They were stunned by Willis's grim report. The FBI were stymied and had lost track of Crystal somewhere north of Laguna Beach, but were headed to a supermarket where she had been sighted.

"I'm almost there now," Wright said, then switched off the car radio. There was no way he was going to tell Willis where they were going. It was still a guessing game. What if Mrs. Anderson was wrong? Then what would they do?

"You were certainly right about Cummings leading Crystal south," Jimmy told Elizabeth.

"Let's hope you're also right about the house where Emily is being held," Wright said.

"She's there, I can feel it," Elizabeth assured him.

"We'll know soon enough," Wright said as he turned off the freeway onto the canyon road which led to Laguna Beach.

XVIII

Crystal stopped in front of Janice Beatty's house. His car wasn't there, but maybe he had left it somewhere else. Perhaps it's in a garage, she thought, as she closed the car door gently and scurried across the road. Miss Beatty's car wasn't there either, which meant she was probably at the Sawdust Festival.

Crystal tried the front door; it was locked. She decided to go around the side of the house, hoping a window was open. The bedroom window was locked, but she breathed a sigh of relief when she found a studio window slightly open. She raised it slowly and climbed inside, knocking over a row of cats. She waited, wondering if anyone had heard the sound, then cautiously moved into the living room.

The house was eerily silent, and dust motes floated in the sun rays that crept through the lace curtains at the windows. The all-seeing eyes of the many cats stared at her, accusing her of trespassing.

Crystal swiftly searched the premises, opening doors, looking inside closets, finding nothing. She returned to the living room and sank into the rocking chair. Why had she thought Emily would be here? What had drawn her back to this house?

Crystal began to weep. Where was her baby? Where was he hiding her? "Dear God," she prayed, "please let me find her."

She rocked back and forth, lost in her sorrow, the minutes ticking away loudly on an antique clock that sat on the fireplace mantelpiece. She finally took several deep breaths, willing her racing heart to slow down.

It was hot in Miss Beatty's house, the air oppressive. Crystal felt clammy, and she was drained of all energy. She snatched some tissues from a box painted with cat faces and wiped her eyes, then the sweat from her brow.

There was no putting it off. She reached for the telephone and dialed the operator. "I want to place a collect call," she said in a heavy voice.

The phone was answered by Neil. "Crystal? Are you all right?"

She noticed the tremor in his voice. "Did you get my message?"

"I've been worried sick. Some girl called from a Safeway grocery store and said you delivered the money and were going back to that cat lady's house."

"I'm here now. I don't know why, but I thought I would find Emily here."

"Crystal. Listen to me," he said excitedly. "Jimmy, and Mrs. Anderson, and Lieutenant Wright left here for Laguna Beach."

"What?" she asked, surprised. "Why?"

"Mrs. Anderson was convinced Cummings was leading you there."

Crystal gasped. Of course; that was it. Mrs. Anderson had felt it too. There *was* a reason why they kept being drawn to this place, but *what*?

"Crystal?" Neil's voice sounded far away. "Stay where you are and call the police. Don't do anything foolish."

Crystal slowly replaced the receiver in the cradle. She went to the bathroom and splashed water on her face, then stared at her reflection. Her eyes were red-rimmed. What had Elizabeth said? Something about eyes revealing the soul. All she could see in her own eyes was guilt. She shook her head and walked outside.

She stood in the middle of the road. What had Emily seen? Where was she? Crystal glanced up the steep hillside. There was a house up above, similar to the many other cottages that dotted the hillside. Its red walls were faded and peeling. Bright red bougainvillea grew below the house. A window, high in the wall, had been clumsily boarded up. Why? A chilling thought crossed her mind. Could Emily be in that room? What had Elizabeth said? Something about Emily's not being able to see any longer. Crystal could hear her heart pounding in her ears. That had to be it!

She began climbing the hill, grabbing at roots and tree stumps, mindless of the rocks which cut into her bare hands, arms, and legs. She grunted, slipping and sliding, forcing herself to continue upward. The ground was hard and overgrown with weeds, but she ignored the scratches and the dust that filled her mouth. She reached the top and crouched behind a pile of logs, breathing heavily.

Crystal finally looked around the wall of the carport and saw the blue Ford that Cummings had been driving. He was here, and she could sense that Emily was inside. She stole to the door and pressed an ear to the pane of glass. She couldn't hear any sounds.

She bit her lower lip, wondering what she should do. Dare she enter the house? She frowned, hesitating, knowing she had to go inside. Emily was here, and she was in great danger.

She turned the door knob and found it wasn't locked. She cringed as she slowly opened the door, its hinges squeaking noisily. She entered the kitchen and saw the red satchel and the money strewn on the table. Yes, he was here. She crossed to the table, her heart thumping wildly, and fingered the money, wondering what she should do.

"Son of a bitch!" Richard exploded behind her.

Crystal whirled around, stumbling back against the table. She turned white, frightened.

"How the hell did you find me, you stupid bitch?"

Crystal cringed from the hatred she saw in his eyes. She found her voice. "Where's Emily?"

Richard slapped her across the face. "I asked you how did you find me? Where are your friends in the green car?" he demanded as he crossed to the back door and looked out the window.

She knew she had to outwit him. "I don't know who you mean," she said, tossing her head proudly, trying not to show her fear.

Richard slapped her again. "Where are the FBI fellows who were tailing you?"

This time Crystal's hand went to her cheek as tears clouded her vision. "You should know," she gulped. "I left them behind in Newport."

"Then how'd you find me?" he demanded.

Crystal knew she couldn't explain about Elizabeth. He would never believe her. She would have to be convincing, and above all, she couldn't let him know the police were aware of his identity. She had to think of Emily. Perhaps she could persuade him to let them go.

"I heard the dog bark at the Safeway store and saw you drive away. I got back into the car and followed you."

Richard's eyes narrowed to tiny slits that distorted his once-handsome features. He wondered if she was telling the truth. He had thought there was no one behind him. How careless of him; and how stupid of her. He certainly hadn't counted on this happening.

Now there would have to be a change in the ending of this affair. He would have to kill Crystal, too, since there was no way he could let her go. The question was, how the hell was he going to do it? He had the gun, but it would be noisy. Should he chance it? First things first. He would have to tie her up.

He studied Crystal. She was even more beautiful than when he first met her. She had been so innocent then—and gullible. But that was long ago. He knew she was smart, and conniving. It took guts to get to the top, and she had done it. Was she lying to him?

"Are you telling me the truth?"

"Yes, of course I am. I saw you get into the car and followed you here," she repeated. "Alone. Now where, for God's sake, is my daughter?"

"I had intended to drop her off at your place this evening," he lied.

"She's here, isn't she. This is where you've been keeping her." Crystal started for the living room. "Emily. Are you here, Emily?" she shouted. "It's mommy . . ."

Richard grabbed Crystal's arm, twisting it forcefully. "Come back here."

Crystal screamed in pain. "Stop it. You're hurting me."

Richard pulled both her arms behind her back and laughed. He was excited by her, by her smell, by her fear. He clamped his mouth down on hers, his teeth grinding cruelly on her lips.

"No," she managed to gasp, fighting to get away from him.

Richard tightened his grip, inserting a knee between her thighs as his other hand reached inside her swim-suit to caress her breast. "God! Remember how you and I used to get it on? Let's do it now," he said, half-dragging her to the living room sofa.

"No, please," she pleaded, struggling in his arms. "Let me go. I'll never tell anyone. I just want my daughter back."

Emily listened at the door. It was her mother. "Mommy? Mommy?" she cried, beating on the door with her fists.

Crystal found the strength she needed. "Emily, darling, I'm here," she shouted as she swiftly kneed Cummings, pushing him back on the sofa.

Crystal ran to the door, unlocked it, and crouched down to gather her daughter in her arms. "Oh, baby! Are you all right? Did he hurt you?"

"Mommy," Emily sobbed, wrapping her arms around Crystal's neck. "I was so afraid."

Richard rolled in pain on the sofa, outraged. "Bitch," he screamed as he reached for the gun on the coffee table. He pointed it at Crystal and Emily.

"Don't move, or you're dead," he grunted.

Crystal whirled around, shielding her daughter. "You must be insane. You wouldn't dare shoot us."

"No? Why not? You didn't really think I was going to let you go, did you?" He laughed cruelly. "If you hadn't been so stupid, you wouldn't have gotten yourself into this mess. Now you've got to die, too."

"What did I ever do to you?" she asked. "Why can't the money be enough?"

"Remember a few weeks ago? I asked you then for a loan, but oh, no. Miss high-and-mighty was too good for her old friend," he spat out at her. "All I needed was a few lousy bucks and maybe a few words in the right ear, and I could have gotten back on my feet."

"So take your money and go," Crystal cried. "Just let us leave here, for God's sake."

"Sorry, sweetheart. The minute I walk out that door, you'll be off to the police and telling them who I am, and that won't do at all. You see, Crystal, the penalty for kidnapping is the same as for killing, so I don't give a damn what happens to you."

Crystal's eyes were filled with terror. "But the police already know it's you."

Her words shocked him. Could it be true? How could they know? He had been careful. "I don't believe you," he said, laughing at the thought.

Crystal realized she had made a mistake. She shouldn't have told him, but it was too late now, and the information might help her. "It's true. We've known for days it was you. The gardener saw you and heard Emily call out your name. They're looking for you now."

"Shut up," he commanded. "I have to think."

He leaned back on the sofa, the gun still pointing at her. He hadn't counted on this happening. It was just like Crystal to screw up things for him.

"Let Emily go," Crystal pleaded. "I'll be your hostage. We can get away together."

"That's just what you would like, isn't it. So that you could later lead them to me." He struggled to his feet. "Get over here. Both of you." He shoved Crystal down on a straight chair, then turned to Emily. "You sit on the sofa where I can watch you."

"Do as he says, honey," Crystal whispered.

"That's right, Emily. If you try and run, I shoot mommy," he said, snarling at her.

Emily reluctantly went to the sofa. She wiped at the tears on her face, watching Richard warily as he opened a closet door and took out a rope.

"I'm going to tie you up for a while," he told Crystal, "so I can figure this out. Put your arms behind the chair."

Crystal did as he commanded. Richard put the gun into the waistband of his pants, then swiftly wrapped the rope around her several times. He knotted her wrists together, then satisfied that she couldn't move, went to sit on the sofa.

Emily moved as far away from him as she could, hating him. She realized that with her mother tied up, she was going to have to find a way to escape. To get help. If she could only get out the back door, then maybe she could run to one of the other houses.

Richard lit a cigarette and put his feet up on the coffee table. He took the gun out of his waistband. Too bad he didn't have a silencer, he thought, but maybe he could improvise. He'd seen it on television. All you had to do was shoot through a pillow, and the sound would be muffled.

Yeah, it would work, and it wouldn't arouse any of the neighbors' suspicions, but he would still wait until later to shoot them, just in case. Was the hole he'd dug big enough for both bodies? He hadn't made it very wide. Well, he would just have to jam them both in.

He had another problem. He had planned on getting a passport to go to Europe, but the FBI would have his name in the computers now. Still, he could get a fake passport. With money you could buy anything. There was another problem. The cops would be watching the airports. No. He'd have to change his plans. Where could he go? Maybe Mexico, he thought. He could walk across the border at Tijuana. Tomorrow was Saturday, and there would be a lot of tourists. Yes, that was it. He would get lost in the crowd.

Now, how the hell was he going to get to the border? Not the bus, 'cause the cops might be watching for him. He couldn't use Kandy's car, that was for sure. He'd have to buy one, but that would be no problem now that he was rich. Of course it would have to be a used one since it would already have license plates, but what difference did it make if it was new or used. All he needed was transportation to get to the border.

The money. Shit! There was one hell of a lot of it, but he could secure it to his chest and legs with surgical tape, and no one would know the difference. Thank God he had decided to let his beard grow. Maybe he should also dye his hair. Yeah. That would work. He would dye it red. Now all he had to do was wait until it got dark.

There was a car parked in front of Janice Beatty's house half-blocking the road. Wright drove past it and continued up the hill, searching. He rounded the curve and then spotted the blue Ford. "Look," he gestured to Jimmy.

Elizabeth leaned forward. "Yes. There. That's the house." She shuddered, then collapsed back against the seat. "My Lord. Crystal is in there, too. I can feel it."

Wright continued up the road past several houses, then

finally pulled to a stop. He turned and faced Jimmy. "I'm going to check it out. Wait here with Mrs. Anderson."

"That's my wife and daughter in there," Jimmy protested. "I want to go with you."

"Cummings is probably armed."

"All the more reason I should go with you," Jimmy said stubbornly.

Wright shook his head. He didn't like the idea; there was still the possibility that Mrs. Anderson was wrong. He couldn't just barge into people's homes. On the other hand, what did they have to lose? They would just have to chance it.

"Okay. This is what we're going to do . . ."

Crystal had to do something. She was a movie star and should be able to act herself out of any situation. It finally came to her. Would Emily understand? It was risky, but she couldn't think of anything else. She had to try.

"What are you going to do with the money, Richard?"

"Travel," he said.

"Really? Where?"

"Don't know."

"You should go to New Zealand. It's a beautiful country. I went there, and so did Emily and her father. Do you remember, Emily?" she asked her daughter. "When mommy made the movie?"

Emily looked at her mother. She remembered. Just after that was when her father went to live at the Malibu house. "Yes," she mumbled.

"Did you see the movie, Richard?" Crystal asked.

"Which one was that?"

"*Castle Noor*."

"Nah. I didn't see it."

"It was a good movie, and fun to make," Crystal babbled, hoping she could make herself clear to Emily. "Do you remember coming to the set, Emily? I showed you where I was acting in the last scene."

"Uh huh," Emily replied listlessly.

"It was in the barn, with all the animals," Crystal said, hoping Emily would understand.

Emily stared at her mother. That was wrong. The last scene was the one where her mother had to escape from a burning house and kept calling for help. Escape! Her mother was trying to tell her to escape. To get help. "Yes, I remember," she said softly.

"It's a shame you didn't see the movie, Richard," Crystal went on. "Such lovely scenery."

"I don't like that kind of crap. If I go to the movies, I want to see something with action," he said, lighting another cigarette. "You know. Like the ones Sylvester Stallone and Chuck Norris make."

Emily began coughing. "Can I get a glass of water, please?" she asked. She coughed again, harder, hoping she sounded convincing.

Richard nodded. "Yeah. And get me a beer out of the refrigerator," he told her. The champagne had gone flat, and he didn't want to start drinking scotch now. It was going to be a long afternoon.

Emily didn't dare look at her mother. She knew what she had to do: She had to escape. She stood, walked into the kitchen, and turned the water faucet on.

Crystal realized she would have to get Richard off the sofa so he couldn't see Emily. "Could I have a puff of your cigarette?" she asked, praying that Emily would figure out what to do.

"I didn't know you smoked," he said. "Unless you still do pot."

"No, I don't do grass anymore, but occasionally I smoke. It calms my nerves. Please. Just a puff."

Richard stood and walked to the chair, laughing to himself. He offered her the cigarette, thinking it was her dying request, just like in the movies.

Crystal half-rose, lifting the chair, feeling the ropes cut into her wrists. Using all her strength, she butted head-first into Richard. "Run, Emily," she cried as she went tumbling over on the floor, knocking Richard off his feet.

Emily dropped the glass and rushed out the kitchen door. She ran blindly, screaming, "Help! Help!"

Richard shoved Crystal aside, pulling the gun from his waistband and clubbing her in the head. "You bitch," he growled.

He ran into the kitchen and out the door. He saw the flash of Emily's T-shirt as she turned the corner of the house. "Come back here, you little . . ."

"Hold it, Cummings," Jimmy called out from the cover of a tall pine.

Richard sank to his knees and fired a shot at the voice. He ducked behind the trash barrel and began edging back toward the kitchen door.

"You're surrounded, Cummings. Give up," Jimmy shouted.

How many were there? Richard wondered. How come they weren't shooting back at him? He reached the door and crawled inside, slamming the door shut. He stood and smashed the window pane with the gun butt.

"Hey, pigs! I have Crystal Smythe in here. You'd better not come any closer," he shouted.

"Daddy," Emily cried. "Mommy's in there with him."

"Sssh. Stay where you are, sweetheart. Don't move."

Richard picked up a knife off the kitchen table and

returned to the living room. "You stupid bitch. How the hell did your husband get here?" he asked as he cut Crystal's ropes.

"You wouldn't believe me if I told you," she blurted out.

Richard yanked Crystal to her feet. "Okay. You and I are going to walk out of here. If you want to stay healthy and live to see that kid of yours, you'll do what I tell you."

Crystal touched the side of her head. It was bleeding profusely from where he had hit her with the gun. "Give up, Richard," she said. "It's your only choice."

"Shut up," he commanded, pushing her forward into the kitchen. He grabbed the money, shoving it into the satchel, sweating from fear. He walked back to the door and looked outside. It was quiet. The husband had to be alone, and he probably wasn't armed.

"You and I are walking out this door. We're going to get into the car and you're going to drive. You understand?"

"Yes," Crystal whispered, wondering if Jimmy was alone. She doubted it. Lieutenant Wright had to be out there, too. And Mrs. Anderson. They were waiting for her—waiting to see what she would do. Crystal had played dozens of roles, some in which she supposedly had been beaten and had to escape. But this was real life, and in the movies she always had a stunt woman for the actual physical action. What could she do?

Richard cracked the door open. "We're coming out now, and we're going to drive away," he shouted. "Don't be a hero, Mitchelson."

"You've got your money. Let my wife go," Jimmy shouted.

"No way. She's my ticket out of here. Stay clear."

He swung the door back, and using Crystal as a shield,

prodded her forward. "Slowly," he said, as they moved to the side of the car. "Okay, get in."

Crystal knew it was now or never. She put her hand on the door, then yanked it open all the way, slamming it into Richard. She swiftly turned and began running to the road.

He grunted in surprise and regained his feet. "You bitch," he screamed. It was then that he spotted the man behind the bush. He dropped the money satchel and whirled, firing blindly.

Wright didn't wait. He fired four times, wanting the man dead.

Richard screamed once again, but this time in pain. "No, no," he coughed, as blood spewed from his mouth. "No . . ."

Wright came forward cautiously, but wasn't surprised by what he found. He had always been a good shot, and three of his bullets had found their mark. There wouldn't be any need for an ambulance. He turned and saw Emily being hugged by Jimmy and Crystal.

"Daddy. I want you to come back home and live with us."

"I promise, darling," he said, laughing.

"And I'll make you stick to that promise," Crystal whispered, leaning her head on his shoulders, knowing she would never again let anything come between them.

Elizabeth joined the policeman and looked down at the body. "Such a nasty, evil man," she said. "Thank heavens my powers came back to me."

Wright took a crumpled pack of cigarettes out of his pocket. There was only one left, and he had started the pack that morning. Smoking too much, he thought, as he lit up, then smiled, realizing that this one tasted a lot better than any other he had smoked that day.

"You were right all along, Mrs. Anderson," he said,

smiling at the little lady. "You know, I wonder if you might be able to come by my office when we get back to the city. I think I could use your psychic powers. You see, I have this case I've been working on for some time now and . . ."

BIRTHSTONE
Mollie Gregory

Bestselling author of _Triplets_

_"Finely-etched characters, intricate plotting, and raw
human emotion illuminate this rich novel of a
Hollywood family caught in a web of secrets..."_
—Carolyn See, author of _Golden Days_

_"A novel that has it all: Hollywood, opulence and
decadence and primitive passions in high places."_
—Maureen Dean, bestselling author of _Washington Wives_

_Nearly destroyed by a shocking crime of passion, the
Wyman family has triumphed over their tragedy: award-
winning director Sara, noted movie critic Vail, and
their steel-willed mother Diana are in the spotlight of
fame and success. Then, Sara's daughter Lindy returns, forcing secrets out of the shadows, opening old
wounds and igniting new desires._

__BIRTHSTONE 0-515-10704-2/$4.99
